Praise for The Lady Authors

At the Duke's Wedding

"Filled with romance, passion, danger, scandal, and love... A must read!"

— My Book Addiction and More

"A delightful anthology. The four stories are tied together wonderfully... entertaining, fun and heartwarming."

— Romance Novel News

"The best Regency romance I ever read."

— Pam Rosenthal, bestselling author

At the Billionaire's Wedding

"[A] fantastic contemporary anthology."

— Romance Novel News

"[I]ntertwines contemporary romance with some historical twists and nods to Jane Austen; the four stories blend effortlessly into the final pages. With humor and wit, this sexy selection will definitely please romance readers."

— Library Journal

ISBN-10:   0-9860539-3-7

ISBN-13:   978-0-9860539-3-1

AT THE CHRISTMAS WEDDING

Map of a Lady's Heart © 2017 P. F. Belsley

Hot Rogue on a Cold Night © 2017 Maya Rodale

Snowy Night with a Duke © 2017 Katharine Brophy Dubois

Cover design by Carrie Devine/Seductive Designs
Model © FurmanAnna/iStockphoto.com
Background © Elena Pal/Shutterstock.com
Image © Olena Kucher/Depositphotos.com

Published by The Lady Authors

Printed in the USA

At the Christmas Wedding

CAROLINE LINDEN

MAYA RODALE

KATHARINE ASHE

CONTENTS

Map of a Lady's Heart

CAROLINE LINDEN

PROLOGUE

Kingstag Castle

December 1816

A storm was coming.

Viola Cavendish didn't need to look at the sky to know it. She could recognize the signs, all of them ominous, converging upon Kingstag Castle. Even worse, she had a very bad feeling she might find herself at the middle of it.

"I'm sure everything will be fine," said the Duchess of Wessex as she buttoned her fur-trimmed pelisse. The footmen were carrying down the duke's and duchess's traveling trunks, and the coach was outside the door. Viola could see the horses' breath steaming in the cold air as they stood waiting to carry her employers away for at least a fortnight.

The duke and duchess weren't supposed to leave for another month. The duchess's sister, Mrs. Blair, was expecting her first child after Christmas, and everyone at Kingstag could talk of nothing else. Well—all the females at Kingstag were keenly interested in the baby, although Kingstag was mostly populated by females. Aside from the duchess, the castle held the duke's mother, the dowager duchess; the duke's three younger sisters, Serena, Alexandra, and Bridget; and an elderly relation, Lady Sophronia. Since Mr. Blair was a cousin to the Cavendish family, everyone felt some claim upon the child, but especially the duchess, who was eagerly anticipating the visit she planned to make when the child was born.

But yesterday an express letter had arrived from Mr. Blair, saying his wife's labor pains had begun almost a month earlier than expected, and she was begging for the duchess to come as soon as possible. The duchess and her sister were extraordinarily close; without hesitation the duchess declared that she was leaving at once. The duke argued with her—Viola had been ordered from the room, which was rare—but in the end the duchess had prevailed, although only on the condition that the duke would go with her.

That was the moment Viola foresaw the coming storm. As the duchess's personal secretary, she was privy to almost everything that went on in the castle, and there was quite a bit going on at present. Not only was it nearing Christmas, but houseguests were expected, and the dowager duchess was ill. With neither the duke nor the duchess in residence, the position of hostess would fall on Lady Serena, who was young and unaccustomed to presiding. The next ranking lady would be Lady Sophronia, but no one would dare leave her in charge. Lady Sophronia delighted in chaos and mischief , and she always claimed to be pining for a scandal.

Viola could smile at that when she believed the duchess or dowager duchess would be around to prevent anything untoward. Now, though, the dowager duchess was confined to bed with a cold, the duchess was leaving, and Viola had the horrible thought that *she* would end up responsible for whatever disaster ensued.

Not that she could ever express that thought aloud. Her job was to be confident and capable, no matter what was asked of her. That was why the duchess had hired her, and Viola wasn't careless enough to let something like a house party unsettle her—at least not visibly. She gave a poised smile in response to the duchess's assurance that all would be well. "Of course, Your Grace."

"The dowager duchess will surely be on her feet again in a day or two," her employer went on. "Serena's friends are delightful young ladies and I'm sure they'll be no trouble." She paused. "You might have to keep a close eye on Bridget."

Viola fought back a laugh. Bridget was the duke's youngest sister, and could be charitably described as high-spirited. Most of the trouble in the castle could be traced to Bridget.

On the other hand, Viola genuinely liked the girl. Once she had been just as enthusiastic and eager for adventure as Bridget was. Still, she said a quick prayer that Bridget wouldn't go looking for extra adventure and mayhem in the next fortnight.

"Be sure to send the tenants' Christmas baskets by the end of the week," the duchess went on, "and let Serena tend to the decorating; I've already discussed it with Mrs. Hughes and she can assist."

"Yes, madam."

"I expect Serena and her friends will be rather quiet." Worry shadowed the duchess's eyes for a moment. "If they wish to have some entertainment, allow it. Especially . . . Well, encourage it as best you can."

"Yes, madam." Viola understood the concern. Serena was the eldest of the duke's sisters, a charming beauty at age twenty-one. Until several weeks ago she'd been engaged to marry the Duke of Frye, pink-cheeked with happiness and excitement, and then one day the engagement was abruptly over, and no one spoke of why. Even Viola had no idea what had happened. Serena turned pale and silent, and her mother, the dowager duchess, had almost immediately announced a Christmas house party of friends to cheer her.

A burst of noise made both women look up. The duke was coming down the stairs, his secretary close behind. Because of the sudden change in plans, Geoffrey Martin was accompanying the duke, which left Viola even more in charge of the castle. Geoffrey was carrying the large traveling desk that contained the duke's correspondence, and he went directly out to the waiting coach and horses.

The duke came to his wife's side. "Are you ready, my love?"

"Nearly," she told him. "We're leaving poor Viola in a horrible situation, Gareth."

Wessex glanced at her. Viola stood a little straighter under his piercing dark gaze, and bobbed a curtsey. "I'll do my best, Your Grace."

"And that's why I'm not worried," said the duchess firmly, putting her hand on Viola's arm. "I have great faith in you."

"Thank you, Your Grace," she said with another tiny curtsey. Viola tamped down her sense of impending disaster, which was surely just her imagination. The duchess had hired her for her competence, giving her a home and an income when she desperately needed both. It wasn't only her own well-being that depended on it; her younger brother Stephen needed her support until he was old enough to manage it for himself. Viola would be forever grateful to the Duchess of Wessex for giving her such a plum position.

For the past two years she had devoted herself to earning the duchess's trust, and she wasn't about to lose it now. "I shall be guided by Her Grace the dowager duchess in every uncertainty."

"Quite right." The duke gave her a small smile, which did wonders to his face. He appeared very somber and intimidating until he smiled. "We must go, Cleo, if we're to reach Morland today."

The worry in his wife's face deepened. "Yes, I'll be right there." She drew Viola aside as the butler stepped forward with the duke's coat and hat. "Send someone to Morland Park if there's any trouble," she said quietly, naming the Blair home. "It's only ten miles, we can return in a day."

"Your Grace," protested Viola, "I'm sure that won't be necessary—"

The duchess made a subtle shushing motion. "Perhaps not, but if anything untoward happens . . ." Her eyes bored into Viola's, as if trying to convey something too terrible to say out loud. Startled, Viola could only wet her lips and nod.

"Very good." The duchess blew out a breath. "I hope all will be well, both here and at Morland."

"Yes, Your Grace. I dearly hope Mrs. Blair is well." Viola bowed her head. If Mrs. Blair's child was born too early, he might not survive.

The other woman smiled wistfully. "I wish we were taking you with us. I don't know what I shall do without you." She sighed. "I wish we didn't need to go at all yet."

The duke approached with her cloak. "We must go, Cleo," he said again. The duchess nodded, and Wessex folded the cloak tenderly around her shoulders.

Viola followed as they went out to the coach. Footmen rushed before them with hot bricks for the carriage floor. Geoffrey, his muffler pulled up almost to his hat brim, swung into the saddle of a gray gelding. The horses shook their traces as the duke and duchess climbed into the carriage.

"Good-bye," called the duchess, waving as a footman closed the door. The duke touched the brim of his hat, and the coachman lifted the whip and started the horses.

Viola waved back, hunching her shoulders against the cold. Running footsteps sounded behind her, and then Bridget Cavendish was beside her, swinging one arm exuberantly in the air. "Good-bye," she cried. "Give our love to Blair and to Helen!" The carriage rolled on, past the oaks.

Bridget lowered her arm. "I hope Helen has the baby safely."

"Yes," said Viola softly. "I hope so too."

"With Cleo there, I'm sure she will." Bridget turned to her, and Viola finally focused on her long enough to see the gleam in her eyes. *Oh no.* "Cousin Viola . . ."

"No," said Viola immediately. Her late husband had been one of Bridget's distant cousins, and Viola was therefore only a relation by marriage, but when the girl called her "cousin," Viola had learned to be wary of what came next.

"You didn't even hear my idea!" Bridget looked wounded. "It's not rude or dangerous. I'm sure Cleo would allow it, if she were here."

"And yet I can't help but note you did not ask before she left." Viola shook her head with a soft *tsk*. "What is it?"

Bridget brightened right out of her pretend hurt. "A play. To cheer Serena. It will be silly and make no sense at all and she'll be so diverted. Please say we may put it on!"

That didn't sound so dreadful . . . and yet it was Bridget, so Viola wasn't reassured. "Which play?"

"Oh, I'm writing it," was the cheerful reply. "Completely original. Nothing vulgar or inappropriate, I promise."

For a moment she was shocked into silence. It wasn't that Bridget wasn't bright enough or creative enough to write a play, it was that Viola had never seen her sit still long enough to write a scene, let alone multiple acts. "How exciting," she said, recovering. "May I read it?"

"Even better—you'll be in it!" Bridget's eyes glowed as she beamed back. "Everyone will be, except Mama if she's going to be ill for a while, and Great-Aunt Sophronia. They'll be our audience."

Her heart settled into a normal rhythm again. If Bridget meant for her to have a part, she'd have to see the play, and could put a stop to any nonsense before it got out of hand. And if anyone could make Serena smile again, it would be Bridget. For all her madcap ways, the girl was irrepressible in her good humor and wit, with a for making people laugh even in their foulest tempers. And the ess *had* said to encourage entertainments.

"It sounds like a fine idea," she told Bridget.

"Thank you!" The girl clapped her hands and ran back into the house before Viola could say anything more, which was likely for the best.

A gust of wind made her shiver. She wrapped her arms around herself and cast one last look down the long oak-lined avenue; the ducal carriage was already gone from sight. Her gaze drifted upward. The clouds seemed to be growing thicker and grayer by the moment, and the air had a leaden stillness that promised snow.

Viola didn't like storms.

CHAPTER ONE

"How much farther is it?"

Wesley Morane, Earl of Winterton, inhaled slowly and then exhaled even more slowly. If he didn't know better, he would think his nephew was still a child instead of a young man nearing his twenty-first birthday. "A few more miles, I expect."

Justin scowled and slumped by the window. The weak light caught his fair hair and made him look as young and petulant as he was behaving. "Aren't we nearly to Cornwall yet?"

It felt as though they had circled the globe in this carriage. Wes tried to keep his voice calm as he replied, "No." He did not repeat an earlier mistake, of offering to show Justin their progress on the small but handsome leather-bound atlas of England he kept in the traveling chaise. That had not gone well, with Justin fixating on the distance left to travel instead of the beauty of the illustrated map of Dorset.

Several minutes of silence passed. Wes did not fool himself they would continue indefinitely. Time had already seemed to stretch and slow, much like the distance they had still to travel. At one point he wondered if the carriage and horses had become stuck in a vast mud slick, where the hooves and wheels were only churning in place, never making an inch of progress.

"I could have stayed in Hampshire," Justin said abruptly. "Dorset is hideous in winter."

So is Hampshire. Wes managed to keep himself from saying it aloud. He did not manage to keep from thinking about a few places that were not hideous in winter—the West Indies, for example. The winter of 1808 had been splendid there, sitting under thick palm fronds and learning about the spice trade from his father. The islands were a humid swamp in the rainy season, but the rest of the year, it was magical.

"I recall you agitating to leave Hampshire," he said instead. "Your mother told me you were wild to be away."

The boy's mouth pulled sullenly. "Not this far away."

That was what his mother had feared. Anne was Wes's oldest sister, and she knew exactly what her son wanted, so newly grown to manhood and so abruptly possessed of his father's title. Justin had barely finished university when his father died, leaving him the new Viscount Newton. Instead of the Grand Tour he had been promised upon completing his studies, Justin had gone home to New Cross House to console his mother and sisters and lay his father to rest.

But mourning soon grew tiresome for a young man of high spirits and energy. If he couldn't sow his wild oats in Italy or Spain, Justin was determined to sow them somewhere. He fell in with a crowd of young dandies who spent their time racing carriages, dicing, and drinking at the local pub. When the local miller called on Anne to complain of young Lord Newton's attentions to his daughter, Anne wrote to Wes and commanded him to take charge of his nephew before the boy was hopelessly debauched.

He'd gone at once; he had to. Anne might be a decade older than he, but he was still the head of the family. Privately he didn't think Justin was in as bad a way as Anne claimed, but his sister was grieving her husband, and rationality had never been her strong suit anyway. It seemed obvious to Wes that the best course was to separate the restless son and anxious mother.

On impulse he decided Justin should come with him to Kingstag Castle in Dorset. Wes had his eye on a particular old atlas, and he strongly suspected the duke had recently acquired it. The only way to be certain was to see it himself, and his sister's demand that he deal with his nephew provided all the excuse Wes needed to set off for Dorset at once. Not only would it give Anne a respite from worrying about Justin, he reasoned, it would remove the boy from the miller's daughter as well as his wastrel friends for a fortnight, and allow Wes a chance to influence his nephew for the better.

Rarely had he regretted anything more.

"Where did you want to go?" he asked, wondering what had made him think he could act as a mentor to this sulking young man. Had he been this odious when his own father died?

"Italy," said Justin at once. "Rome. My father promised me I would see all the sights."

"That's an even longer journey," Wes pointed out. "Some of it aboard ships, which can be even more beastly than the roads."

"At least the destination is worthwhile," flung back his nephew. "I've nothing to do with the duke—"

"And you can only be civil and cordial to someone you've known for ages?" Wes raised one brow. "You've got a lot in common with Wessex, you know. He also inherited young. You might find him an interesting acquaintance."

The expression on Justin's face was just shy of incredulous. "I doubt it. He's old enough to be my father."

Not quite; Wessex was only a few years older than Wes, if memory served. "Your father would be pleased for you to know him," he said instead.

Justin did not reply. He turned to gaze moodily out the window again. After a few minutes, Wes drew out his travel atlas. He smoothed open the pages and his irritation subsided. The illustrations were remarkable, and he was able to locate their location to within a few miles. The travel guide provided plenty of description of the surrounding countryside, and he lost himself in vignettes of Roman ruins and splendid castles and manors.

"It's snowing," Justin muttered.

Wes turned a page, still reading about the stone circle found not far from here. "We're almost there."

"What if we have to stop and become snowed in at some dreary little inn on the side of the road?"

"I doubt that will happen."

Justin was quiet for a moment, then burst out, "We'll be trapped at Kingstag, won't we?"

Wes glanced out the window. It was indeed snowing, but not hard. "It's not likely, this far south. We're not in Russia."

"Might as well be," was the grumbled retort.

"You have no idea what Russia is like."

"Nor am I ever likely to!"

Wes closed the book with a snap. "Your behavior is the reason," he warned. "This is why your mother wanted you to come with me— I daresay she was sick to death of listening to you complain." He glared at his nephew. "If you wish to be treated as a man of sense, worthy of respect, you might begin acting the part."

Justin gaped at him. "I didn't ask for my father to die!"

"Neither did I," Wes retorted. "I was only five years older than you when my father died. Don't imagine I've forgotten what it was like." He softened his voice as Justin's eyes grew round and his lower lip jutted out. "Life serves us all some hard turns. Carousing at the pub and chasing the miller's daughter isn't something you are owed, and either one can cause long-lasting regret. Do you want to cause your mother even more anguish, on top of her sorrow at your father's death?" Justin jerked his head *no*. "I should hope not." With that stern pronouncement, Wes sat back and opened his book again.

For the next hour Justin said nothing. Once or twice Wes stole a glance at him under pretext of checking the weather, but Justin was simply staring out the window, shoulders hunched. He hoped his nephew managed to comport himself graciously at Kingstag. Wes didn't know Wessex personally, and his mission would be greatly complicated by a surly nephew. If Justin behaved like a moody child and cost Wes a chance to get that atlas . . . He breathed deeply and assured himself that would not happen; he would not allow it to happen. One way or another he would rein in Justin.

Finally the carriage slowed to turn into a winding oak-lined avenue. Wes put the book aside for good; it had grown too dark to read anyway, even with the lamps lit. Outside the window, one of the outriders galloped past on his way to announce them at the house. "I believe we've arrived."

Justin nodded.

"I recognize this is not how you planned to spend your holiday," he went on, trying to be understanding. "A viscount will be subject to duty and obligation, and not all of it is exceedingly pleasant. However, you can make anything as bearable, or as horrible, as you choose by how you approach the matter. Conduct yourself with grace and good will, and you will find yourself master of the situation instead of a victim gnashing his teeth over the gross indignity of everything."

"What am I do to here, Uncle Winterton?" asked Justin plaintively. "I know nothing about atlases or old books. I've never met the duke. It's the middle of winter and I shall miss Christmas with my mother and sisters. It feels like punishment."

"We'll be back in Hampshire by Twelfth Night. If all goes very well, perhaps sooner. And I don't view it as punishment—a change of scene, nothing more." He waited, but Justin merely heaved a silent sigh. He accepted his fate, but without understanding. "Buck up, lad," said Wes bracingly. "When you were a child, you used to beg to come along on my travels."

"The West Indies sounded a great deal more exciting and exotic than Dorset in winter."

Wes laughed. The carriage had reached the front of the house, which was indeed a castle, though one shorn of moat and outer wall. "True enough! But you never know where adventure may be lurking." The footman opened the door, and Wes stepped out.

Justin followed, pulling his greatcoat tightly around him as he peered up at the massive stone walls of Kingstag Castle, doubt written on his face. "In Dorset? I can't imagine."

"Try." He strode forward through the swirling snow. An inch or two had accumulated, suggesting it had been snowing for some time here. With a sharp jangle of harness, the carriage started off again; the coachman would want to get the horses out of the cold as soon as possible. The butler was waiting in the wide open doorway of the house, holding a lantern aloft like a beacon.

The cavernous hall inside was dim, the candlelight no match for the soaring vaulted ceiling above. A footman pulled the tall doors shut with a clang behind them, while another servant took their hats and coats, and a third instantly stepped forward with a broom to whisk away the snow that had blown in with them. The butler bowed. "Good evening, my lords. Won't you come this way?" He led them into a cozy parlor nearby. A fire burned in the hearth, and Wes went to warm his hands, grateful for the heat.

"Are you certain they're expecting us today?" Justin lingered by the door.

Wes turned to let the fire warm his backside. "Why?"

His nephew shrugged. "It didn't seem as though they were." He drifted into the room, fiddling with his watch chain.

Time passed. More time passed. Justin began openly checking his watch, in silent demonstration that he'd been right and this visit was indeed a punishment. Wes grew restive. He had an invitation, damn it, from the duke himself. He had more or less begged for it—perhaps even almost invited himself—but he was still an invited

11

guest. Today had been explicitly fixed as the date he would arrive, and however reluctantly the duke had agreed, he *had* agreed to that. Wes had roamed across half the world, and he knew how to plan and execute a trip on time, with minimal delays. Had it really thrown the duke's household in uproar, or was something more serious going on?

His fingers were reaching for the cord to summon a servant when the door opened at last. A woman stepped into the room—a very attractive woman, with toffee-brown hair and soft green eyes. His hand dropped back to his side in surprise.

"Lord Winterton," she said, dipping a curtsey until her dark blue skirts pooled around her. She raised her head and looked him in the eye with a warm smile on her lovely face, and Wes would have sworn the floor rose and fell under his feet like a ship on the sea in a squall. "I apologize that you've been left waiting."

His eyes fixed on her, Wes bowed. "Were we? I hardly noticed." Justin made a quiet noise behind him, and he started. He'd forgotten his nephew was in the room. "My nephew, Viscount Newton," he said, motioning toward the young man.

She made another graceful curtsey. It made her bosom plump up beautifully. "Welcome to Kingstag, Lord Newton."

"Thank you, ma'am." Justin's voice sounded deeper and more interested, which perversely annoyed Wes. This woman was too old for his nephew. Not that she was old by any stretch. In fact she looked to be just about perfect. But when he shot a glance of veiled rebuke at Justin, the boy was gazing attentively at the newcomer.

She came forward, her skirts swaying attractively. "I am Mrs. Cavendish, private secretary to the Duchess of Wessex. I'm afraid I bring unfortunate news. His Grace is not in residence now."

It took a moment for the words to penetrate Wes's brain. His attention had snagged on the way her lips shaped the words. "We had an appointment," he said.

She bowed her head. "I apologize, my lord. His Grace was called away rather abruptly. I believed Mr. Martin to have written to anyone expected, requesting a postponement."

"There's a snowstorm," protested Justin. "The roads are a nightmare."

Her face blanked for a split second, then turned pink. It was entrancing, and completely distracted Wes from the urge to correct

Justin's rude statement. "Oh no," she said, her lips curving into a rueful smile. "I didn't mean you must leave, certainly not in this weather. You are very welcome to stay. I regret that I cannot tell you when the duke may return, though."

If someone had told him an hour ago that the duke would be away and his trip would be for naught, Wes would have snarled in frustration. Now, he stared at Mrs. Cavendish's smile and forgot all about atlases and the long carriage ride and the snow. "That is very kind. I hope Wessex wasn't called away on a tragic matter."

Her expression flickered for a moment. "Nothing of the sort. Her Grace the dowager duchess bade me welcome you, and convey her regret that she's unwell and unable to receive you herself."

Wes bowed his head and murmured a wish for the duchess's health. Both the duke and the duchess were away on urgent business—there could be no other kind that required them to leave in such weather—and the dowager duchess was confined to her bed. There must have been quite a search to find someone to tell him the bad news.

As it happened, he was not sorry Mrs. Cavendish had been the one chosen.

"Withers is having rooms prepared for you," Mrs. Cavendish went on. "May I send for some refreshment? You must be chilled and tired after your journey. The family dines in an hour, if you would care to join them."

"Thank you." Wes shook himself out of his daze. He was dumbstruck by a secretary; what a fine example to set for his nephew. Hypocritical, too, after warning Justin away from the miller's pretty daughter.

The door opened behind her before she could reply. A young woman, about Justin's age, slipped in. "Viola, may we—?" She stopped short at the sight of the two men, her mouth hanging open. "Are you a friend of Frye?" she asked Justin suspiciously.

Justin blinked. "Who?"

"The Duke of Frye," said the young woman with a trace of disgust, earning her a dismayed glance from Mrs. Cavendish. "The scoundrel."

A deep blush suffused his face. "N-No." He sucked in a quick breath and added, somewhat boastfully, "I am Lord Newton."

She brightened. "Oh! Are you joining the house party? You didn't tell me anyone else was coming, Viola."

Mrs. Cavendish put up one hand. "Lady Bridget, please." She turned back toward Wes. "Lord Winterton, Lord Newton, may I present Lady Bridget Cavendish, His Grace's youngest sister. Lady Bridget, the Earl of Winterton and Viscount Newton."

"A pleasure to meet you," said Lady Bridget cheerfully as she curtseyed. Her attention immediately swung back to Mrs. Cavendish. "We need a ladder, loads of white feathers, and something that could portray a ghost—a tablecloth, perhaps."

"What? Why?" asked the other woman in some alarm, before she held up her hand again. "Never mind. We shall discuss it later."

Lady Bridget rolled her eyes. "But—"

"Later," repeated Mrs. Cavendish with a small shooing motion of her hand. Reluctantly, Lady Bridget went.

"I beg your pardon," said Wes. "I'd no idea there was a house party."

Mrs. Cavendish shook her head, but with a betraying flush on her cheeks. "It's only a few guests—friends of Lady Serena, the duke's sister. I shall urge them to stay out of your way. The castle is quite large enough for all."

There was really no choice. Night was falling, as was the snow. "Thank you," he said again, revising his plan. Perhaps it wasn't the worst thing to have an extra day or two without the duke at home. He could examine the atlas at leisure, to be sure it was the one he wanted. If not, he could take his leave and go without a fuss; he would say he needed to return Justin to his family in time for Christmas celebrations, as his nephew wished.

But if it *were* the atlas he wanted . . . This could be an invaluable chance to plan his strategy. The duke had not wanted to sell it, and had only agreed to let him look at it when Wes pushed all boundaries of politeness. It would take some persuading to get Wessex to part with the atlas, and any insight he could glean before the duke arrived home might prove vital. And he suspected the lovely secretary would know her employer's mind . . .

Yes, it suited him quite well to have missed the duke.

"We would be delighted to dine with the family," he said. "In an hour, you say?"

14

"Yes. Withers will send a man to attend you, if you've not brought your own . . . ?"

Wes shook his head. He'd got used to doing for himself on short journeys, and Justin didn't have a valet to bring.

Mrs. Cavendish excused herself and left. Wes turned to his nephew. "Well, that's quite a turn."

"What?" Justin was staring at the closed door, and flinched at his remark.

"That Wessex isn't here." Justin looked blank. "You shall get your wish to be home with your sisters for Christmas."

"Oh. Yes." The young man cleared his throat. "The house party may prove diverting."

Wes glanced at him with sudden suspicion. "Oh?" He could almost hear his sister's voice in his ear, urging him to deliver a lecture about proper behavior toward young ladies. Wes quieted it for the moment. Lady Bridget seemed full of high spirits, but the dowager duchess, who must be Lady Bridget's mother, was in residence. He wanted to be a mentor to Justin, not a nagging conscience.

And of course, he'd had a few improper thoughts about Mrs. Cavendish himself. If he scolded Justin for being mesmerized by a pretty female, he'd be the biggest hypocrite in Britain. He said nothing.

But when the butler appeared soon afterward to conduct them to their rooms, things took another turn for the worse. They hadn't even made it across the hall before a patter of footsteps and a rustle of skirts heralded the arrival of not one, not two, but four young ladies, including the mischievous Lady Bridget at the rear.

"Lord Winterton," said one of them, who seemed to be the leader from the way she stepped forward. Tall and slim, she was striking rather than beautiful, with very dark eyes and hair, but fair skin. "Lord Newton. Welcome to Kingstag Castle." As one, all four of them curtseyed, and Wes and Justin bowed. "I am Lady Alexandra Cavendish. My cousin Viola tells me you are here to see my brother Wessex, who has been called away."

"Yes," Wes replied. "We shan't intrude."

"Oh no." Her gaze moved to Justin, who seemed to be holding himself unusually erect, his chest puffed out a little. "We would be delighted to have you join our party. We're putting on a play, you see, and haven't enough gentlemen to fill all the parts."

"A capital idea," said Justin before Wes could speak. "Thank you, Lady Alexandra, we would be honored."

She smiled. "Excellent. Bridget will assign you lines." She curtseyed again. "Until dinner, my lords."

Justin stared as they left in a troop. Lady Alexandra glanced over her shoulder once to smile at him. Wes took one look at his nephew's face, and began shaking his head. "We're leaving tomorrow." He'd have to come back later in pursuit of the atlas. Making the trip twice was far preferable to spending his time watching Justin like a hawk. The last thing he needed was a scandal between his nephew and one of Wessex's sisters. The duke would never sell him the atlas then.

"No!" Justin grabbed his arm. "Please not, Uncle." He cleared his throat. "And, er, I just gave my word to be in the play."

"You've no idea what the play is."

"Does it matter?"

Wes ran one hand over his face. Four very pretty young ladies, without enough gentlemen to fill all the parts. His sister, Justin's mother, would be calling for the carriage—for the sleigh, if necessary—immediately.

But. On the other hand, the young ladies were obviously well-born. Wes would have to keep a close eye on his nephew, but perhaps this would motivate Justin to improve his manners. The Newton viscountcy made him an eligible match, after all, even if his sullen behavior did not. It might be a good lesson for the boy to see what sort of behavior appealed to decent young ladies.

And then Mrs. Cavendish's face flashed through his mind. Cousin Viola, Lady Alexandra called her. Not merely a secretary after all. She seemed to be in charge of the place. Staying for a few days would probably thrust him together with her, as the only adults supervising this play . . .

"Very well," he said. "We can stay."

CHAPTER TWO

Viola personally took the dowager duchess's dinner to her on a tray. The duchess had been sick in bed for a few days now, but still insisted every evening she would be on her feet in the morning. Tonight Viola said a fervent prayer that it was true this time.

"Good evening, Your Grace." She set the tray on the table near the bed.

"Thank you, Viola." The duchess's voice was hoarse from coughing.

"Some visitors arrived today." Viola tidied the tray and uncovered the dishes. "The Earl of Winterton and his nephew, Viscount Newton. Lord Winterton had an appointment with the duke."

"Oh dear." The dowager coughed, and Viola handed her a cup of steaming tea. "Wessex will not be pleased to have missed him."

Nor was Viola especially pleased to have two more guests to entertain. "I thought Mr. Martin would have written to cancel their visit, but they must have set out before his letter reached them."

The duchess made a sound of dismay. "How regrettable."

Viola brought the tray over to the bed. The dowager was propped up on a number of pillows, looking older than usual. Her face was pale except for the flush of fever in her cheeks, and her eyes looked sunken and glassy. She'd fallen ill several days earlier and seemed to be in the worst of it. "Ma'am, perhaps we should send for the doctor—"

The duchess gave her a wan smile. "So says Ellen," she murmured, referring to her maid. "I've seen what doctors do, you know. I prefer to take my chances with the fever."

17

Viola frowned in worry. "Yes, ma'am, but . . ."

The duchess pushed herself a little more upright and pulled the tray toward her. "I have no plans to succumb to it, mind you. If I go into a decline and hope begins to wane, you and Ellen may send for the doctor, but as long as I have my appetite and can sleep, I intend to brave it out." She inspected the tray and sighed. "More blancmange. Tell Cook I would like something with flavor next time."

"Yes, ma'am." Viola hesitated. "What ought I to do with Lords Winterton and Newton?"

The duchess blinked. "Oh yes. I suppose they must stay the night."

She wet her lips. "It's snowing, Your Grace, and it shows no signs of stopping. The roads may not be fit for travel tomorrow."

"Then they must stay until the roads are fit." The duchess gave her a reproving glance. "You didn't think otherwise, surely?"

Viola blushed. She'd already told the gentlemen they were welcome to stay. "No, no. I only worried about the inconvenience to Lady Serena and her friends."

Something of the older woman's usual perception returned. "Are these gentlemen by any chance handsome, rakish fellows?"

"Rakish! Oh my, I've no idea," Viola babbled. "But . . . Lord Newton is rather young—near Lady Alexandra's age, I would suppose—and he is a handsome gentleman."

"Oh dear." Another fit of coughing seized the duchess, and Viola hurried to fetch a clean handkerchief. "And Winterton?" rasped the duchess a moment later, reaching for her tea. "Tell me he's a somber older gentleman capable of keeping his nephew in check."

"Er." Viola shifted her weight, picturing the man in question. "I wouldn't call him *much* older . . ."

The duchess closed her eyes and leaned back against the pillows. "Is there a Lady Winterton? Send Ellen to fetch *Debrett's*, Viola."

Viola rang for the maid, who returned a short time later with the tome listing all the aristocracy of Britain. She paged through it to the Earl of Winterton's entry and read it aloud to the duchess. "Wesley Edward Fitzallen Morane, Earl of Winterton, Viscount Desmond, Baron Lyle; born August 31, 1784; succeeded his father, Allen, the late earl, on March 12, 1810."

"No countess," said the duchess on a sigh. "And he's handsome." Viola opened her mouth to protest that she'd never said that, realized it was true, and said nothing. The earl was a man who drew the eye—at least her eye—with coal-black hair and vivid blue eyes in a lean, tanned face. He looked like a man of bold action and passionate interests.

"I shall have to recover." The dowager ruined this determined statement with another bout of coughing, and Viola refilled her teacup without waiting for permission. "There is no way Serena can maintain order. Even if these two gentlemen arrived as the very souls of dignity and propriety, Sophronia would corrupt them into the biggest scoundrels in England within a week. I shall be out of this bed by morning if I must be carried on a litter to do it."

Viola took one look at the dowager duchess, pale and weak and still feverish, and knew there was no way she would be recovered by the morning. "You mustn't risk your health, ma'am." She took a deep breath and girded herself. "I shall do everything I can to assist Lady Serena, and I'm sure we can manage between the two of us."

"Are you?" The dowager held up one hand to forestall a protest Viola wasn't making. "I know my daughters. Bridget, in particular, can be . . . willful."

Viola knew that all too well. This play of Bridget's was beginning to worry her; despite asking twice, she had yet to see a single page of it, and Bridget's odd requests were growing alarming. A ghost? Feathers? She said a silent prayer that she wasn't about to make a promise she couldn't keep, which might well lead to the duchess dismissing her from her post, and gave a decisive nod. "Of course. I'm very fond of Lady Bridget, and I'm confident I can guide her."

"Well," said the dowager, her voice heavy with doubt, "perhaps . . ."

"There's little choice, I fear," Viola added. "The roads will soon be impassable." She'd checked on the snowfall right before bringing the dowager's tray. The snow was four inches deep and still falling heavily. John the footman reported that Hugh, the head gardener, was predicting a great deal of snow, based on his observations of the squirrels at Kingstag Castle. Hugh claimed he could predict the weather by the animals' behavior. Viola wasn't convinced of that, but given the way her luck had run the last few years, this storm would be an epic blizzard that brought all of Dorset to a standstill.

The house was full of young ladies and gentlemen, with more expected, who would grow bored and restive if trapped inside for days on end.

Not one but two additional handsome gentlemen had arrived on the scene, soon to be trapped in that same house.

The duke, who could deal with the visiting gentlemen, was away and not expected to return soon.

The duchess, who could organize activities to keep the young ladies occupied, was also away.

The dowager duchess, who could maintain order and decorum by sheer force of will, was confined to bed for several more days at least.

Lady Serena, nominally the hostess in her mother's stead, could hardly be expected to supervise the friends who had been invited to cheer her after her recent heartbreak.

And that meant Lady Sophronia, who loved chaos and scandal more than she loved breath, would be in charge.

Viola recognized that she was the only person at Kingstag with any hope of preventing both chaos and scandal. She had expected that the duchess's absence would offer her a bit of a reprieve from work, when she might have some time for herself. With no small amount of regret, she realized that instead of enjoying some cozy afternoons by the fire with a good book or writing letters, she would be keeping a keen eye on Lady Bridget's play rehearsals, as well as on all the guests, especially the young ladies. Her heart sank at the futility of that endeavor. Perhaps she ought to keep her eyes on the gentlemen . . .

Then she blushed, thinking of keeping an eye on Lord Winterton. That wouldn't be a hardship. Keeping her eyes *off* him would be harder. But he didn't look like the sort to cause trouble with young ladies barely half his age—if anything, Viola thought the young ladies would be causing trouble over him.

Lord Newton, though, had gazed at Bridget with such interest, and Viola sighed.

"With luck the snow will be gone in a few days, and the gentlemen can be on their way—presuming His Grace hasn't returned by then, that is. In the meantime, I'm sure there will be no trouble. I shall keep a keen eye on the whole party."

The dowager still looked doubtful, but also relieved. "If you are confident you can maintain order, then I see no cause for alarm."

"I can," she promised the duchess with more confidence than she felt. "I give my word."

A servant directed Wes to a large formal drawing room before dinner. He hadn't seen Justin since shortly after they arrived, but he heard his nephew's laugh as he approached the drawing room doors. Since he hadn't heard Justin sound that happy in months, Wes's step quickened in a mixture of interest and alarm. What could have pleased him so much?

The sight that met his eyes was both wonderful and confounding. Justin wore a blindfold and was seated on a chair in the midst of several young ladies. He wore a wide grin. A handful of other people stood about the room, some watching the spectacle with amusement, some with disapproval. Wes's main concern was his nephew; what on earth——?

"Good evening, Lord Winterton," said a woman beside him, and he instantly forgot all about Justin.

He bowed. "Good evening to you, Mrs. Cavendish."

She smiled. Tonight she wore a stylish green dress that matched her eyes and displayed her figure beautifully, and he felt a stir of dangerous interest as he looked down at her. "Some of the ladies begged Lord Newton to play a game with them."

"He appears to be enjoying it." Justin said something, too quietly for Wes to hear, but a burst of laughter from the group indicated his nephew was in excellent humor tonight. "Very much," he added wryly.

"The aim of every hostess." She said it lightly, but Wes caught a note of something else in her voice. Tension? Alarm? Good God, what had Justin done? They'd only been here an hour. "May I present you to the other guests?"

"That would be very kind of you." He offered her his arm, partly out of manners, but mostly out of eagerness to draw her a little closer. She blinked as if startled—and then laid her hand on his sleeve. Even that slight pressure sent a shock wave through him. Wes inhaled deeply, and almost went light-headed on the scent of her: rosemary and lemon. It made him think of Italy, and the hot Tuscan sun above the villa where he'd spent a glorious four months several years ago. He let her lead him across the room.

By the time he made the acquaintance of Lady Serena, the ostensible hostess; Viscount Gosling and Mr. Jones, two visiting gentlemen; Lady Jane Rutledge, a neighbor; and a brother and sister called Penworth who were apparently Cavendish cousins, Wes felt distinctly old. Mrs. Cavendish might be near his age, and Lady Sophronia, an elderly relation, was far older, but everyone else was much more Justin's peer.

That could be taken in two ways. First, advantageously, as it seemed they had stumbled into the exact sort of party that might bring out Justin's more polished side and encourage him to behave in a more appropriate manner.

But second, it also meant far more temptation for his rash and headstrong nephew, and therefore greater risk that Justin would forget himself and do something stupid. Wes felt every one of the eleven years he had on Justin.

"I apologize again for intruding on the party," he told his companion, watching as the young people continued their game.

Her cheeks were the most entrancing shade of pink. "Please don't think of it as an intrusion! I feel certain that if the duke were here, he would have urged you to stay. And I must say, your arrival was very welcome to the young ladies, especially Lady Bridget."

"Yes, she seems very cheerful."

To prove his point, the girl in question let out a shout of laughter, clutching her belly as she did so. "Bravo," called Lady Sophronia, sitting on a sofa nearby.

Wes ducked his head closer to Mrs. Cavendish. "What game are they playing?" he murmured. The bright scent of lemon was driving him to distraction. He wanted to breathe her in forever.

"One of Bridget's inventions, I believe." She wore a slightly apologetic expression. "I'm not certain I can explain all the rules very well—or at all—but the main point is that the blind man"—she nodded at Justin, who still wore the blindfold and a beaming grin—"is presented several clues, and must guess the mystery subject."

"How does one win?"

"By guessing correctly on the fewest clues."

"Ah." He glanced at his nephew. It was clear to see that Justin was enjoying being the center of so much attention. He sat with his hands on his knees, his elbows out, making his shoulders as wide as possible. As Wes watched, Lady Alexandra came up to him and placed her palm against his cheek. Justin flinched, but his smile grew wider than ever.

"Sleigh riding," he said, and the young ladies erupted in applause and giggles.

"Well done," declared Bridget. "Although we should deduct points after Alexandra cheated."

"It's not cheating," protested her sister. "My hands were cold! The clue was cold!"

Justin peeled off the blindfold. "It was the best clue of all," he assured her in his strangely deeper voice. Alexandra smiled, and Bridget rolled her eyes.

"Who shall be next?" She scanned the room. They had clearly been playing a while. "Cousin Viola!"

"No," said the woman next to Wes. "Absolutely not."

"Spoken like a chaperone," he murmured.

"As I am," was her low reply. "Perhaps you should play."

She hadn't said it loudly, but Lady Bridget heard. "Oh yes! Please do, Lord Winterton. We've all had a turn and it's still a quarter hour until dinner."

"Do, Uncle," added Justin with a fiendish gleam in his eye.

Wes glanced at Mrs. Cavendish. Her eyes had widened in surprise, but she recovered quickly. "It won't hurt," she whispered with a rueful little smile. "If you feel adventurous."

God. The blood roared in his ears. That smile did him in, captivating and intimate. Wes heard himself agree before he could think twice. "If it will amuse you." He couldn't resist leaning closer and adding a quiet plea. "But you must give me some hint of what to do."

Bridget hurried over to thrust the blindfold into Mrs. Cavendish's hands. "We'll be sure to choose something clever this time," she said. "Sleigh riding! We can do better . . ." She darted back across the room to huddle with the other young people.

Wes caught the gleeful look Justin sent his way. He turned to Mrs. Cavendish. "Help me," he whispered.

She laughed as they crossed the room to the chair. "It's not difficult." Wes took a seat and she lifted the blindfold, settling it gently over his face. He closed his eyes and took a deep breath as she moved behind him, her fingers stirring his hair as she knotted the cloth. "They will give you clues to the word or saying they've thought of," she said, her voice soft and very near his ear. Wes's imagination began to wander dangerously, conjuring up other ways she could be behind him, her lips near his ear and her hands in his hair. He wondered if the scent of lemons came from her hair or from her skin.

"After each clue you make a guess," Mrs. Cavendish went on. "Lord Newton required nine clues to reach the correct answer, which is the best so far tonight."

"So to win, I need to guess after eight or fewer clues."

"Yes." Now blind, he could still tell she was smiling. "The wittier or more ridiculous the guess, the better."

"Ridiculous?" He turned his head toward her voice. "What do you mean?"

"Lady Bridget thrives on the ridiculous," she murmured.

He would have asked more, but a querulous voice snapped, "Viola! Cease flirting with Lord Winterton and come sit by me. I cannot hear what everyone is saying and you must tell me."

"Of course, Lady Sophronia," replied Mrs. Cavendish. "Good luck," she whispered to him. Wes heard the swish of her skirts as she moved away.

Flirting. He should be ashamed at himself for thinking so, but he wouldn't mind at all if Mrs. Cavendish did flirt with him—blindfolded and otherwise.

"We have decided," announced Bridget then. "Are you ready, sir?"

Wes thought of Justin's little smirk, and Mrs. Cavendish's rueful smile, and of how fiercely he'd played cricket at school. He flexed his hands and said firmly, "I am."

The first clue was *maps*. Still thinking of Viola Cavendish's lemon and rosemary scent, he said, "Italy," which elicited snickers and a hearty "Wrong!" from Bridget.

The second clue was *fire*. Wes puzzled over it until he remembered the admonition to be witty, so he replied, "Christopher Wren." Wren had remade the map of London after the great fire. But his inquisitors only giggled and told him he was wrong again.

The next clue was a dreadful screech, emitted right near his ear, rather like a seagull whose tail was being plucked out. Wes almost bolted out of the chair, but Justin's muffled laughter stayed him just in time. He thought for a moment, decided to be ridiculous, and said, "A history professor who's fallen asleep over his pipe, and set his robes afire."

Lady Bridget hooted with laughter, and the others joined in a moment later. "Better, but still wrong," Justin told him. Wes would have blinked, if his eyes weren't bound shut. Had that been approval in his nephew's voice?

Fourth clue: a gust of air in his face. He thought hard, and said, "A phoenix." There was a moment of silence, which made him hopeful, but then someone said, "Incorrect."

The fifth clue was *Odysseus,* which pricked his interest. Now he began to concentrate in earnest. "Cyclops," he guessed, only to be told he was once more wrong.

The sixth clue took a moment. Wes's mind worked the whole while. Maps, fire, Odysseus, wind, and shrieks. He suspected Justin had put forth this mystery item, to stymie him, and now he was absolutely determined to win. It didn't hurt that he'd caught Mrs. Cavendish's voice saying something quietly, no doubt to Lady Sophronia. It was idiotic and foolish, but he wanted to tear off the blindfold—after he won—and see her smiling at him, surprised and impressed. She was the duchess's secretary, only a few steps up from a servant, but she had the most marvelous green eyes, like the sea in the West Indies after a storm . . .

He was so lost in contemplation of her eyes, it was a total shock to receive a splash of water right on his cheek. Quite a lot of water, actually; it ran down his face and wet his cravat, and there was a dismayed gasp as he reached up to wipe his face. "Bridget," moaned a female voice.

So much for impressing anyone. But the water made him think of the sea in the West Indies after a storm—hang it, also of maps of the ocean, especially medieval ones with illustrations on every corner, and when he said, "Sea serpent," a startled hush fell over the room.

"Am I wrong again?" he asked after a moment.

"Er—no," said Justin, sounding a little nonplussed. "You're correct."

"Near enough, anyway," said Lady Bridget. "It was 'sea monster.'"

"I ought to receive an extra point, for being more precise." Wes pulled off the blindfold, and found he was staring directly at Mrs. Cavendish. She was leaning toward Lady Sophronia but gazing at him, her eyes wide and her lips parted. Their gazes collided and lingered for a moment, then she turned away, a faint pink in her cheeks.

"Well done, Lord Winterton." Lady Bridget stepped forward and offered him a towel. "You trounced Lord Newton and won the round. And I do apologize for throwing a bit too much water."

"I told you no boy would outsmart a man in his prime," crowed Lady Sophronia from her perch beside Mrs. Cavendish. "Didn't I, Viola?"

Her murmured reply was too low for him to hear, alas, as it came just as the butler entered to announce dinner. Lady Bridget bounded forward. "Hurrah! I'm famished!"

"Winterton, you may lend me your arm," announced Lady Sophronia, rising from the sofa. Wes obeyed the command immediately, taking the chance to exchange a quick glance with Mrs. Cavendish. Her eyes glowed with mirth and when she stepped aside to make way for Lady Sophronia, her skirts brushed his leg, sending a charge up his spine.

Good Lord, what was happening to him? Wes tried to focus his attention on the elderly lady clinging to his arm. She was giving directions to all the other guests, pairing them up in no discernible way. She told Justin, a viscount, to give Lady Alexandra his arm, while Lady Serena was assigned to Mr. Jones, a mere gentleman. But no one seemed willing to argue with her, and they went in to dinner.

As he pulled out Lady Sophronia's chair, Wes scanned the table, confirming his suspicion. Sophronia hadn't told Mrs. Cavendish what to do; he'd hoped it was because there weren't enough gentlemen present—counting himself, there were only five, while there were seven ladies—but it appeared Mrs. Cavendish would not be joining them for dinner.

Which was unaccountably disappointing.

CHAPTER THREE

The next morning Wes was determined to see if the Duke of Wessex owned the atlas he coveted.

Logically, the most likely place was the library. Even better, at this time of morning he should be able to explore it in solitary peace. Wes had a vague notion that ladies never emerged from their bedchambers before noon, and judging by the silent stillness of the wing where he and Justin had been settled, neither would his nephew. Excellent.

After a quick breakfast in the dining room—barren of all other guests, but laid out with enough dishes to feed a regiment—he asked the butler to direct him. The Kingstag library was on the ground floor, set at the rear of the house. It was a long, narrow graceful room, with tall windows looking out on the snow, still falling thickly beyond the glass. Fires were burning in the hearths at each end of the library, and there were comfortable-looking chairs and sofas arranged at artful intervals. At the far end of the room stood a pair of large globes behind a settee, which immediately caught his eye. He made a note to examine them at a more opportune moment.

Because, unfortunately, he had not discovered the room quiet and deserted. There were a large number of people already there. On the settee before those globes sat Lady Alexandra, smiling and laughing with one of the young ladies Wes dimly recalled meeting last night, and—to his surprise—Justin, who hadn't willingly risen before ten any morning since they'd left Hampshire. Today his nephew seemed quite pleased to be awake, smartly attired and freshly shaved and vying for the ladies' attention with another young dandy. Nearer the doorway where Wes stood, Lady Bridget was pacing, waving her arms as she spoke to Mrs. Cavendish, seated on a chair in front of the windows and studying some pages in her hands.

No one looked up at his entrance.

Wes paused in indecision. Retreat in silence and return later, when he could examine any atlases in the room at leisure? Or stay to see what had put that charming little frown on Mrs. Cavendish's face?

"It makes no sense, Bridget," Mrs. Cavendish said. "You've written lines for a *swan.*"

"Does art need to follow every dictate of logic? *No,* I say," declared Lady Bridget. "It is supposed to transport one's soul."

"Obviously," murmured the other woman. "But you must have some sense of story—"

"It's a farce, Viola. They don't need to make sense."

The expression on Mrs. Cavendish's face—perplexed, thwarted, and amused all at once—made Wes want to laugh. He did laugh, in fact, a bare catching of breath in his throat, but it made the lady look at him, her green eyes wide with surprise. He tried to cover it with a cough, then thumped himself on the chest. "I beg your pardon," he said.

"Good morning, my lord." Mrs. Cavendish got to her feet and handed Lady Bridget the pages with a speaking look. The young lady took them to the desk and began writing, scribbling out one long line. Perhaps the swan had lost his part. "Were you looking for someone?"

You. The unexpected thought caught him off guard, and Wes coughed again, a little too hard. "No," he rasped. "I was looking for the library."

She smiled. "You've discovered it! As have most of the other guests. Lady Bridget is working on her play."

"Farce," said the girl, sotto voce.

Mrs. Cavendish closed her eyes for a second. "Were you seeking something in particular?"

"Er . . . A book," he said, unable to think of anything more intelligent to say.

She gave him a patient look. Anyone looking for the library would naturally be seeking a book. "Of course. Have you anything in particular—?"

"No, no, I'll just have a look around. Don't mind me," he said hastily. He strode to the nearest shelf and frowned thoughtfully at it.

"I don't say that the play must be a model of logic and wit, but even a farce has some sense to it." Mrs. Cavendish returned to her conversation with Lady Bridget, her voice lower but still audible to Wes's alert ears.

"This scene has sense! See, the pirate arrives to find the swan sick with love for the lonely spinster, which stokes his own affections for her."

"But on the next page you've got a ghost arriving to deliver a prophecy."

"That also makes sense. He's a ghost because he drowned in a flood. As there's a pirate and a swan, a flood would affect both of them."

Wes choked on another laugh, trying again to make it into a cough. He could just picture the struggle Mrs. Cavendish was undergoing. The ladies behind him fell silent. He realized he was staring at a selection of books about sheep farming, about which he knew nothing and cared even less, and walked to the next bookcase.

Their conversation resumed, even more quietly. "But Bridget, the prophecy is about who shall marry the prince. Where is the prince?"

A gusty sigh, presumably from Lady Bridget. "Viola, there must be a prince."

"Why?"

"I don't know, I haven't written that part yet!"

This time he coughed so hard to cover his amusement, he felt light-headed. It would serve him right if he fainted right here in front of everyone because he'd been eavesdropping. Justin was glaring at him in incredulous outrage, and by the time Wes fished out his handkerchief to mop his stinging eyes, Mrs. Cavendish was beside him.

"I will ring for the maids to dust," she said. "I do apologize, my lord, I'd no idea it was so unpleasant in here."

"Not at all," he croaked through dry lips. Hoist by his own damn petard.

"Then let me send for a cup of tea," she suggested. "I could have it sent to your room, if you wish."

"Yes, Uncle, I do think that would be a good idea," Justin put in from across the room. "You must mind your health, after our long journey here."

Wes glared at him as he stuffed the handkerchief back into his pocket. *Mind his health,* indeed, as if he were a feeble old man. He might look deranged after this, but he was not feeble. "Entirely unnecessary, Mrs. Cavendish. Some fresh air is all I need. Perhaps I'll take a turn in the garden."

"It's snowing out, you know," put in Lady Bridget. "Absolutely pelting down. The doors are probably frozen shut. Tea in the morning room would be far more comfortable."

"Serena and Mr. Jones are in there," said Lady Alexandra.

Bridget's head came up. "Arguing?"

Her sister looked surprised. "No, silly, why would they be arguing? Serena despises him. I think they're rehearsing lines for your ridiculous play."

"Farce," said Bridget.

"A talking swan is ridiculous." The young man beside her raised his brows, and she gave him a teasing smile. "Yes, Lord Gosling, I know you play the swan. I'm sure you shall do your best, but you must admit it *is* ridiculous."

"Not in the slightest," declared Lord Gosling, executing a gallant bow toward Lady Bridget. "All the best actors have played swans. I hope to give the premier portrayal." Lady Alexandra and the girl beside her burst into laughter.

Bridget's mouth thinned. "I shall write something even better for you, Alexa."

The other girl rolled her eyes at Justin, who laughed indulgently. Wes could see very well what was happening there: Lady Alexandra was lovely, and competition always sparked a man's spirit. He tried to send Justin a look of warning, but his nephew deliberately avoided his gaze.

"Are we all to get special parts, Lady Bridget? I could fancy being a prince," Justin said. Casually he propped one foot on the base of the globe beside Lady Alexandra's settee, and rested his elbow on his knee. Wes scowled at the rakish pose.

"It depends." Her gaze moved to Wes. "Lord Winterton, what sort of character would you like to play?"

"I?" he asked, startled.

"Yes, I'm considering adding an elderly king, in the vein of King Lear. I expect he'll have to die so his son the prince can become king. Would that suit you? How would you like to die?"

Justin snorted with laughter. Lady Alexandra smiled, and the other young lady giggled.

"*Bridget,*" gasped Mrs. Cavendish. "My lord, perhaps you'd like to see the house?"

He ought to stay to keep an eye on his nephew. He burned to search the shelves for the Desnos atlas. He did not want to walk away from all the slights on his age and health without protest or at least a show of vigor. Instead he looked into Mrs. Cavendish's desperate green eyes and said, "Thank you, I very much would."

"I hope you feel better, Uncle," said Justin, as Wes followed her toward the door.

"Have some tea," added Lady Alexandra. "Cook makes splendid tea cakes."

"And stay indoors!" Lady Bridget said just as Mrs. Cavendish pulled the door shut behind them with a bit of a bang.

$\mathcal{V}$iola heaved a heartfelt sigh and rested her forehead against the door for a moment. It was silent and cool in the corridor, although perhaps it only seemed that way to her. What had got into Alexandra and Bridget?

Never mind—she knew very well. Lord Gosling was nothing short of beautiful, and had the most perfect manners she'd ever seen. Viola suspected the dowager duchess had invited the young viscount in case Serena and Frye never made up their estrangement, but Alexandra seemed to have taken matters into her own hands. Add in the also-handsome Viscount Newton, and things could only get dangerous. Viola devoutly hoped the other young people would join them soon and defuse the subtly competitive air between the two gentlemen.

In the meantime she had to deal with the Earl of Winterton, who had just been insulted and practically ordered out of the library. Bracing herself, she turned to face him.

He had a right to be very put out; instead he was grinning, and as their eyes met, he began to laugh. In sheer relief, Viola gave a gasp of laughter herself.

"I'm sorry," she began, trying to regain her dignity, but the earl waved one hand.

"For being a sensible adult in a room full of silly young people? I assure you, your offer of a tour could not have come at a more opportune moment." He made a face. "I could almost feel myself aging and sinking into senility. In a few more moments I would have been relegated to dozing in the corner with a cap on my head, tended by a nurse."

She laughed. She couldn't think of anyone less likely to be found dozing in the corner in need of a nurse than Lord Winterton. Today he was even more handsome than before, if that were possible, his blue eyes dancing with mirth. "The young ladies are a trifle high-spirited at times."

Winterton assumed a tragic expression. "I suppose I've forgotten what it's like to be young and full of life."

"It looks very tiring," she replied in the same grave tone.

His grin returned, and the rogue even winked at her. "For those around them, perhaps."

Viola laughed again in spite of herself. She was astonished at her young cousins' behavior, and was enormously relieved that the earl wasn't taking them much to heart. She ought to have guessed that Lord Winterton, who appeared to be an intelligent and educated man, would seek out the library once confined to the house by the steadily falling snow. Tomorrow she would banish everyone from the room. Perhaps Bridget, if left to write her play without the sly goading of her sister, would embrace some form of sense, or at least hurry up and finish the silly thing.

"If you wanted a particular book, I shall have a footman brave the room to fetch it," she said. "The Kingstag library is exceptional, and I'm sure it can supply something to suit you."

Winterton stared at her with those blue, blue eyes for a long moment. "I rather fancy a tour of the house, as you suggested. If you wouldn't mind."

"Oh," said Viola in surprise. She'd offered in desperation, to escape before Bridget said or did anything to give actual offense. "Of course not." She gestured with one arm. "Shall we?"

He fell in step beside her, hands clasped behind his back. Viola tried to ignore the awareness that rippled through her. She had given many tours of the castle in her two years here; the duke and duchess entertained a steady stream of guests. This should be no different . . . but it was.

"The oldest parts of the castle date from the fifteenth century," she began. "The first duke was given the land for his service to the crown. He was by then a rather elderly gentleman, but his grandson, the second duke, built the central part of the castle."

"The Cavendish family has been in Dorset a long time."

"Yes." Viola opened the door they had reached. "This wing of the castle is relatively new, added only fifty years ago and hence quite modern. Here is the billiard room. Some of the young gentlemen have taken to playing in the evening."

"A fine room," the earl said approvingly, studying the carved mahogany table. It was a very masculine room, done up in the highest quality. Viola remembered her first reaction on realizing the castle held a room dedicated solely to one game—a game no one in the family played much—and quietly closed the door.

"I couldn't help but notice your name is also Cavendish," Winterton remarked as they walked onward.

Her shoulders stiffened involuntarily. She was used to this question, but he must know the answer. She was hardly the first poor relation to be taken in by a family, but it still stung, that reminder— even unintentional—that she had once been mistress of her own home instead of a servant in someone else's. "Yes. My late husband, actually, was a cousin of His Grace." She lowered her voice and gave a rueful smile. "A very *distant* cousin, not one tenth as grand."

"Ah—no. I didn't mean . . ." He grimaced, but with a sheepish grin that made her want to smile back. "I was contemplating how difficult it is to speak to my nephew, and wondering if perhaps you had any suggestions to offer me, since you seem to be in a similar position. Having to advise and reason with your younger relations, I mean."

"Oh!" She made a small motion with one hand, embarrassed but also pleased. "I wish I could say yes, but it's not really the same at all. We're only distant relations, the young ladies and I, and they rightly look to their mother the dowager duchess, or even to the duchess herself, for advice."

"But they don't openly wish for you to leave the room," he pointed out. "At least not in your hearing."

Viola laughed. "Perhaps that's because I have no real authority over them. It renders me utterly powerless to spoil any schemes or plots they may have."

The earl tipped his head in thought. "Perhaps there's something in that. On the other hand, Newton has only held his viscountcy for a few months. He's in desperate want of counsel, whether he admits it or not."

"I have long noticed that often, the more desperately someone needs guidance, the better it is to wait for him to ask for it. Urging your excellent thoughts and ideas upon him only gets the bit between his teeth, so to speak, and sets him against everything you say."

"I see." He gave her an appraising glance. "And do you sit by and watch as they make a muddle of things?"

Viola smiled. As if she had any choice, when it came to Serena, Alexandra, and Bridget. "I find it helps me hold my tongue if I think of the things I did and said when I was that age. It usually quashes my righteous disapproval."

"Good lord," he murmured with a rueful expression. His lips quirked as he gazed at her. "Quite right it would."

Viola could have stood there all day smiling back at him. The realization made her blink and turn away; *do not be too familiar with an earl,* she told herself. She opened the wide double doors to the gallery. "The formal gallery. It contains a portrait of every duke and duchess as well as many other family portraits and mementos. Would you care to see?"

He inclined his head, so she led the way into the long, narrow room and opened some of the shutters for light. No doubt he had a similar room at his own family seat, but he gave every appearance of interest. In the best of circumstances it was a dramatic room, reflective of the wealth and power that had concentrated in the person of the Duke of Wessex over four hundred years. Today it was gray and dim, the snow casting its pall through the tall windows. Viola returned to the door as Winterton strolled the gallery. She didn't want to spend any more time in the chilly room—no fires had been laid in here—but a wicked part of her also took advantage of the opportunity to watch the earl openly.

It was unfair for one man to be so handsome. Lord Gosling was beautiful in a boyish way; the Earl of Winterton was a mesmerizing man in the prime of life. His dark hair was a rumple of unruly waves today, curling over his brow like a classical statue. He paused in front of a portrait, raising his chin to study it, and Viola's eyes skimmed over the lines of his profile. His nose was straight but not large, his jaw firm. He turned to continue his circuit of the room and her gaze drifted lower over broad shoulders, clad in a royal blue coat. His hands, still clasped behind his hips, were elegant, long-fingered and strong. Viola tore her eyes away but not before noticing that his backside was also rather perfectly shaped. She fixed her gaze on the vase on the mantel and kept it there as his footsteps echoed softly in the silent room. *Do not ogle an earl,* she scolded herself. What had come over her?

"A veritable museum of Cavendish history." Lord Winterton returned to her side.

Viola smiled. "Yes. The dowager duchess take a particular interest in maintaining it."

"The lady above the fireplace, I take it." He turned toward the portrait in question, and Viola's attention snagged once more on the sensual set of his lips before she yanked her gaze away.

"Yes. Miss Alice Penworth, when that was painted soon before her marriage." In the painting the dowager duchess was young and beautiful, glowing with love and happiness. It was no secret her marriage to the late duke had been one of love, which had ended tragically some seventeen years ago with the duke's sudden death, when Bridget was a baby.

"Her youngest daughter has her looks."

Viola nodded. "All the young ladies do, to some extent. They have their father's coloring. His Grace looks very like his father, though."

"Does he?" He scanned the walls. "Which is he?"

She glanced at him in surprise. The portrait of the late duke looked almost exactly like the current duke; Wessex was the image of his father, from his deep-set eyes and stern face to his height and build. "There." She indicated the portrait between the windows, at an angle from the dowager's. The arrangement and their respective poses made it appear that the late duke and his wife were gazing in adoration at each other across the room.

35

"Of course." Winterton went to stand in front of it. "It's very like Wessex, you say?"

Slowly she followed him. "To the life." She hesitated. "Are you not acquainted with His Grace, then?" She had assumed he must be a rather close friend, for the duke to invite him to Kingstag at Christmastime. Wessex was devoted to his family and guarded his time with them closely. The dowager duchess was the one who had planned the house party, and only then because of Serena's recent heartbreak.

"Not really, no," said the earl. He seemed absorbed in the painting. "He's a stern man, I take it."

Oh dear heaven. Had she let a perfect stranger into the castle? The earl claimed to have an appointment, but he'd offered no proof and Viola had never heard warning of his visit from Mr. Martin, who normally kept her apprised of things like that. The duke and duchess preferred their schedules be kept aligned. Her spine stiffened and she said, "I suppose you'll have to form your own opinion."

"Our correspondence was cordial," he said. "And the rumors I heard paint him a passionate, romantic fellow."

The rumors were probably about how the duke had married. Before he met his duchess, Wessex had been engaged to another woman—Miss Helen Gray, now Mrs. Blair. That wedding had been called off at the very last minute, and within days the duke married Cleo and Miss Gray married Mr. Blair. Viola had heard many versions of the story from the Cavendish girls, but she wasn't sure how much truth lay in them. Bridget declared her brother fell in love with his betrothed bride's sister at first sight and pined away until Helen took pity on him and released him from the engagement. Serena believed the sisters had worked it out between the two of them, which one would become the duchess, with all its duties and responsibility, and which one would get James Blair, who was a great favorite of the girls. Alexandra claimed Mr. Blair challenged the duke to a duel over Miss Gray, whom he had been secretly in love with for ages, and the duke stepped aside because *he* was secretly in love with Cleo.

It all sounded highly melodramatic and very unlike the reserved, practical duke she knew. Privately she suspected it had been an arranged marriage between Wessex and Helen Gray in the first place, and once they had a chance to know each other a bit they had realized how wretched their union would have been, a disaster averted in the nick of time. Viola had had many opportunities to see Wessex and Mrs. Blair together, and there was no chance, in her opinion, that either of them could have believed they would suit each other.

On the other hand, one could all but hear the passion crackling between Wessex and his duchess, while the Blairs were the picture of bliss. Whatever had happened, it had certainly ended happily for all of them.

Not that she would ever tell the Earl of Winterton any of that.

"You must judge for yourself," she said again. *Please let the duke and duchess return early,* she silently wished. "Would you like to see the rest of the house now?"

The earl couldn't miss the coolness in her tone. He turned to her, his azure eyes brighter than ever, and smiled—warmly, as if to reassure her. "Very much, Mrs. Cavendish."

CHAPTER FOUR

$\mathcal{W}$es went down to dinner more curious about Mrs. Cavendish than about the location of the Desnos atlas.

His tour of the house had been cut short when a servant came to inform Mrs. Cavendish that the dowager duchess wanted to see her. From the alarm that flashed over her face for a moment, Wes guessed that his absent hostess was keeping an eye on things from afar. But the end result was that his companion excused herself, and he didn't set eyes on her for the rest of the day.

It left him free to amuse himself, and he did try to redirect his thoughts toward the Desnos. After a calculated delay, he returned to the library. This time only Lady Bridget was in the room, pacing and muttering to herself. At his entrance, she stopped short.

"I beg your pardon," Wes said with a slight bow. "Mrs. Cavendish was called away, and I hoped to find a book to read."

The young lady pressed her lips together, but curtseyed. "Of course. I was about to go to the drawing room anyway. Do come in, sir, and help yourself to any books you fancy." She went to the desk, gathered her papers, and left.

Wes stood back as she went by him. He hadn't meant to chase her away, but he wasn't about to protest being left alone in the library for a while. He headed straight for the globes, presuming any travel books would be there.

An hour of hunting did not turn up the Desnos, nor any atlas which might be mistaken for it. He stood drumming his fingers on the table, wishing he could ask Mrs. Cavendish. She must know. She appeared to know everything that went on in the house.

And yet he doubted she would tell him, even if she knew precisely where the Desnos was. He had been mesmerized by her, and felt an unwarranted eagerness to take a tour of Kingstag Castle when she offered. But he hadn't missed the chill that came over her demeanor after he revealed that he didn't know the Duke of Wessex personally. She wasn't merely the duke's employee, she was also a relation. The widow of a distant, lowly cousin, in her telling, but one who clearly took her familial connection seriously.

Wes had distant relations who turned to him for support or assistance. He supposed he employed some of them; he'd been away from Winterbury Hall so much, he wasn't entirely sure. He *was* certain none of them were members of his personal household, and he was quite sure none of them were remotely as attractive as she was.

Mrs Cavendish, though, was a member of the family here. He eavesdropped on her easy conversation with Lady Bridget with amusement, but also envy. His discussions with Justin were never so affectionate or so . . . so . . . peaceful. It was genuine curiosity in part that drove him to ask her advice.

Wes didn't think too much on the other reasons he felt like seeking her out.

When he reached the parlor where the guests were gathered before dinner, Justin gave him a severe look. Wes ignored it. Mrs. Cavendish was engaged in conversation, so he skirted the throng of young people, biding his time, and as he did so another lady caught his eye.

"Good evening, ma'am." He bowed before Lady Sophronia.

She looked him up and down. "Winterton! It's about time. You may sit with me; all the handsome men do."

Amused, he took the seat next to her on the sofa. Lady Sophronia was tiny and must be over ninety, but her hair was still elaborately arranged, and dyed an unnatural shade of red. Unlike many elderly ladies who clung to the fashions of their youth, she wore a modern gown, although with the most unusual cape over her shoulders.

She noticed him looking at it. "Otter," she confided, stroking it gently. "A gift from my second fiancé. Such a fine man he was; Russian, you see, and so virile."

Wes blinked. "Indeed."

"Have you been to Russia?" She nodded at Lady Alexandra, who was holding court for Justin and some of the other young people by the windows. "Alexandra tells me you're quite a world traveler."

"I have been to Russia, ma'am, though only once, and not for long. I prefer climates warmer than England, not colder."

She gave a snort of laughter. "Missed your mark this time! There hasn't been this much snow at Kingstag in decades. I should know, I've been here for seven of them."

"Have you really?" he said in admiration. "You must know everything there is to know about the castle, then."

Her gaze turned sharp. "More than likely. What's sparked your curiosity?"

Unconsciously he glanced at Mrs. Cavendish. She was speaking to the eldest Cavendish girl, Lady Serena. "Nothing specific," he said absently. "Mrs. Cavendish very kindly took me on a tour of the house today."

"Did she? Viola's a good girl." Lady Sophronia nodded. "Wretched luck, of course, but she's got spirit. I like her."

"Wretched luck?" Wes tried to look only mildly interested, even though he'd gone tense and somehow concerned. Did Sophronia only mean that she was a widow? Reduced to working for wages? What bad luck had Viola Cavendish suffered?

The elderly lady shook her head and wagged her finger at him. "It's not my place to tell you her life story. If you want to know, you'll have to get it from her."

Wes sat up a little straighter. "Indeed, Lady Sophronia, I meant no offense—"

She cackled with laughter. "No, of course not! You can't keep your eyes off her. I may be old but I'm not blind. She's a pretty girl . . ." She paused, her head tilted thoughtfully to one side, and gave a small shrug. "Not a girl, I suppose, but certainly young enough to be foolish about some things. Well, I'll tell you this: her husband—a good lad, James, but no head for money, and a man without money is hardly worth marrying—was Wessex's third cousin. Their great-great-grandfather was my uncle, and a duller person you never met. He was a Calvinist and as a consequence never spent a farthing on anything frivolous in his life. What a waste!" She shook her head, looking piqued. "He left his children provided for, but James . . . The men in that branch of the family are handsome as

40

anything, but idiots, all of them, each in his own way. Thank goodness Wessex inherited some sense with his title, or we'd all be living on turnips and roasted squirrels. Have you ever eaten a squirrel?"

"Er." Wes blinked at the diversion. "No. A crocodile once, on the banks of the Nile. But James . . .?" For once he had no interest in talking about his travels.

Sophronia seemed pleased. "Crocodile! How exotic." She gave him a triumphant smile. "I knew you were not a dull person. I have no patience for dullards. You must tell me more about Egypt, and your visit to Russia. I always longed to see Sergei's homeland. A Cossack shot him before we could marry. Such a cowardly thing to do. A proper duel with swords would have been at least romantic and exciting."

"Of course," he said, trying once more to get the conversation on more interesting topics. "I take it Wessex was close to his third cousin?"

"What? Oh no, he barely knew the boy." She frowned. "Such a pity. James's grandmother was my bosom friend. We had such times together! But she had a weak heart, as did all her family; they died young, every one of them I can remember. Naturally Wessex would look after James's widow, but Viola was the one who insisted on a position."

"She seems part of the family." He watched as the woman in question spoke quietly to Lady Serena, who smiled warmly in return and clasped her hand for a moment. "Quite warmly received."

Sophronia scoffed. "She knows how to make herself useful! I do admire that in a person, you know; people who know how to do things are wonderful to have around."

"Then it seems a very fortunate thing for all, that she's here."

"Indeed," said Sophronia. "As for how long she'll stay . . ." She raised her shoulders. "Well, necessity will guide that, I suppose."

Wes tried to look only politely curious. "Necessity?"

Sophronia glanced around furtively, and lowered her voice. "Oh yes, she has very good cause to stay for now. Later? Who can say. But she'll likely not see reason, not where *he's* concerned."

"Ladies and gentlemen, shall we go in to dinner?" Lady Serena blushed and smiled prettily as she made her announcement. At her side, Mrs. Cavendish gave a tiny nod of approval, and even the butler looked proud.

Wes mustered a smile and helped Lady Sophronia to her feet. She waved him away and summoned Lady Bridget, who hurried over, and they began a quiet but animated conversation.

He strolled off, wondering what she'd meant. Who was *he*? Why was Mrs Cavendish only in her post because of *him*, and why was she unreasonable about him? All in all, Lady Sophronia had only inspired more questions than she'd answered.

Well. Perhaps he was unreasonable for being so interested. If he wanted to know more about the lady, he ought to own his interest honestly and speak to the woman. He was nothing but a gossipy bore if he pried into her history from afar and never made an effort to know her. And if he became less interested as a result of that effort, then he neither deserved or needed to know every detail of her past.

He would just have to keep reminding himself of that every time she smiled at him.

CHAPTER FIVE

$\mathcal{F}$or the first few days of the party, Viola felt confidently in control. Serena was doing an admirable job as hostess, Bridget's ideas for entertainments stayed within the bounds of propriety, and even Sophronia was behaving herself. Every day she reported to the dowager duchess that all was well.

By the third day, the novelty of the deep snow began to wear off. Alexandra snapped at Serena, who told her to go sulk in her room if she couldn't be civil. Lord Newton and Mr. Jones got into a testy argument about sleigh racing. One of Serena's dearest friends, Miss Kate Lacy, arrived at last after being delayed by the storm, but so did a mysterious young man called Conte Luigi Mascapone. Viola knew he was not on the guest list and despaired of what to do with him, but Lady Sophronia clasped him in her arms, declared he was the grandson of a dear friend of hers, and invited him on the spot to stay for the party. Viola could do nothing but send the housekeeper to prepare a room for him.

Lord Winterton seemed to be either hiding from the young people, which Viola could somewhat understand, or fascinated by Kingstag; more than once she bumped into him in some unusual part of the house. He claimed to be lost, which was reasonable, but she was beginning to wonder how such a world traveler had such a poor sense of direction.

The last straw was catching Bridget doing something suspicious in the library on the fourth day.

Viola didn't actually know what Bridget was doing. She went to inquire how the play was progressing—by then she was in desperate search of anything to occupy the rest of the guests, and Bridget had holed up in the library promising to have a new act ready before dinner for people to rehearse. But when she opened the door, Bridget was not at the desk, writing diligently on her play. She was standing in front of an open French window, letting powdery snow blow into the room.

"Bridget!"

With a startled motion the girl slammed the door. The glass shuddered so hard Viola feared it would break.

"What are you doing?" Viola hurried across the room. Snow was blowing against the glass, and the wind blew loudly against the castle walls, throwing up white powder that sparkled in the weak winter sun.

"Getting some fresh air." Bridget widened her eyes innocently and went back to the desk. She dropped into the chair and bent over her papers, scribbling away.

Suspicious, Viola scanned the terrace outside. She could see no one, but were there footsteps in the snow leading from the door around the corner? It was hard to tell in the glittering breeze. "Was someone here on the terrace?"

"In all this snow?" Bridget scoffed. "Who would traipse through it?"

"That isn't an outright denial."

Bridget made a face, her pen still skimming across the page. "I suppose if you think someone might decide to wander through the snow to chat through an open window, there's nothing I can do to dissuade you. Go out and search, if you like."

Viola was certain the girl was lying, but there was nothing she could do. She turned the lock on the French window just in case, and went back to the desk. "How is the play coming along? Everyone is quite anxious to have more scenes to rehearse."

"It's bloody brilliant," said Bridget with satisfaction. "Original and ridiculous and everything a farce should be. Read this." She pushed some pages across the table.

Viola picked them up and began reading, only to catch a slight motion from the corner of her eye. Bridget had slid something beneath the blotter. Her eyes narrowed, but she kept her mouth closed. She'd got into a battle of wills with Bridget before and always ended up completely routed. There was no one here, and as Bridget had said, the snow was much too deep for anyone to have snuck into the Kingstag gardens and up to this terrace.

That said, Viola would have wagered a week's salary that Bridget had been talking to someone through that open door.

"It does sound ridiculous," she commented after reading the scene Bridget had given her.

The girl beamed. "Doesn't it? And so fitting for Serena."

Viola read again. "That she's pursued by a swan?"

"Well, that's what Frye is," Bridget replied. "Handsome but cruel."

"But Lord Gosling plays the swan, not Frye."

"Drrr!" Bridget rolled her eyes. "Obviously I could not write a part for Frye, because he's not here. Gosling will do just as nicely, though. I don't care for him."

"Because . . ." Viola couldn't even think of a reason.

"He's too agreeable! Whatever odd thing I write for him, he smiles and carries on. Agreeable men are so very disagreeable, don't you think?"

She laid the pages back on the table. "If you say so . . ."

Bridget beamed again. She knew she'd won.

On the fifth day things slipped a bit further out of control. Lady Sophronia had taken over supervising the play rehearsals, with Bridget's help when the latter wasn't off in the library writing, and Viola was shocked to see her almost encouraging Mr. Jones, playing a pirate from Shropshire of all places, to kiss Serena, playing a maiden—or, as Bridget insisted on calling her, a Lonely Spinster. The kiss wasn't called for in the script, although the pirate did bear away the maiden at some point, but Viola was alarmed by this. She managed to insert herself into the direction and even the acting twice, but finally Sophronia pinned a gimlet gaze on her.

"Dear Viola," she said, "I have not seen Lord Winterton in an age. The poor man, he must be feeling very put out to arrive and have no one to look after him."

Viola blinked. "Lady Sophronia, he's quite comfortable. He assures me so every morning." Viola looked forward to those brief meetings over breakfast; it was easily the most pleasant conversation she had all day. Her worries about the earl had subsided. He might not know Wessex personally, but he was clearly a gentleman and had behaved with the utmost propriety.

But he *had* been strolling all over the castle, and Sophronia's words planted a seed of doubt. Perhaps she had neglected him. She could hardly blame the man for avoiding the antics of the young people, who were scouring the castle for props and costumes and— Viola was sure—a bit of mischief whenever possible.

"Balderdash," said Sophronia bluntly. "A man won't say when he's bored, Viola, he shows you. Winterton has been wandering the corridors like a lost child. I'm very much afraid he shan't give a good report of our hospitality to Wessex."

Viola's lips thinned at this transparent effort to get her out of the drawing room. "I am sure Lord Winterton understands the circumstances."

"But do you want to chance it?" Sophronia looked past her as Viola reeled. "Bridget! What have you got for us today?"

"A new scene, but we lack any suitable props." Bridget plopped onto the sofa beside her great-aunt. Sophronia leaned her head close to see the pages she held. Viola had long since decided that Bridget was Sophronia reborn, exuberant and irrepressible. "Viola, could you help locate them? Everyone else is busy rehearsing."

She shifted uneasily. The pair of them were looking at her so innocently, it immediately put up her guard. "What do you need?" Perhaps it could be found swiftly and she could be back before anything untoward happened . . .

Bridget consulted her pages. "A large book, a cape—preferably red velvet; what do you think, Aunt Sophronia?"

"Oh yes, definitely red velvet," said the old lady in delight.

"A set of goblets that may be thrown around and not break, and an iron chain."

Viola, having listened in growing dread, blinked at the last. "An iron chain?" she cried. "Bridget, what's in this play?"

"A ghost," said Bridget patiently. "I've told you that for days. But we haven't got a chain, or a crown—"

"A crown?"

"He's the ghost of the king."

Viola put one hand to her temple. "You said the ghost delivered a prophecy *about* the king."

"Yes. And then the king dies and becomes another ghost." Bridget smiled as if she'd just answered every question. "And the prince becomes king after that, you see."

Viola stared helplessly. "Of course."

"There must be a chain and a crown somewhere in the house," Bridget went on. "It is a castle, after all. Ask Mama if you cannot find them on your own." She paused, then added, in a markedly offhand manner, "Perhaps Lord Winterton would help you look."

Viola glanced at Sophronia, who merely gave a tiny smile and nod, and knew she was stuck. "Very well, I shall ask him. But you must promise to behave," she added in a lower voice.

Sophronia waved both hands. "Of course! Of course!"

"No more kisses on stage," Viola added, casting a glance at Serena and Mr. Jones. Serena was talking to Lord Gosling, but Mr. Jones was watching her with a strangely pensive expression. She was afraid the kissing would give the poor man ideas, which would be unfortunate. Frye might be despised as a scoundrel by Alexandra and Bridget, but Viola knew the dowager duchess still hoped Serena's erstwhile suitor would return and persuade her to mend the broken engagement.

Bridget rolled her eyes. "We need the chain desperately. Otherwise Mr. Penworth will have no way to rehearse his scene, which is vital to the plot."

"We cannot have that," said Sophronia at once. "Viola, I am certain no one can find these things as quickly as you can."

Viola very much doubted there was a plot to this play, but she couldn't overrule Lady Sophronia. She nodded and went to find the earl.

He was in the small parlor near the grand hall, admiring a book of engravings laid out on a table near the windows. He glanced up as she came in, and a broad smile crossed his face. "Mrs. Cavendish. How does our grand entertainment progress?"

"I cannot speak to its grandiosity, nor to it being entertaining," she said wryly. "I have been sent in search of props, and hoped I might enlist you as well."

"Of course." He closed the book and faced her. "What are we in search of, and where should we begin?"

"That's why I need help," she replied. "A most ridiculous list, and I haven't the first idea."

His eyes lit up and he grinned. "Excellent! An adventure."

"That it will be," she agreed, and they set out.

One item was easily accomplished. A visit to the kitchens and a few words with the cook unearthed some tinware that the actors could throw and not break. Viola told a footman to take it to the drawing room where the play was being staged, and they went in search of the next item.

"A scarlet cloak," mused the earl. "Surely one of the ladies has a suitable one?"

Viola hoped so. By good luck they ran into Miss Penworth on her way to the music room. She was very talented on the pianoforte, and Bridget had assigned her the task of choosing and playing dramatic music for the play. Viola had lost all reserve by now, and spurred by Lord Winterton's suggestion, she asked Miss Penworth if she or any of the young ladies had brought a red cloak. Fortune smiled on her; the young woman had brought such a cloak, and promised to send it to the drawing room.

"Thank you," said Viola fervently. "I hope Lady Bridget's play does no harm to it."

Miss Penworth laughed. "I've known Bridget all my life," she confided. "If it does, I am already well aware that His Grace will replace the cloak. He replaced my doll when Bridget drowned it in the lake, two bonnets lost to escapades planned by Bridget, and more hair ribbons than either of us could count."

Viola breathed a sigh of relief as they left Miss Penworth to her practicing. "Two down, three to go."

"What's next?" the earl wanted to know.

"A crown, a large book, and an iron chain." She shook her head. "A chain! Perhaps in the stables?"

They paused before a window overlooking the park in front of the house. The snow had stopped and the sun had come out, but the scene was no less daunting. It looked like a foot of snow drifted over the grounds, with only a few tamped paths through the glittering whiteness. Getting to the stables, down near the lake, would be cold and slippery.

"Perhaps in the attics?" The earl cocked his head toward her, his eyes dancing and a wry smile on his lips. "Or the dungeons?"

"There is an armory, but no dungeons I know of." She tapped one finger on her lips, thinking.

"Dare I ask why a chain is required?" The earl appeared in no hurry to keep searching. He clasped his hands behind him and stood watching her. "It seems an odd item in a farce."

And that is why Bridget wants it, Viola thought. "There was mention of a ghost—two ghosts," she amended. "One will be the dead king—hence the crown—and one will be ... another ghost." His lips curved. Against her will, Viola's did the same. "I've absolutely no idea why she wants a chain," she confessed.

"Is that the weak, infirm, dead king I'm to portray?" he asked, as if dreading the answer.

She tried to stop it, she really did; but a gasp of laughter escaped her, then another. "I'm terribly afraid so," she said, her voice shaking.

Winterton sighed and hung his head as Viola bit her lips to keep the laughter bottled inside her. "At least I'm to be a weak, infirm, and ultimately dead *monarch*. Having been here a few days, I now know it could have been so much worse. A dead night-soil man, or a pickpocket."

"Well. Yes." Viola tried to speak normally. "But the king leaves a crown for the prince, while a pickpocket ..."

"That depends on his skill at picking pockets, don't you think?" The earl grinned impishly. "He might leave a ruby the size of a hen's egg."

She laughed again. "Or a tatty old handkerchief."

"Ah, but it's the chance of something more exciting that renders it interesting. I think Lady Bridget would agree with me."

Viola shook her head, but still smiled. "No doubt. Bridget would write a scene having him pick the pocket of a mikado or a rajah, as simple as you please, in the heart of Westminster."

"A rajah! Now that would be an interesting role." The earl's face lit up. "I've been talking to young Mr. Jones about India, as he intends to take a diplomatic post there."

"Does he?" Viola hadn't heard that about Mr. Jones, only that he was friends with the scoundrel Frye and therefore must be hateful, according to Alexandra. She also claimed he'd said something very unkind about Serena, but from Viola's observations, he hadn't meant it.

"Yes. He asked for my advice on the journey there. I gather Newton has told everyone I've traveled to every corner of the globe, and can't bear to set foot in England." He said the last with a grimace.

"Have you?" Viola blushed when he looked at her in surprise. "That is, I did hear that you are a great traveler. I've never been out of England, and can't imagine what it's like in India."

"Do you long to see the world?" he asked, sounding interested.

She thought for a moment. "A little," she replied at last. "Yes, I suppose I do. I never had the chance of it." A clock chimed in the room behind them, making her guiltily aware that she was doing nothing, just standing in the corridor talking to the earl. "Shall we see if there is a suitable large book in the library?"

"Of course."

"It's not true that I can't bear to set foot in England," he said abruptly as they walked. "I've been home for almost a year now."

"So long," she murmured.

"So few people truly get to see the world," he went on, almost as if trying to persuade her. "There are places so vastly different from England, one can hardly describe them. People so different than Englishmen. Art and food and music. I would hate to spend my entire life without seeing anything other than the village I was born in, perhaps a few other villages, and then only London for exotic sights."

That rather perfectly described Viola's own life. "How very fortunate that you were able to see more." She opened the doors of the library. Bridget had completed most of her play, so everyone was off rehearsing in other rooms. The library was quiet and empty.

"I do feel fortunate." The earl went to the French windows, opened the drapes, and gazed out at the snow. The wind had died, and the view was dazzling. "Those who have the means and the ability and the desire to travel ought to do so, to bring those far corners of the world home to those who stay."

"So it's your duty?" She smiled to take the sting off the words, but he still shot her a sharp glance. Viola put up her hands. "I don't judge, my lord. You have the means and the desire; therefore it's entirely your choice whether you stay or not."

"Wouldn't you go, if you could?"

Her smile turned wistful. "Perhaps. Perhaps not. Everyone dear to me is here in England. It hasn't felt like a great loss to remain home."

He recoiled as if struck. "I didn't mean it's a loss to stay home."

"And I didn't mean it's an indulgence to travel." She hesitated. "Lord Newton is young. Life seems to pass so slowly when you're young. You feel you will go mad if you can't escape the ordinary drudgery of home and family. It's only when you're a bit older that you realize how easy it is to lose those things, sometimes without noticing until it's too late.

"I expect he's told everyone you're impatient to be gone because *he* would like to explore the world—at least a bit of it beyond England's shores—and because of his father's death he cannot. He sees you as free to do as you please, and if he were free to do as he pleased, he would be on the first packet to France." She stopped at his expression. "That is only my guess at his feelings."

"No," he said slowly, still staring at her. "No, I believe you're correct."

Viola felt her face heat. "You know him much better than I—"

"I doubt it." Winterton's eyes were piercing. "I've only seen him a dozen times since he was a boy."

"Well." It was astonishing how flustered she felt, just from him looking at her. "Perhaps you'll become better acquainted with his thoughts and feelings during this visit." She chewed her lip and changed the subject. "A large book. Perhaps an atlas would do?"

He tensed. "Pardon?"

"An atlas. Bridget said it must be a large book, and an atlas is the largest book I can think of." She went to the bookcase and surveyed the selection behind the finely carved wooden screen. "Perhaps this one. It's large and looks impressive." She pulled it from the shelf and opened it on the wide table.

The earl stepped up beside her. "Absolutely not."

"Why not?"

"It's Cellarius's *Harmonia Macrocosmica*, and shouldn't be trusted to Lady Bridget's farce. I'm astonished Wessex keeps it here among the other books."

Viola gaped as he took the book and turned gently through a few pages. His face was bright and sharp with interest. "This is one of the most beautiful examples of celestial cartography in the world. Look—" He laid one page in front of her. "The northern sky."

It was a beautifully illustrated page, in vivid colors with constellation figures sketched over a background of stars. "It is lovely," Viola whispered in awe. "I'd no idea it was particularly valuable."

"I suppose not everyone would think so." He closed the book reverently and put it back on the shelf. "Is Wessex a collector?"

"I'm not privy to that. The duchess has a fondness for maps, but I've never heard her speak of the stars."

Winterton went still, as if startled. "Maps?"

Viola smiled. "Yes." Before her marriage, the duchess had owned a prosperous draper's shop in Melchester, and she'd stocked a good number of exotic fabrics from around the world. Viola had seen the map that used to hang in the shop offices, with pins pressed into the countries where she got her fabrics: fine cottons from America and India, silk from China, jacquard from France. Now that she was mistress of Kingstag, someone else ran the shop, but she still took an interest in it.

"I also have a fondness for maps." Winterton turned around, his head cocked curiously. "I've never met a duchess who shared it. Does she collect them?"

"Do you?" Viola asked brightly. On no account would she discuss the duchess's personal interests with him. "I suppose you must, on your travels."

"I do have a number of them," he admitted with a grin. "Atlases and maps are marvels—an entire worldview contained in one page or one book. I have an atlas of the world that doesn't include any hint of America, because it wasn't known. Another ancient map is centered about Jerusalem, per the church's preference. And others— such as this Cellarius—are maps of things we can never possibly visit."

"Yes," she murmured, struck by his enthusiasm. "But you would like to."

"To visit the stars? No." His gaze grew distant. "But they are a traveler's dearest companion. The same stars that shine above home in England also shine above the West Indies, the Americas, and China. Every sailor learns to chart his way using them as a guide. In that respect, a map of the stars is more valuable than any map of the land."

Viola couldn't stop a small wistful sigh. She was perfectly happy here in England—mostly—usually—but the excitement in the earl's face as he spoke of sailing the seas and seeing exotic lands and people did plant a tiny seed of envy in her heart. Just to have the chance to go on such a journey would be incredible.

But she did not have that chance, and probably never would.

"You find the prospect appealing," said the earl, his gaze returning to her with keen discernment.

"A little," she allowed. "Well—yes, I do. Perhaps not to travel all the way to China, but to see Paris, or Venice, or some of the mountains in Switzerland . . . *yes,* it does sound thrilling." She turned back to the shelves to break the moment. *Do not be tempted by a wealthy earl's questions,* she told herself. "What would you suggest we give Bridget, if none of these are suitable to being props?"

The earl turned to the bookcase. "Are these all the atlases at Kingstag?"

"Yes." Too late Viola remembered that the duke had bought another recently as a gift for the duchess. It was a finely bound atlas, with all the trading routes around the globe marked, and the duke thought his wife would be charmed by the drawings and engravings of items from far-off lands. It mirrored the map she had kept of where her goods came from.

But that was to be the duchess's Christmas gift, and as such could not possibly be flaunted in Bridget's play. Viola had been sworn to secrecy by Wessex, who was quite pleased with himself for thinking of something so unusual for his wife.

The earl seemed disappointed by her answer. A thin line appeared between his brows as he stared at her for a moment, almost as if he knew her answer wasn't entirely correct, but he said nothing. After a moment he pulled a book from the shelf. "This one."

"An almanac of last year." Viola grinned. "No one will be tempted to read it during the play, I suppose."

Winterton's mouth twisted ruefully. "Not in the least."

$\mathcal{W}$es didn't know what to do. For a moment he'd thought he would finally get a look at the Desnos atlas, to see if it was the one he sought.

There were only a few known editions of the Desnos atlas, all dated from the previous century. They were handsomely illustrated and annotated, which would have made one desirable enough to a wandering soul like his. But the particular atlas he sought had belonged to his father.

Wes had spent hours poring over those maps, listening to his father's tales of the sights he'd seen in those remote and exotic locations. When the late earl died, the atlas has been mistakenly sold with some other books and Wes had been searching for it ever since, making inquiries of collectors and dealers all over England. After years of no success, he'd heard the Duke of Wessex might have it. The duke's reply to his queries had been vague and not very encouraging, but Wes was undeterred. He'd learned the duke was a family man, which meant there was a chance he could be persuaded to sell it by Wes's story—and that was enough chance for him to travel to Dorset, in winter, with his surly nephew in tow. He was determined to have that atlas again.

But it was not in the Kingstag library, and now Viola Cavendish had just said there were no other atlases in the castle. Her face, though, had gone blank for just a moment after she said that, as if remembering something. Perhaps she suspected there was another?

He thought hard about it as they went about the remaining tasks. They delivered the almanac to the players in the drawing room and found the housekeeper, who promised to send a footman to the stables in search of a chain. He trailed after Mrs. Cavendish as she scoured a storage room, finally holding up a battered piece of metal with a pleased exclamation.

"Will this serve as a crown, do you think?" she asked, lifting it above her head.

"Hmm? Yes." He had to know about that atlas, but was it better to ask her now, or wait until Wessex returned and ask the duke directly?

Some of the humor left her face at his curt reply, and Wes immediately regretted it. "A fine crown indeed," he said more heartily, reaching for it. "Does it suit me, since I'm to be the doddering old king who wears it?" He set the thing on his head and crossed his eyes.

She smiled uncertainly. "Very well, sir."

"Then a crown it is." He took off the cylinder, which had probably once been part of a chandelier, or perhaps a base for a glass dish. It was tarnished and bent now.

"We should get Lady Bridget's approval before congratulating ourselves." She headed toward the door.

"Mrs. Cavendish?" She paused, but didn't look back. "I apologize," Wes said. "For my abruptness."

"Oh no, my lord," she began, but he made a low noise in his throat and she fell silent.

"May I confide in you, ma'am?"

Slowly she turned to face him fully. "Yes, but . . ."

"But your loyalty lies with Wessex; I know." He smiled wryly. "You must have wondered what brought me to Kingstag in the middle of winter." She said nothing, but her green eyes were fixed on him. Wes thought he might drown in those eyes, and knew he was doing the right thing by being honest with her. "I am looking for a particular atlas Wessex may own. He may not, but neither of us knows for certain. I came to Kingstag to see if it's the one I desire, and if so, if I can persuade Wessex to sell it."

"What sort of atlas?"

Wes's face softened in memory. "A very dear one, to me. It's a Desnos atlas, which are not common, but neither are they very rare. But this one was once my father's. He died while I was away— Tahiti—and by the time I returned home, it had somehow been consigned with other old books and sold. My mother didn't know it was anything special, but that was the atlas he showed me when I was a small boy. It inspired my interest in foreign lands, from the wild Americas to exotic China. I would like to have it back, for the notes he wrote in the margins, his observations of other peoples, tales from his voyages—" He stopped, unexpectedly overwhelmed.

"Was he a great traveler as well?" she asked softly.

Wes nodded. "Not as much as he would have liked. He took me on my first voyages around Europe. My mother and sisters stayed home, but he took me, a raw stripling without two ounces of sense." He grinned, shaking his head at the memories. "As I grew older I went with others and sometimes off on my own, while he returned home to manage Winterbury Hall. Much as I did when he died."

Mrs. Cavendish crossed the room. "I'm very sorry you lost him, sir."

"Call me Winterton," he said, savoring the blush that colored her cheeks. "And thank you."

"I understand why you wish to reclaim the atlas," she went on. "I probably shouldn't say so, but the duke recently bought an atlas, as a gift for the duchess. He isn't likely to sell it, whether or not it was your father's. Are you certain the one you seek isn't among the others in the library?"

"I had a look the other day," Wes admitted, "and didn't discover it. The bookseller I contacted in London said he'd sold a Desnos atlas only recently to Wessex."

Mrs Cavendish looked at him with compassion. "I don't think he'll sell it," she said again.

Wes mustered a smile. "I shall have faith as long as possible."

"Perhaps it's not even the same one."

"Perhaps." But he suspected it was. "I don't suppose you could show me the one Wessex bought recently?"

She drew back. "No. I don't even know where it is. His Grace asked me a few questions when he was searching for a gift for Her Grace, but I had nothing to do with it otherwise. I know nothing except that he thought the maps and illustrations in it would appeal to Her Grace."

"The Desnos atlas does have splendid illustrations."

She chewed her lip for a moment. "I'm sorry I cannot help you."

Wes opened his hands wide. "I didn't expect you to do more than you have. I shall have to wait until Wessex's return to see if it is my father's old atlas, and if I can persuade the duke to part with it."

"I wish you luck," she said softly. "His Grace is devoted to his family. He might understand."

Wes couldn't help smiling back. "Thank you, Mrs. Cavendish."

There was an odd moment as they stood there beaming at each other. Even though she'd all but driven a stake through his hopes, confirming that Wessex likely did have the atlas while at the same time making clear why the duke was very unlikely to sell it to him, Wes found himself feeling happier than he had since arriving in Dorset. There was something about her face that made him want to smile every time he caught a glimpse of her. She was lovely, but it was more than that; her face was full of kindness and humor and so expressive, he could gladly sit and watch her without saying anything at all. But when she smiled *at him* . . .

Good lord, he was in trouble.

"We should present the crown to Bridget," she said.

"Right." Wes put the makeshift crown on his head, tilted it to a rakish angle, and folded his arms. "As the late, desperately unlamented ruler of this realm, I command it."

Her face lit up and she laughed. Her nose wrinkled a bit when she did, and his heart gave an odd thump. "You're taking your demise very well, my lord."

"Given that I have no choice, I shall accept my fate gracefully, as befits a monarch." He took the crown from his head. "Perhaps it will serve as a good example for the prince." As hoped, Justin had been given the part of the prince, although Wes still had no idea what that role entailed. Not that he knew what his own role entailed.

"Lord Newton has made himself very agreeable." Mrs. Cavendish closed the storage room door behind them as they headed back to the drawing room.

"He is improving," Wes admitted. Justin had been in excellent spirits since they arrived. Perhaps Anne was wrong to keep him at home so much. Wes certainly hadn't wanted to be at home when he was twenty. He'd gone to Egypt with two of his mates from university that year.

"He's charming," said Mrs. Cavendish diplomatically. "I daresay the young ladies are very pleased you brought him to Kingstag."

Wes laughed. "At least I did something to redeem myself!"

"Oh no! You are most welcome, Lord Winterton!" She put her hand on his arm. Wes stopped in his tracks, as did she. He stared into her sea-green eyes, and again his heart took a strange leap.

Good lord, he was in trouble . . . and it was exhilarating.

With a muffled gasp she snatched her hand away, and without thinking Wes caught it. "Thank you," he whispered, raising it to his lips for a kiss. "For I find myself very pleased that I came."

CHAPTER SIX

*A*fter the electric moment with the earl, when he caught her hand and looked at her as if he'd like to pull her back into the privacy of the storage cupboard and kiss her senseless, Viola tried to busy herself with dull tasks in the distant reaches of the castle. Not because she feared the earl actually would pull her aside and kiss her senseless, but because she was coming to hope he might.

Her hand had tingled for an hour where his lips brushed it. After she delivered the makeshift crown to Bridget, she fled the drawing room, even though it left Sophronia completely in charge. The earl had watched her go—Viola could swear his gaze made her feel warm and giddy from all the way across the room—but thankfully he didn't follow. That was proper, she told herself; she was a servant and he was a gentleman of leisure.

So she ended up sitting in the small room off the duchess's private parlor where she normally worked, staring out at the snow and wondering about the foreign lands Lord Winterton had been to. Had he seen the ancient pyramids in Egypt, which Stephen said were marvels of engineering? Had he been to India and seen elephants? Lord Newton had told the young ladies fantastical tales of his uncle's journeys, and as much as Viola reminded herself it was not her place to know, she burned to ask him about all the places she had read of, but would never see herself.

It was true that everything and everyone she held dear was in England. Even more, the dearest person in the world to her, her brother Stephen, relied upon her being prosperously employed, and that was easiest to accomplish in England. She had neither means nor opportunity to go abroad, whether she wished to or not. Unlike the earl.

She sighed, brushing her fingertips over the knuckles he had kissed. Everything about her life was unlike the earl's. She was an idiot to sit here thinking a kiss on the hand meant anything. He was being polite, or flirting, or even trying to persuade her to help him locate that atlas. Not that she didn't understand his desire to have it. She'd made sure Stephen got their father's astrolabe and sextant, and she'd kept her mother's pearl necklace, which would have paid for a term at Cambridge.

But whether or not the duke would be willing to sell the atlas, if he even had it, Viola knew she ought to stay out of the matter. Her growing sympathy for and interest in Lord Winterton could only get her in trouble.

She was still torn when she went down to dinner. It was part of her duties to help oversee dinner and entertain the guests in the drawing room before and after the meal, but she was not expected to dine with the guests. When it was just family, she was often invited to join them, but during this party she receded to her proper place.

Naturally the first person she set eyes on when she reached the drawing room was Lord Winterton. No one else was in the room yet, so she felt safe enough returning his smile.

"How did the rehearsal progress?" she asked.

His eyes closed for a moment, as if in pain. "Apparently I die a very bloody death, though thankfully off stage."

Viola giggled before she could stop herself. "I trust you're quite regal and imposing before that."

"Pompous and boring, I should say. 'Let not my subjects make merry,'" he intoned. "'There is too much frivolity in the kingdom, and I will have an end to it.'"

"Oh my." Viola wondered what on earth Bridget was thinking. "To what end?"

"Solely to *my* end," he replied dryly. "My role is to be pompous and boring, die savagely, then return as a ghost after the prince becomes a far more beloved king, to penitently pronounce that I was wrong to be so pompous and boring, but now I shall rest in peace because the new—much better—king has brought such joy and merriment to my former kingdom."

Viola burst out laughing.

59

"I do not recall actually agreeing to be in the play," the earl went on, although he was smiling now as well. "I suspect my nephew wrote my entire part, and I can only be grateful the rest of the guests shall be actors in the play as well, and not sitting in the audience watching."

"I am so sorry," Viola gasped, wiping at her eyes. "Lady Bridget is quite fanciful . . ."

"And Lady Sophronia is even worse!" he exclaimed quietly. "I shouldn't say this, but I believe she patted me on my—er—hindquarters."

Oh merciful God. Viola herself had noticed, more than once, that Winterton had exceptionally fine—er—hindquarters. And she knew Lady Sophronia had an eye for such things. "Perhaps it was inadvertent," she suggested weakly.

Winterton gave her a look. He didn't think so.

God save her. Viola could feel her face turning red. "I'm so sorry," she said again, her voice shaking as she tried desperately not to laugh again. She could picture exactly how Sophronia would have lined it up.

Winterton's face eased. "I took no offense. She reminds me greatly of my grandmother, who used to say she appreciated a pair of muscular calves on a man. She paid her footmen a bonus if they were strong runners, and not because they could deliver her messages faster. I hope I live to such a great age, when I may say what I like and not care a whit what others think about it."

"I suspect Sophronia reached that age seventy years ago," murmured Viola. "Thank you for being such an excellent sport about the play."

He grinned. "When one travels, one learns to accept the unexpected and make the best of it. Often those surprising turns lead to the most memorable experiences of the journey. I find Lady Sophronia charming."

Viola let out her breath in relief. No wonder Sophronia had patted his bottom; she must have recognized Winterton would let her get away with it. "I do as well," she whispered, "but not everyone does."

Winterton laughed. His eyes were so blue and friendly, and Viola found herself smiling back at him. Again.

The other guests came in then, discussing the play rehearsal in good spirits. Bridget had somehow procured a bucket of white feathers, and stuck them all over a coat and cap for Lord Gosling to wear in his role as a Lovesick Swan. The effect was quite ludicrous, but Gosling took the teasing in stride with a smile, declaring that he thought it a very handsome costume since Lady Bridget had made it herself. Bridget rolled her eyes at his flattery, but Viola could tell she was pleased. Bridget was pleased whenever anyone embraced her mad ideas.

When the butler announced dinner, Lord Winterton made sure to offer Lady Sophronia his arm. Viola's heart gave a funny little jump at the easy way he had with the older woman. Sophronia *was* charming and amusing, when approached the right way—any sign of shock or indignation, and Sophronia would dig in with relish, purposely being even more shocking and inappropriate.

Viola went to take her own dinner before it was time to return to the party, to instill some order and decorum to whatever after-dinner activities Bridget persuaded Serena to do.

Tonight it was charades, which was perfectly acceptable. Viola settled at the side of the room and watched in amusement. As usual, Bridget's riddle was ridiculous and took a very long time to guess. When Serena finally called out "chalk figures for dancing" and Bridget nodded, a small cheer went up.

"I wondered if anyone would ever solve it," said a voice beside her.

Viola glanced at Lord Winterton. "Someone always does," she assured him. "Lady Serena knows her sister well."

They both turned to watch Serena, taking her place at the front of the room and pondering her riddle. She looked happier, Viola realized. The grave quiet air she'd worn for weeks after her engagement ended had vanished, and when she smiled at something Miss Penworth said in jest, it was open and warm. It brought a small curve to Viola's own lips; all three Cavendish girls had become like younger sisters to her, and she took their sorrows and joys very much to heart.

"I heard she was recently disappointed in love." Winterton sat on the settee beside her, his voice low enough no one else could hear. "She seems to be recovering."

"Happily, she does."

The earl glanced at her. "I heard the cruel young man was even invited to this party."

Bridget, Viola reflected, had no discretion at all. "He's not cruel," she murmured in reply. "He's young." Young, handsome, and a very dashing duke. She didn't know why the Duke of Frye had ended his engagement, but she couldn't believe he'd done it to be cruel to Serena. Their families had been close for ages. And Serena didn't look very brokenhearted anymore . . .

"Is there no chance of reconciliation?"

Winterton's question startled her. "Oh! I'm sure I don't know. But Frye hasn't arrived, as you can see, so at the moment I rate it very low odds. He can never be forgiven if he never comes to beg forgiveness."

He grinned. "Nor should he be." For a moment they watched as Serena delivered her riddle. "Do you have an interest in the stars, Mrs. Cavendish?"

Viola blinked. "Stars in the sky?"

"Yes."

"A little." It made her think of Stephen. She had to blink back a sudden tear at the thought of her brother.

"Come with me," the earl said. "It's terribly cold, but the sky is beautiful. I thought you might like to see it."

Her lips parted in surprise. And delight. After all, her brother might be looking at the same stars tonight. It was two days before Christmas, and it was the closest thing to sharing it with him she might have. "All right," she said.

She cast one glance over the room as they slipped out. Everyone was absorbed in charades. Sophronia was watching from her usual chair near the hearth, and there was a great deal of mirth and laughter. A little devil on her shoulder whispered that no one would miss her for a few minutes.

Viola followed the earl to the doors at the back of the hall. In the summer they often stood open, presenting a beautiful vista over the gardens, bowling green, and the ancient oaks that lined the road to the stables. Tonight all those sights were covered in piles of snow, and the raw air made her eyes water as they stepped out. She clasped her arms around herself and stayed close to the door, sheltered from the wind.

"It's a bit cold," said the earl sympathetically, looking unaffected by the temperature himself. "But look." He raised his arm and swept one hand across the skies.

She put back her head and gasped. It had been snowing heavily all evening, but now it almost looked like a hole had opened in the sky. Clouds still ringed the horizon and hovered over the tops of the trees, but directly above them was a jeweled canopy of stars, sparkling against the black velvet of the night.

"There is Polaris," said the earl, pointing. "And there is Sirius." He pointed toward the far left horizon.

"Goodness," breathed Viola. "You can see everything! There—look—the Cork Nebula lies there!" In excitement she pointed as well.

Winterton looked at her in amazement. "The Cork Nebula! How do you know that?"

"My brother is studying mathematics and astronomy at Cambridge," she said, still gazing raptly at the stars. "The Cork Nebula is at the heart of Perseus. There is Pegasus, and Lyra, and—oh—such a beautiful view of Vega!"

The earl's eyes moved back to the sky. "I have no idea which stars are in Pegasus," he said after a moment. "I only know a few points of navigation."

"That's not even one star in a thousand," said Viola with a laugh.

"What else do you see?" He stepped closer, until their shoulders were touching. Viola felt the warmth of him beside her like a roaring fire.

Stars. She focused on the sky and pointed east. "There is Pollux." It was easy to find, nice and bright. "And there south of it is the belt of Orion. The Spanish call them Las Tres Marias. The ones in asterisms are easier to find."

"Marvelous," murmured the earl, his head tipped back, giving her a perfect view of his profile.

"Stephen would have spent every night outside, pointing them out to me. Our mother made him come inside, and he would sleep under an open window, even in the dead of winter." She smiled in memory.

"Mathematics and astronomy. How impressive."

She nodded. "Stephen's brilliant. I wouldn't be at all astonished if his name is as famous as Mr. Herschel's some day."

The earl was staring at her. "I'd no idea you had a brother, Mrs. Cavendish."

"Only one, younger." She raised her brows in fun. "Ought you to know all my family?"

He laughed ruefully. "Forgive me. Of course not. I have inflicted my family on you, and that really should be enough."

"Inflicted! Lord Newton is hardly that bad . . ." She paused at his expression. "Perhaps writing a painful death for you as king was a bit much."

He snorted. "What is your brother like?"

"Brilliantly clever," she said at once. "We knew from the time he was six that he should go to Cambridge. My father was a sea captain, and he taught Stephen how to navigate by the stars."

"A sea captain! And you never had the desire to go away?" The earl clasped his hands behind him and studied her with interest.

She smiled wistfully. "I never had the chance! Females, I was told, are not very welcome on ships . . . But Stephen went on a few journeys with him, where he noticed nothing but the stars overhead. Once my father showed him how to use the sextant—well! My brother barely pays attention to anything on earth now when an idea seizes him. His passions are stars and nebulae and planets, how they move and how they change appearance, and how he might possibly improve his telescope so that he can see them better. When he's working on a calculation, he forgets to speak to anyone, to eat, even to sleep."

Winterton shook his head in amazement. "I always admired those fellows at university."

"I can't even imagine an entire college of them," she said honestly. "Stephen alone amazes me."

Winterton chuckled. "I doubt one chap in ten at Cambridge works that hard at his studies as all that. But here—you're shivering."

Viola realized she was. "We'd better go back inside."

He opened the door and touched her back lightly as she went back in. Viola felt that touch through all the layers of cloth between them. *Do not make anything of it,* she told herself. "Thank you," she told the earl as he bolted the door behind them. "For showing me the sky."

"It may be snowing again by morning."

"I know." Viola smiled. "But it was beautiful for that moment."

His blue gaze felt like a caress on her face. "Yes. Very beautiful." She flushed with pleasure, as if he'd paid her a great compliment. He reached up and gently brushed a few flakes of melting snow from her hair. "Like the night Of cloudless climes and starry skies; And all that's best of dark and bright . . ."

Kiss me, she thought, feeling herself falling into his mesmerizing eyes. Viola stopped breathing as the force of the thought hit her. "Marlowe?" she asked breathlessly, trying to jolt herself out of it.

"Byron, I believe." He fingered a loose curl of her hair, studying it for a moment before smoothing it behind her ear. "We could check, in the library."

The library would be dark and deserted and private now. Anything might happen there, just between the two of them. She should go back to the charades, remember her duty, and not let poetry and starlight go to her head. Slowly she nodded. "Yes. Yes, we could."

Something shifted in his focus. He knew what she meant. He offered his arm.

Do not be stupid, Viola told herself. But she put her hand on his arm and went with him.

CHAPTER SEVEN

$\mathcal{W}$es's pulse seemed to be pounding against every inch of his skin. Her hand was on his arm, and her eyes were glowing like emeralds, and he'd never seen anyone more beautiful than Viola Cavendish, standing in the frigid night, head thrown back to gaze at the stars. Her lips had parted in wonder, and Wes had nearly kissed her right then and there.

It was all he could think about now. That, and her hand on his arm as she went with him on the most specious errand ever invented. He knew very well it was Byron's poetry he quoted, but for a half hour alone with her, he'd happily check every book of poetry from Marlowe, Jonson, and Shakespeare. If they weren't distracted before locating the poetry books, that is . . .

They reached the tall double doors of the library. She picked up a lamp from a nearby table as Wes reached for the doorknob.

But a lamp already burned inside, on the desk by the near hearth. The two people in the room looked up, startled, and in a flurry of movement flew apart.

Not, though, before Wes saw who they were and what they were doing. Lady Alexandra was frantically smoothing her dress back into place. Justin ran one hand through his disheveled hair, but seemed to realize it was hopeless. His jacket was off, his cravat was askew, and he gave Wes a glance that was half sheepish, half defiant.

Wes shut the door with a bang.

"Uncle, let me explain," began Justin.

"Close your mouth," said Wes in a deadly soft tone. "I will speak to you later. Lady Alexandra, are you hurt?"

Her flush was visible even in the low light. "Not at all, sir."

"What is going on?" Mrs. Cavendish finally found her voice.

Lady Alexandra looked frozen. Justin cleared his throat. "It was not nearly as bad as it looked."

"No?" Mrs. Cavendish turned a frigid gaze on him. "What was it, then?"

Justin opened his mouth, seemed to realize the problem, and closed his mouth.

"It was only a kiss," said Lady Alexandra in a quavering voice. "Just a little one."

Mrs. Cavendish looked pointedly at Justin's white shirtsleeves. They must have been alone here for some time. Wes could have smacked himself for not paying more attention to Justin's interest in the girl. How long ago had they snuck away from the party in the drawing room? Alexandra had been sitting on the desk, Justin's hand on her knee—thankfully on top of her skirts—and her arms around his neck. It probably *had* only been a bit of kissing, but Lady Alexandra was the daughter of a duke, a young lady who was expected to make a very good marriage and have a spotless reputation.

And if that reputation became tarnished and stained by Wes's feckless nephew, there would be hell to pay.

"I hope your mother Her Grace agrees," Mrs. Cavendish told Lady Alexandra.

Alexandra shot her an agonized look, but nodded. Viola reached for her arm and drew her firmly toward the door.

"Mrs. Cavendish . . ." Justin's voice was hesitant. "Truly it was my fault. I asked her to come away from the party . . . Blame me."

"I do, sir," she said bluntly. "But it is not my response you need to be concerned about." She swept Alexandra out the door.

A full minute of silence reigned in the library. Justin didn't seem to know where to look. Wes counted to ten to save his temper from erupting. "What the devil?"

He must have mastered himself better than he thought, because a slight smile crossed Justin's face. "She's very pretty."

Wes stared at him stonily.

"She's great fun too."

Wes maintained his stare.

Justin began to wilt. "It was naught but a little kiss."

"Don't you ever say that to me again!" Anger finally boiled over. Justin flinched as Wes advanced on him in a fury. "Go to your room and stay there. Do not speak to anyone. Do not ring for a servant to remove your boots. Do not do *anything* but sit quietly in your room. If I can't trust you to do that, we leave tomorrow morning even if we must climb through snowbanks higher than our heads, carrying our baggage. Do you understand?"

"Yes, Uncle," Justin muttered.

Wes continued to glare at him. "I will attempt to smooth things over as much as possible. If you leave your room before I come speak to you, I shall find a switch and thrash you like the boy you clearly still are."

"Yes, Uncle," Justin whispered.

Wes grabbed his jacket from a nearby chair and flung it at him. "Go."

Justin's ears were red as he tugged his jacket back on and ducked out of the room.

Wes paced for a few minutes. Bloody hell. Was that boy's head completely empty? What was he thinking?

He had to stop himself there. Of course he knew what was in Justin's head; much the same desire had been beating away at Wes's own brain. If not for Justin, he might be kissing Viola Cavendish right now . . .

But that was a totally different situation, he argued to himself. He was not a green boy and she was not an innocent young lady. They both knew what they were doing. If he kissed her, if she kissed him, it would be because they both wanted it . . .

He sighed. It didn't really matter. And he suspected that how he handled Justin's indiscretion would have a large impact on whether he'd ever get another chance with Viola.

*V*iola kept a firm grip on Alexandra's arm as she hurried down the corridor toward the dowager's apartment. The only way for Alexandra to head off any trouble over the kiss was to confess it immediately to her mother, before a careless comment or whisper could blow the whole thing out of proportion. Viola also hoped the experience would leave a lasting impression on the girl and prevent her from doing it again.

"Viola, I'm sorry." Now Alexandra was full of contrition. "But it was only a little kiss! Nothing more. Surely you don't think I'd forget myself enough to do worse."

"I don't know anything. You slipped away with a man and went into the dark library, which looks very guilty. Girls have been ruined for doing that."

"Ruined! It was nothing!"

Viola stopped. "A little kiss is nothing. But what would have come next?"

Alexandra blinked. "Nothing! Newton would never—"

"Perhaps not, but you don't know him well enough to be certain of that. I would hate to see you make a terrible mistake next time."

Alexandra flushed from her neckline to her ears. "Next time?"

"If you can do it once, you can do it again. The next time a handsome man whispers pretty words in your ear and begs you to sneak out with him, you'll be more likely to go. After all, you got away with it before and bore no consequences." Viola raised her brows at Alexandra's shocked expression. "Don't tell me it's impossible. In London there will be many handsome men wanting to dance with you and kiss you, and some of them will not have restraint or honor."

"But I never have a chance to do anything!" the girl protested, tears thickening her voice. "I'm always behind Serena, waiting for her to find a husband. Well, now she's been jilted and I'm still waiting. All the gentlemen look at her first—next spring even Bridget will be out with me, and I shall just be the Cavendish sister in the middle. I'll end up like Aunt Sophronia—"

Viola rolled her eyes. "Only if you wish to."

"Newton's very handsome! And eligible! Don't you think Gareth would approve of him, if he knew?" she argued.

"If he knew," repeated Viola with meaning. "I shan't speculate on what your brother might do or say, *if he knew*, since neither you nor Lord Newton took the time or trouble to seek his approval before sneaking off for a bit of kissing. What do you think he'd say now?"

Alexandra bit her lip. "I shall explain to Mama. Mama will understand."

"I hope so." Viola was relieved that Alexandra had grasped the import of this moment. If the dowager could see that it was a harmless kiss, nothing much would come of it. No one else had seen anything, and even if the other guests had noticed Newton and Alexandra leaving together, that was proof of nothing. Viola could even say she had been with them, if it came down to it.

Of course, if the dowager grew upset that her daughter had been able to sneak off with a gentleman, there was one person to blame for failing to chaperone her: Viola.

They had reached the dowager duchess's suite of rooms now. Viola put her hands on the girl's shoulders and gave her a firm squeeze. "Chin up. Your mother was once a young woman, hoping to fall in love, flattered by a handsome young man's attentions. She will surely understand what you're feeling. But that's no excuse to be foolish, and risk your reputation for a few moments of excitement. And don't blame Lord Newton; unless he carried you off to the library against your will, you are as much to blame as he. You are a young woman now, Alexandra, and must take responsibility for your own actions. Be honest and true with your mother, and I have faith she'll treat you fairly."

The girl stared at her with dark, worried eyes. "Isn't it monstrously unfair that such a trifling thing could cause such trouble?"

Yes. Viola felt uncomfortably aware of all the impure thoughts she had had about the Earl of Winterton recently, and how easily she could have been the one caught kissing in the library. He found her attractive; she sensed that if she gave him any sign, he would kiss her. Perhaps do more. Perhaps she had even agreed to go to the library with him because she knew he wanted to kiss her, and she wanted him to do it.

But she had even more to lose than Alexandra did. "Yes, but that won't change anything. 'It's not fair' is rarely a winning defense."

A spark of pique animated her face for a moment. "It should be. Lord Newton won't be judged so harshly over a trifling little kiss."

Viola sighed. "His uncle looked very displeased with him. But that doesn't affect you, which is why you must speak to your mother before anyone else does. Own your mistake and learn from it, so you don't make a worse one later."

Alexandra wilted. "All right." She put back her shoulders and knocked on the door. It opened almost immediately, and Ellen let her in. Viola waited until the maid had closed the door before she let out her breath.

CHAPTER EIGHT

*V*iola dutifully returned to the drawing room, but thankfully everyone else was ready to go to bed. No one asked where Alexandra or Lord Newton had gone, although Sophronia did murmur something about Lord Winterton with a sideways glance at her. Viola let it go. Tonight had been hard enough already.

So she did something she rarely did and helped herself to a bottle of port from the tray in the drawing room, then climbed the stairs to her rooms and shut the door.

Just looking at her apartment gave her a pang. The duchess had given her a luxurious room by servants' standards, a comfortable bedroom with an adjacent sitting room. It was small, but it was private and it was hers. Even more, it wasn't on the servants' floor but tucked at the end of the corridor where the duke and duchess had their rooms, almost like a member of the family. That was to make it easier for her to answer the bell that hung discreetly near her bed, of course, and it was right next to the servants' stair, but it still made all the difference. She could pretend that she was more Cavendish than servant.

It was shocking how quickly her happily settled life might go to pieces.

With a sigh she dropped onto the chair near the hearth and poured herself a glass of port. What were the odds the dowager would be upset? Viola had always admired the dowager duchess's levelheaded approach to things, but there was no telling what she might do when one of her children was in trouble. The poor woman was still ill, growing frustrated at her inability to recover, and every day she peppered Viola with ever more detailed questions about the party's progress. She was very annoyed that Frye had not arrived yet. The match between Serena and Frye had been arranged by their fathers years ago, and the dowager duchess still clung to hope that Frye would arrive, fall on bended knee to apologize profusely for breaking the engagement, whereupon Serena would graciously forgive him and fix a date for the wedding.

Now Viola faced the possibility that the dowager was about to be greatly disappointed by two daughters instead of one. Serena displayed no interest in Frye's attendance, and Alexandra was sneaking off to kiss a young viscount she'd only met last week. Anyone would be upset in these circumstances, and Viola knew she was the most likely person to bear the blame.

What would she tell Stephen if she got sacked? She took a large sip at the thought. Her poor brother. If she could have held on for another two years, he would have been able to finish his studies and become eligible for a post at the university. That was where Stephen belonged, among the books and scholars and ancient stone buildings that had harbored the likes of Isaac Newton. What would he do, out in the real world? He was brilliant enough to be a professor and witty enough to be a dean . . . except when his brain went off on some wild and wonderful journey through the realm of astronomy and mathematics. She'd known him to stay awake for three days straight, barely eating, working away until his hands were black with ink and he looked like a wraith from the grave. She'd given up scolding him about it years ago; he told her it was like a hurricane in his head, and he would have no peace until it blew itself out. Nor did he want peace from it—on the contrary, he reveled in those storms of thought that swept him away from her and everyone else on earth, into the exotic and thrilling world of numbers and stars and all sorts of things that enchanted him, but bewildered everyone else.

Alas, hurricanes of thought didn't pay well. James, her dear James, had been so fond of Stephen. His affectionate kindness for Stephen, then only a gangly lad, had been what initially endeared him to Viola. When she married him, James had pledged to pay for Stephen's schooling, and off her brother went to Cambridge.

But that came to an abrupt end when James's heart gave out. His income was only for his life, and it turned out he hadn't saved much for his widow—not that he'd had time, dying before his thirty-seventh birthday. Viola had been staring poverty and ruin in the face, and Stephen the loss of his place at Kings College.

The Duke of Wessex offered her a small stipend when she applied to him for help, as James's most illustrious relation, but it wouldn't have been sufficient to support both her and Stephen. Viola had swallowed her pride and asked for a position instead, with a regular, higher salary. As a secretary, she was able to send to Stephen enough for his school fees and books. If she instead had to pay for her own lodging and keep . . .

The tap on her door roused her from her growing anguish. She went still, suddenly gripped by fear that the dowager duchess might be sending for her already.

"Mrs. Cavendish?" called a low voice. "Viola?"

She gasped in relief, and went to open the door. "Good evening, sir. Do you require something?"

The Earl of Winterton stood there, looking penitent. "I wanted a word, if I may."

Viola dipped a shallow curtsey. "If you please, sir, perhaps Mrs. Hughes or Withers—"

"No!" He lowered his voice and ran one hand over his hair, ruffling it into unruly dark curls. "I wanted to talk to *you*."

She gripped the doorknob. The servants at Kingstag Castle were expected to be as respectable as the family. Socializing and romantic attachments were permitted, but only when conducted with propriety and decorum—and inviting the earl into her private rooms would be neither proper nor decorous. And she had just scolded Alexandra for doing much the same thing with Lord Newton.

On the other hand, letting the earl sit on her sofa for a few minutes could hardly make things worse, if the dowager duchess decided to sack her. She opened the door wider. "Then you might as well come in."

Winterton frowned. Viola gave a small shrug and went back to her chair. She propped her foot upon the fender and waved one hand toward the tiny table by the fireplace. "Have a glass of port, m'lord."

Slowly the earl stepped into the room. "You're upset."

Viola tilted her glass at him. "No," she corrected him, "I am resigned."

"To what fate?" He closed the door behind him.

Viola looked hard at that closed door, decided it didn't matter enough to protest, and sipped her port. "The duchess left me in charge of the household. Yes, Lady Serena is acting as hostess," she acknowledged as his brow dipped. "But she's not accustomed to maintaining order in a household this size. Naturally Her Grace the dowager duchess is, but she's still stricken in bed. Hence, the duchess entrusted me with the running of the house in her absence."

"That's a weighty responsibility."

She laughed weakly. "Isn't it? I assured her I could manage, even with the guests and the snow and Lady Sophronia being let off her lead. And I *was* managing well enough, until—"

"Until my nephew and I arrived," he finished when she didn't. "I will speak to the duke. Newton will speak to the duke and he will do whatever the duke deems proper and necessary."

Viola felt herself droop. "Proper? You know as well as I do what that normally means, my lord. But you are not acquainted with the Duke of Wessex."

Winterton hesitated. "No, I've never met him."

"Then allow me to offer you some advice, when you do meet him." She rearranged her feet on the fender. The fire was very warm. "He adores his sisters. He will throw over propriety and every rule of society to protect them, and a viscount who's still wet behind the ears will be no match for him."

"What are you saying?"

"I am warning you to tread carefully, and for heaven's sake tell your nephew the same. The duke will not be pleased to learn he trifled with Lady Alexandra."

"I imagine not." The earl came another step into the room. "May I?" He gestured at the sofa. Viola waved one hand in assent, and he took a seat. Any fluttering awareness she had of the man should be entirely overwhelmed by the disaster that loomed before her.

Still, he sat very near her. When he stretched out his own legs, his boots brushed her skirts. As if from a distance she watched the fabric sway, then settle. Goodness; the port must be having an effect on her after all. She turned her head to look at the earl, and discovered him watching her.

She guessed what he would say. *What ought I to do to keep the duke from calling out my nephew?* Viola had not seen the Duke of Wessex in a temper often, but he was not a meek or indecisive man.

"What will happen to you?" Winterton asked instead.

It took a moment for the question to sink in, which then caused her to sink lower in the chair. "Me? I might be sacked."

"Why?"

"You know why," she said softly.

"Hear me out," he responded, calm and unruffled. "Lady Alexandra has been flirting with Newton all week. Putting them together in the same house for days on end in a holiday spirit was bound to foster some interest between them. It's only natural."

"And it's only natural that His Grace will be furious." She sipped more port.

"But why would he sack *you?*"

Viola swirled her port, then drained the glass. "I ought to have kept a closer watch on Lady Alexandra."

"And I on Newton." Winterton blew out his breath. "His mother will have my head for this, you know. I thought I'd outgrown my fear of her, but tonight I am discovering that I have not."

She peeked at him. He looked glum but serious. "His mother is your older sister?"

"By several years, and she entrusted her son to me on the condition I would teach him some restraint and dignity." He grimaced. "She'll box my ears and slap my face, just as she did when I scalped her favorite doll."

Viola's eyes went wide. "Scalped!"

For a moment something like guilty enjoyment flickered over his face. "I fancied myself an American savage, like the ones I read of in travel diaries. They cut off their enemies' hair, did you know? Anne can be a bit . . . managing, and at the age of six I decided she was my mortal enemy. Obviously I could not cut off her hair, but her doll . . ." He flexed one hand and shrugged. "It seemed a good idea at the time. She was too old for dolls then, yet she took it oddly to heart."

Viola laughed. It was wrong to laugh, both at the story and because she might still be in an ocean of trouble, but once she started, she couldn't stop. She laughed until her sides hurt and she was gasping for breath and her eyes were wet. And when she finally recovered enough to catch her breath, she discovered she'd crossed the line into sobbing at the end.

The earl had gone down on one knee in front of her. He held out a handkerchief without comment. Viola took it and blew her nose, loudly and miserably.

"Is there a chance you're underestimating Wessex's understanding and compassion?"

She rolled the damp handkerchief into a ball. "Perhaps. It will depend, I suppose, on what Lady Alexandra tells her mother. If the dowager duchess takes umbrage, she will urge the duke to do the same."

"What will Lady Alexandra tell her, do you think?"

Viola thought of the set expression on Alexandra's face as she went in to see her mother. "I expect she'll say it was a trifle; some harmless flirting, a stolen kiss."

"As it most likely was," he pointed out.

Viola sighed. "She's a proper young lady, the sister of a duke. She's not at liberty to flirt with and kiss any young man she chooses."

"No." He looked down. "If I may repeat my question . . . What will you do?"

"If I'm sacked?" He gave a slight nod, and she put down her glass. "Look for another position." She looked sadly around the room. "I'm very fond of this one, though. It will be hard to leave Kingstag."

He nodded, rubbing his hands on the arms of her chair. Viola covertly watched. He had lovely hands, strong and big. "Would it reassure you," he said very slowly, "if I promised you a similar position at the same salary?" She jolted, and he raised those lovely hands as if to calm her. "Only if you cannot find one more to your liking. I hate to think you might be brought low by my nephew's actions, and thus by my own. I blatantly invited myself to Kingstag, and then I brought Newton with me. If there is blame to be laid, I must accept my share."

"You don't need to do that, my lord," she murmured.

"But I want to." One corner of his mouth tilted upward. "I want to very much, actually."

Viola turned her gaze to the corner of the fender where her feet were propped. *Do not become enamored of an earl,* she told herself. Especially not this earl, with his strong hands and endearing grin and an offer that could easily lead her to forget herself and do something very wrong, like flirt with him. Encourage him. Let him kiss her, and kiss him back, repeatedly, until she ended up in bed with him, begging him to make love to her. She didn't want that, she really didn't, even though part of her *did* want it, despite it being a terrible idea and—

A knock at the door startled her out of those thoughts and sent her leaping to her feet. She looked in alarm at the earl, who had also risen. There was no way to excuse his presence in her private room.

Without a word, he pointed at her bedroom, brows raised. Viola gave a quick nod, ignoring her conscience, and he stepped quietly inside, closing the door behind him. Straightening her shoulders, Viola went to the main door and opened it.

Alexandra stood there. Her eyes were a little wet, but she managed a smile. "May I come in?"

"Of course." Viola stepped aside and followed her to the tiny sofa.

"Mama said I must apologize to you," the girl began. "I put you in a very bad spot, and betrayed your trust. Mama was terribly upset that I took advantage of your distraction to steal away, when she's been so sick and you've had to do so much more than usual." She sucked in a deep breath. "But I want to apologize for myself. I know it was wrong, and even though nothing very improper happened, I'm sorry I did it. As soon as I saw your expression, I felt so stupid." She pleated her skirt, her whole figure drooping. "I hope you don't think less of me."

"Of course I don't." She clasped Alexandra's hand. "I understand exactly—what's more, I agree that it isn't fair a mere kiss should be judged so harshly. But I don't make the rules, and I would hate it more if you suffered. I may not be your sister—or your brother— able to protect you in other ways, but you are very dear to me, Alexandra."

Alexandra gave her a grateful smile. "As are you to us, Viola. I told Mama several times it was not your fault, and she agreed it was all mine." She made a slight grimace. "Jane always says her mother would sack a companion who allowed her to get into trouble, but I won't let Cleo think ill of you. I don't want you to go, and I shall try very hard not to put you in that position again." She paused. "What you said, outside Mama's door . . . Thank you. I had been feeling rather put out lately—everything has been Serena, Serena, Serena. I *want* her to be happy, I do . . . and I shall never forgive Frye for breaking her heart, *never* . . . but I was beginning to feel impatient with all the fuss over her. This whole party was arranged to cheer her up, and she doesn't even seem sad to have lost Frye." Her mouth quivered. "I shall try to be a better sister."

Viola pulled her into a hug. "You *are* a good sister. What happened to Serena was dreadful, but she shall survive it—as shall you survive this little to-do." Alexandra smiled. Viola squeezed her hand. "I fear we're all going a bit mad, trapped inside by all the snow. Who knew it could snow so much in Dorset? I've never seen the like . . ."

Alexandra laughed at last. "Nor I." She got up. "Mama said she doesn't want to make a fuss over a kiss—as long as I have learnt my lesson. I shall keep Lord Newton at a distance and be more conscious of my actions."

"Very good. That's all any of us can do." Viola walked her to the door. "Good night, Alexandra."

"Good night." Alexandra left, and Viola closed the door, feeling vastly relieved. If Alexandra escaped this with nothing worse than a scolding and chastened spirits, all would be well.

She had not forgotten that the Earl of Winterton was in her bedroom. He must have heard her conversation with Alexandra, and his mind must be at ease about his nephew. If the dowager duchess saw no reason for upset, there would be no need to tell the duke. That would put her own mind at ease, of course; if she didn't lose her position at Kingstag, there would be no need for her even to think about Winterton's offer, and what it might lead to, and why he'd said he wanted to propose it to her very much.

She opened the door and paused. It was a small room, barely big enough for the bed and a washstand, with a clothes cupboard in one wall. Consequently, Lord Winterton had stretched out atop her bed, his long legs crossed, his arms folded behind his head. There hadn't been a man in her bed since James died two years ago. The sight sent a shock of desire through her, hot and so powerful she had to cling to the doorknob to keep herself steady.

"She's gone," she said, shocked by the low husky quality of her voice.

He sat up and swung his feet to the floor. "I heard. All will be well?"

He was relieved the duke wouldn't thrash his nephew. "It seems so."

Winterton nodded. He still sat on her bed, far too big and masculine for her widow's room. Viola was trying without much success to stifle the wicked thoughts drifting through her mind like snow, a veritable blizzard of sinful images threatening to swamp her composure. She shouldn't have drunk that port; it had shot her good sense to flinders.

"Then you won't be sacked," said the earl.

Viola cleared her throat. She hadn't even been thinking of that. "I feel less anxious on that score."

He smiled again, that roguish grin that made her heart skip beats and her mind go blank. "And vastly relieved you shan't have to address what I said earlier."

She was too distracted by the sight of him sitting on her bed, his large, lovely hands clasped between his knees and his coal black hair rumpled as if he'd just woken . . . in her bed . . . "Yes, of course."

He got to his feet and came toward her. It only took two steps but they seemed very momentous and significant steps to Viola, still gripping the doorknob. "I'm relieved as well. I think you misunderstood what I meant. It wasn't an improper offer."

"No, of course not," she said. *Do not disagree with the earl,* she told herself. It would be rude. Or silly. Or . . . something, she wasn't precisely sure what, but she didn't want to argue with him now. Not when he was close enough that she could see the faint shadow of whiskers on his jaw and the pulse in his neck and the three different shades of blue in his eyes.

"If I had caused you to lose your position, it would have been my duty to see that you had another," he explained. Almost idly he reached out and took her hand. "But I don't really want to employ you."

"No," she agreed. As if she would get anything done if she saw him every day.

"Do you know why?" His voice was growing softer with each word. His thumb stroked over her knuckles. Viola's knees were softening, and her heart was booming against her ribs.

"I think . . ." She had to wet her lips. "I suspect so."

"Would it be unwelcome to you?"

No. She wanted him to kiss her more than ever, even after she'd just scolded Alexandra for letting a man kiss her, even though she'd been racked with anxiety at the thought of losing her position. Or perhaps that was *why* she wanted him to kiss her, because she'd thought she was on the brink of disaster and had been saved. Because she'd felt on the brink of disaster for most of the house party, and didn't have the will to resist the temptation that was *him* any longer.

For answer she lifted her face to his and leaned forward. Winterton met her halfway, his lips brushing hers like the softest feather. "Winterton," she whispered. "Please—"

"Viola." His hands cupped her jaw. "My name is Wesley. Wes, really."

She smiled in surprise. "Wes?"

"It rhymes with *yes*," he whispered, a laugh lurking in his tone, and then he was kissing her again, not so lightly this time, nor so briefly. Viola moaned when he teased her lips apart and his tongue swept into her mouth. His fingers curled into her hair, loosening the pins until it fell down her back. She arched against him, shivering when her breasts met his chest.

The earl—Wes—made an inarticulate sound of pleasure and gathered her closer. Viola realized she was on her toes, straining against him, clinging to his jacket. She felt drunk with desire, reveling in every shuddering breath he drew, every touch of his hands on her face, her shoulders, her back, her waist. No more was she a mere secretary and he a wealthy earl. In this moment they were simply man and woman, mad for each other.

"Viola." He broke the kiss, his chest heaving. "Viola." He pressed one more hard kiss on her mouth. "God above, I should go."

"I know." She burrowed into his embrace, wrapping her arms around his waist. He was so male and strong and he smelled so good, she had to swallow back an invitation to stay the night here with her. She hoped it was the port making her reckless, but she feared deep down it was far more than that.

"Can I see you again?" His thumb rolled over her lower lip, followed by his own lips in a lingering kiss.

"Every day, my lord," she said breathlessly. "Until you leave."

He went very still. "Can I see you again like this—Viola and Wes, not Winterton and Mrs. Cavendish."

Until you leave, she thought again. "Yes."

A wolfish grin flashed across his face and he kissed her once more, his lips lingering. "God," he moaned. "God help me, I want to stay but I am *going.*"

"Good night," she whispered.

His eyes seemed to glow. "Good night, love."

$\mathcal{W}$es returned to his own room with jaunty steps. What a bloody brilliant idea it had been to come to Kingstag Castle. Thank God Wessex had been away, and was still away. At the moment he didn't even care if the Desnos atlas were here, either. He'd kissed Viola Cavendish, and she had kissed him back. He couldn't wait to do it again.

He tried to check his racing pulse and remind himself to keep his wits about him. She was no society matron, looking for a fleeting affair to amuse herself. She was also not his equal, socially, and she would be cruelly hurt if their attraction to each other caused trouble. The last thing on earth he wanted to do was hurt Viola.

A slight frown crossed his face. How was he to manage this? Wes knew what his mother would do if a female servant at Winterbury were discovered in an affair with a guest. Of course, Viola was not really a servant, and even servants had some rights to personal relationships. She was the duchess's personal secretary, a position of some importance, independence, and status. What's more, she was a Cavendish cousin, and he . . .

Wes's steps slowed to a halt. She was a respectable woman—not quite a lady but not so far beneath him. He needn't be ashamed of his attraction to her. Why, who knew—in time, he might even—

"What happened?"

The tense question gave him a violent start of surprise. "Good lord, Justin," he snapped. "What do you mean shouting at me?"

His nephew blinked at him in astonishment. He was peering through his barely-opened door. "I didn't shout. You were standing in the corridor staring at nothing. Am I in terrible trouble?"

Right. Justin had been kissing Lady Alexandra. Wes's heart settled into a more normal, if rapid, rhythm. He glanced over his shoulder and motioned for his nephew to let him in. "We'll discuss this privately."

"Well, what happened?" Justin demanded again once Wes was inside and the door was safely closed. "Shall I apologize to the duke? Lady Bridget told me he's not but ten miles away. I could manage it, with a sturdy horse."

"Calm yourself." Wes waved one hand at the chair, but Justin stayed stubbornly on his feet, his hands in fists. Wes shrugged and dropped into the seat himself. "Lady Alexandra has spoken to her mother, who agrees it would be idiocy to make a scandal out of this. I believe Wessex is very protective of his sisters, but with the dowager duchess's support, I don't think you need to fear being called out or marched to the altar."

Justin's face broke with relief. "Thank you, Uncle."

Wes gave him a hard look. "Don't for one moment believe you won't suffer any consequences. Even if Wessex doesn't care a fig for what you did, I care, and so will your mother."

"Mother!" the boy exclaimed. "Why would you tell her?"

"Because this is twice now you've been kissing females without honorable intent." Justin's mouth fell open, and Wes nodded. "I didn't say you had *wicked* intent, but you know perfectly well that if you go around kissing young ladies, you'll find yourself married to one of them before long. Is that what you want?"

"Well—no, not precisely . . ."

Wes rubbed his hands over his face at Justin's cagey tone. "If you think the solution is to kiss maids and tavern wenches, be assured I shall punish you for that. A gentleman doesn't trifle with women, be they noble or ordinary."

His nephew scoffed. "*Some* women—"

"Those are whores," he said bluntly. "If you can't keep your trousers fastened, you'd best be prepared to pay for the pleasure. Whores are willing because you pay them, not because of your charm and grace, but at least a whore expects nothing but payment from you. Seducing a girl like Lady Alexandra . . ." Wes shook his head. "I couldn't save you from Wessex's wrath in that case—in fact, I'd step up to whip you after he did. You'd do the honorable thing by her, and then spend the rest of your life being a decent husband to her."

Now Justin was offended. "Of course I would! That is, I didn't seduce her—it was only a little kiss—but I am a gentleman and I know my duty—"

Wes rose. "And your desire is to be married before you're twenty-two, before you've had a chance to go to London and meet dozens of pretty girls? Before you've got a chance to travel and see something of the world? Marriage is for the rest of your life, and you've been telling me for days and days that you were so bored in Hampshire you might run mad from it. Now you're ready to become head of the family, bring home a bride, and settle down?"

Justin had flushed progressively redder as Wes spoke. Now he squirmed. "No—not yet, not all that."

"Then mind your behavior. And if you can't, I'll thrash you until you can. Gentlemen have far more freedom than ladies, and therefore greater responsibility to exercise it wisely. Being young and stupid does not excuse you from the consequences of your actions."

Justin scowled, but wiped it away as Wes raised one brow in warning. "Yes, Uncle."

Wes put one hand on his nephew's shoulder. "We've all been young and stupid, every man one of us," he said in a kinder tone. "It's one thing if you fancy the girl and can see yourself married to her. If you can't . . . you shouldn't be kissing her. Even if you don't get caught by her outraged papa, you give her cruel and misleading ideas about your intentions. You're a cheat and a rogue if you let a girl fall in love with you just so you can steal a few kisses and embraces."

Now thoroughly sobered, Justin nodded. "I understand. I never thought of it that way, but . . . yes, I see."

"Good man." Wes clapped his shoulder. "I don't think you'd like a lady to lead you on, only to refuse you once you were wild for her."

"Not at all." Justin appeared appalled by the thought.

"Then don't do it yourself." Wes let himself out and returned to his own room. Thank God Kingstag was large enough that he and Justin didn't need to share rooms. He needed some peace to think.

The first realization he came to was that he would need to take his own advice, regarding Viola. He did not want her to draw any wrong conclusions from his actions. The second realization, following close on the first, was that he *did* fancy her, more than usual. He liked talking to her. She was sensible and clever and beautiful, and she made him laugh. Wes had no time for idiots or people who were frivolous, and he couldn't recall the last woman he'd looked forward to seeing the way he did Viola.

So what were his intentions?

He pondered the matter as he prepared for bed, and hadn't reached any definite answer by the time he fell asleep. The only thing he knew for certain was that his interest in her was neither shallow nor fleeting. And he was determined to kiss her again.

CHAPTER NINE

The next day Viola decided to carry on as if nothing had happened and hope for the best. She'd lain awake until late at night, wondering if she would be called into the dowager's rooms to explain herself, but a summons never came.

Alexandra seemed to have decided the same thing. Every time Viola caught sight of her, she was behaving as she should—well away from Lord Newton. The young viscount, for his part, seemed cowed and quiet as well, and spent most of his time with the other gentlemen.

"Good morning, ma'am." Lord Winterton appeared before her. "May I join you?"

"Good morning, sir. Of course." She had covered a table with evergreen branches and was plaiting them into garlands, an activity that would allow her to monitor the play rehearsal and everyone in it.

Lord Winterton pulled up a chair opposite her. It gave her a splendid view of him, and his lovely mouth that had kissed her so tenderly and magnificently last night. Had that really happened? Covertly she studied him as he poked at the mountain of evergreens on her table. She'd had enough brought in to make a garland that would stretch from here to London and back.

Then he looked up and caught her watching him, and a faint smile touched his lips. Viola flushed warm all over her body. Oh yes, it had really happened. The Earl of Winterton had held her close and kissed her until she could hardly breathe. He leaned forward. "Viola," he whispered.

Blushing, she also leaned forward. "Yes?"

"I missed you at breakfast," he said, almost inaudibly. "I never realized how much I looked forward to seeing you every morning until you weren't there."

She couldn't stop herself from smiling. "I had work to do." She motioned at the greenery.

"And then? Will you be free to walk out with me and see the sky again? I believe the snow is finally ending."

Viola glanced at the tall windows. The sky was brighter today, but snow still fell. "Perhaps, but I must keep an eye on rehearsal."

"Of course." He picked up a branch and twirled it. "How does one make a garland?"

Her eyes widened in astonishment. "You want to make garlands?"

"I want to sit with you," he said with a searing look. "And I am willing to make garlands to do so."

Oh my. There was a tiny burst of joy in her chest, and her fingers shook as she showed him how to pull apart the branches and twine them around each other to form a long rope. The drawing room was full of people by now, leaving little chance of conversation without being overheard, so they worked in companionable silence. At one point Wes stretched out his legs beneath the table, and Viola lightly rested her slipper on top of his boot. His blue gaze shot to hers, and she almost melted at the hunger in them.

The day flew by. Viola was called away several times to supervise some aspect of costuming, for the play was to be in a few days. Wes had to go perform his scenes, which sent Viola into gales of silent laughter. A large tea was served midday, and the entire company gathered around the table to consume every crumb of it. Her heart swelled with happiness to see Alexandra laughing and whispering with her friend Kate Lacy, and she felt a rush of relief that Lord Newton seemed more interested in discussing horses with Lord Gosling than in flirting with anyone. All of the guests were in good spirits, and it felt like a sign from above that the party was a success after all.

By the time everyone retired to dress for dinner, Viola had woven a mile or more of garland. She looked at Wes, who was frowning over his much shorter garland, and grinned. "Well done, my lord."

"I haven't done anything worthy of that compliment today, ma'am." He put his hands on the table and half rose from his chair. "Come here."

Viola glanced nervously at the door, but everyone had left. She leaned toward Wes. He closed the distance and brushed his lips against hers. "That's better," he breathed. "Although I might not have done it well enough . . . Let me try again . . ." He kissed her once more, lightly and tenderly, and something inside Viola sang with joy.

Wes sat back, looking pleased with himself. "Much better. I've been waiting all day for that."

Blushing and beaming, she laughed. "Ought you go prepare for dinner?"

He surveyed the greenery piled between them. "I am utterly worn out from all this garland making."

"I hear there is to be dancing after dinner," Viola remarked. "Miss Penworth has agreed to play."

"Dancing!" His face lit. "I feel energized already. Will you dance with me, love?"

Her heart leapt for one wild moment before her brain reminded her to be cautious. "Perhaps. I must speak to the dowager." He blinked, and she quickly explained. "To let her know how the party is proceeding."

"Is her health improving?"

Viola nodded. "I hope she'll be able to join the guests soon." And take her place as hostess, which would be a vast relief.

He grinned. "I hope so as well. But . . ." He reached for her hand. "You didn't answer my question."

About dancing with him. She hesitated, but the temptation was too great. "Yes."

This time his smile was sensuous and intimate. "That's all I care to know."

They went their separate ways. Viola spoke to the housekeeper about arranging the garland in the hall, then braced herself and went to the dowager's apartment.

It went much better than expected. The dowager was vastly improved, even sitting in a chair by the fire today with a hot brick under her feet. "I have promised Bridget I will attend the play," she told Viola. "Thank heaven I shall be able to."

"I'm very pleased to hear it, ma'am," said Viola fervently.

The dowager smiled. "Has Alexandra kept her word to behave today?"

"Perfectly, Your Grace." She hesitated. "And so has Lord Newton. I believe his uncle spoke to him very strongly about what occurred."

"Very good. Tell me about Lord Winterton."

Caught off guard, Viola jumped. "What?"

"Bridget tells me he fancies you." The dowager's gaze was sharp. "Alexandra says you and the earl discovered her with young Newton, and that she didn't believe that discovery happened because you were searching for her."

Viola could only sit with her mouth open in shock.

The older woman leaned forward. "He's a very eligible catch, and Sophronia tells me he's not one of those society fribbles. Is he an honest fellow?"

"Y-yes," she stammered.

"Do you, in my daughter's words, 'fancy him'?" Viola couldn't speak. Her answer must have shown on her face, for the dowager sat back. "Remember you are a Cavendish, Viola. Demand that he treat you as such, or Wessex will have his head."

Startled, Viola gaped. "You're—I'm not—That is . . ."

"Am I upset you've caught a gentleman's eye?" The dowager smiled. "No. I know Cleo values you immensely, but you're far too young to spend the rest of your life tending to someone else's family and household. I am not at all surprised, my dear."

"But . . . he is an earl." So far above her.

The dowager's expression softened. "We never know where love may grow. I was the third daughter of a viscount, no one to speak of, and certainly not worthy of a duke. But my dear, I knew it was meant to be the first time Wessex asked me to dance. Do not be afraid to seize happiness when you find it."

"Thank you, Your Grace," she said softly.

Heart soaring, she left. It wasn't quite a mother's blessing, but the dowager's words had been kind and reassuring. It gave her hope. And confidence.

Somehow Wes endured dinner and the blessedly brief round of port among the gentlemen. Every man seemed keen to rejoin the ladies, and when they entered the ballroom Miss Penworth was already seated at the pianoforte.

He tried to disguise his interest in Viola. She sat next to Lady Sophronia, watching as the other guests laughed and danced. Wes asked Lady Alexandra to partner him first, and then Lady Serena. Both were excellent dancers, but he barely registered a moment of it. He was only biding his time.

After two exuberant airs, someone called out to Miss Penworth to play a more sedate country dance so they might catch their breath. Wes seized his chance and approached the settee.

"May I have this dance, ma'am?"

Lady Sophronia's eyes gleamed as she looked him up and down. "If I would grant anyone a dance, it would be you, Winterton. But I haven't danced since Frederick, my fourth fiancé. He was the finest dancer, and spoiled me for every other partner."

Wes grinned and turned to Viola. "I'm sure I could never live up to him. Perhaps Mrs. Cavendish will step out with me, then?"

"Go on, Viola," said Sophronia, wonderful woman. "Dance with the man."

She took his hand, and Wes felt a charge leap up his arm. She gave him a smile, and it was as though the sun had come out. They took their places and he barely remembered what steps to do.

There was no real chance of conversation. Wes was content to gaze at her when they separated. With her dark hair piled up on top of her head and her green eyes alight with happiness, she was entrancing. Every time they clasped hands, her gaze met his, warm and deep and smiling, and he could hardly breathe from how much he wanted her.

When the dance finally ended, he was both relieved and annoyed. Relieved because it ended the torment of watching her without being able to speak to her. Annoyed because now he didn't even have an excuse to watch her. She moved among the guests with quiet grace, suggesting the next dance, helping turn the pages for Miss Penworth, graciously accepting Lord Gosling's invitation to dance. Wes's gaze followed her helplessly around the room, like a smitten boy's. Everything seemed right when she was around—not only because she had a way of putting everyone at ease, not only because her good cheer never wavered, but because she was the most sensible person Wes had ever met.

After a decade of traveling around the world, Wes had a deep appreciation for people who were able to get things done without fuss or drama. Viola seemed to think of everything and took care of problems before they even happened. The one lapse, Lady Alexandra's stolen kiss with Justin, had happened because he lured her away from the party. Otherwise . . . every arrangement had been pitch perfect. He could tell Lady Serena was somewhat overwhelmed by the demands of being hostess, and Lady Sophronia simply didn't care to mind the details. It was Viola who recognized that Miss Penworth's fingers were growing tired, that Lady Sophronia had nodded once too often, that Lady Bridget was drooping in her chair, and murmured a word in Lady Serena's ear that it was time to end the evening.

Back in his room after everyone had gaily bid the others Happy Christmas and good night—for it was Christmas Eve—he stared into the fire crackling in his hearth, unable to sleep. Was she still working, arranging things for everyone tomorrow? After which she would quietly withdraw into the background, when she deserved to be celebrated as the mastermind of the entire party. Was she enjoying a little sip of port, her mouth rosy and shiny from the wine as she contemplated her work? Had anyone told her how invaluable she was, or how thankful they were she was there?

It was beginning to bother Wes that she was neither hostess nor guest, neither family nor servant, yet everything seemed to rest on her shoulders. Someone ought to thank her, and show appreciation for her unfailing good humor, grace, and charm. Someone ought to make sure she had a happy Christmas, when she had done so much to make it happy for the rest of them.

He wanted her to feel treasured and appreciated. Not only for the way she saw to everyone else's comfort and amusement, but for the way her nose wrinkled when she laughed. For the way she took everything with such good humor and grace. And for the starry look in her eyes when she was well kissed.

He jumped up from the chair and strode to the wardrobe. After a minute of rummaging, he found what he sought. It wasn't much, but he thought she might understand.

His heartbeat seemed to boom in his ears as he made his way through the quiet castle. It was late, nearing midnight. It was almost Christmas Day. When he reached her door, he tapped very lightly and held his breath, waiting.

The first thought through his brain when she opened the door was that her hair was down. It reached below her shoulders, one long curl lying on her breast. Wes's eyes fixed on that curl, on that plump swell of flesh, and his mouth went dry.

The second thought through his brain was that she was in her dressing gown and nightdress.

"Wes," she said softly, and he jerked his eyes up. "What—?"

He cleared his throat. "May I come in?" Her lips parted—damn, how her mouth entranced him. "I have a gift for you," he added.

She blushed the most endearing shade of pink. "Oh no, that's not necessary."

Wes's lips quirked. "Please."

She let him in and closed the door. Without comment he handed her his travel atlas. Viola looked up at him, startled.

"It's not much," he said apologetically. "I've had it with me for years. When I am away from England, it reminds me of home, and when I am in England, it's got splendid maps."

"It's yours? You must keep it—"

"I want you to have it." He shoved his hands into the pockets of his dressing gown. "It also has descriptions and engravings of scenic vistas all over England and Scotland, so you may see a bit of the world even if you never go beyond Kingstag Castle." He gave a lopsided grin. "Happy Christmas."

Her face went still as she gazed at the book, letting it fall open to an engraving of the cliffs at Dover. Then she looked up at him. There was a lovely flush on her cheekbones, and he could feel her every breath. "Thank you. It's beautiful."

His body roared to life, desire pulsing through him like a tidal wave. Before she could say more he kissed her softly, then harder as her hand went up his chest, around his neck, into his hair.

Every thought fled Viola's brain except the smell and taste and heat of him. Wes pressed her back up against the wall and let his hands roam over her waist, her hips, up to her breasts. She sucked in her breath as his thumb went over her nipple. Wes paused, giving her a searing glance. It was all Viola could do to nod; *yes,* she wanted to say, *more.*

He'd brought her a gift, one of his own atlases. She was still clutching it, the worn leather smooth and soft. Normally she and Stephen exchanged small gifts, or at least a letter, but the snow had kept the mail coach from Kingstag for days. The Duchess of Wessex always gave the staff generous gifts, but Viola knew to expect the same thing the housekeeper would receive. Only Wes had given her something personal, something very dear and valuable to him and therefore wonderful to her. She'd never had her own atlas, nor any need for one. Only Wes looked at her as Viola, who yearned to see the world, not merely the secretary who made everything run smoothly. Only Wes . . .

Looked at her as if she were beautiful and fascinating.

Do not be afraid to seize happiness, echoed the dowager's voice in her head. Viola knew she should be afraid. Not only because he was an earl and she was practically a servant, not only because an affair could cause her to become an unemployed almost-servant, but because Wes could break her heart. Somewhere in the last several days she'd gone and fallen in love with him, with his laughing blue eyes and droll sense of humor and wonderful wicked hands, which were currently exploring her body with exquisite effect.

But instead of choosing the prudent course, she dropped the atlas on the sofa beside her and clung to him, kissing him back with every fiber of her being. Being busy from morning to night as the duchess's secretary hadn't made her forget what it was like to want a man, to be wanted and held and loved by a man.

"Viola," he breathed next to her ear, "I want to make love to you so desperately . . ." His hand cupped her breast, a heady sensation through the soft linen of her dressing gown.

She wasn't afraid. She wanted to seize happiness. Even if just this once, she wanted to feel loved by him. She bit his earlobe gently, making him shudder, and whispered, "Please do."

His hands shook as he unbuttoned her nightgown until it gaped open to her belly. She leaned her head back against the wall, breathing unevenly as he drew the sturdy linen apart, baring her to him. Her pulse felt like a drumbeat between her legs.

"Such beauty," he whispered, his fingers tracing her collarbone. "Such sweetness." His touch drifted lower, swirling over her breast.

Viola moaned. "Such passion." He brushed her ribs and Viola quivered. "Viola, I . . ."

She made her eyes focus on him. His hair was wild—from her hands—and his eyes burned as blue as flame. A fine sheen of sweat covered his brow, and he was breathing even harder than she was. "Take off your clothes," she said.

He blinked, and a wicked grin curved his mouth. Without a word he stripped off his dressing gown, his waistcoat, his cravat. He kicked off his shoes and stepped out of his trousers, then pulled the shirt over his head. Viola's throat closed up as he shed his undergarments to stand before her completely nude.

The Earl of Winterton was magnificent, lean and strong and bronzed all over. Only one part of him was untouched by the sun, and her gazed fixed on it. His erection stood straight and thick, and the pulsing between her legs grew stronger.

"May I?" Unabashed at her staring, he fingered the edges of her nightgown. Viola managed to nod, and he slid the garment off her shoulders. "May I?" he whispered again, his hands sliding around her hips. Again she nodded, and he lifted her against him. She put her arms around his neck and hiked her legs around his waist, and he carried her through the open door into her bedroom and rolled them both onto the bed.

He drove her wild with light, teasing touches, then firmer strokes that made her twist and writhe in his arms. He kissed her everywhere, his mouth hot and potent. Viola was the one who finally reached between them and wrapped her hand around his erection. "I want you," she gasped breathlessly. *"Wes."*

Wes moved over her. His arms bulged as her hand slid up and down his length. Her body humming, Viola guided him between her legs and hooked one leg over his hip. His entire body was taut, and she thought she might burst into flames if he didn't take her then.

He pressed inside, making her gasp. He slid almost out and licked his thumb. "You're so beautiful," he rasped. "I'm about to spend myself just looking at you." He touched her as he slid deep again. Viola arched off the mattress and gripped handfuls of the linens.

Again Wes pulled back. "Open your eyes." His voice had gone ragged. His body was shaking. Viola forced open her eyes and saw that his face was tight with strain. "I want to see the moment when you find your pleasure . . ." He stroked again, his hips moving in slow, hard time with his thumb. Viola stared into his eyes until she couldn't, until the waves of climax made her vision go dark and her body convulsed. She clutched at him and he thrust hard and deep as he kissed her. Dimly she felt him shudder in his own release, but he kept kissing her until she felt soft and exhausted.

"Viola," he murmured as he nuzzled her ear. "I want to stay the night with you."

So he could make love to her again. So she could make love to him, and wake up with his arms around her. Viola gave a sleepy smile. "Please do."

CHAPTER TEN

𝒱iola had never had a happier Christmas Day.

She woke with Wes stretched out in her bed, looking down at her with a wicked smile. He made love to her again, and only left when the full light of day shone through the small window.

Breakfast was quiet. Withers told her the Cavendish girls had gone to eat with their mother in her apartment, and the other guests were sleeping late. She drank her tea leisurely, wallowing in the memory of every wicked, sensual thing Wes had done.

The rest of the day passed much the same way. Bridget cajoled everyone into one last rehearsal for the play, and dictated several notes for improvement to Viola, but the sun had come out and the young people wanted to go outside. It was cold and bright, and before long the company was throwing snowballs at each other, the ladies shrieking in glee and the gentlemen roaring about battlefield honor and glory. Lord Gosling took a large snowball to the face and Bridget laughed so hard she went head over heels backward into a snowdrift. Lady Alexandra threw one at Lord Newton, who seemed to enjoy it very much. By then Miss Penworth and Lady Jane had dug a hollow under a tree, and began throwing snow at everyone from the safety of their fort. Viola managed to hit Wes in the shoulder with a snowball, and in retaliation he chased her into the garden, out of sight of everyone, and kissed her among the snow-covered rosebushes.

Tonight Viola was invited to dine with the guests. She wore her best green gown and her mother's pearls, and felt Wes's admiring gaze as if it were a physical touch. When he tapped lightly at her door late that night, she was waiting, ready to spend another night in his arms.

Boxing Day brought a return of duty for Viola. Lady Charlotte Ascot finally arrived, after being snowed in at a roadside inn. The dowager was well enough to come down, swathed in shawls, to present the servants their gifts and thank them. Viola accepted her gifts happily—a length of blue silk, oranges from the hothouse, and five gold guineas—and belatedly sat down to write her brother a letter. She had to share her happiness about Wes with Stephen.

It led to a surprising discovery.

She found Wes in the billiard room with his nephew and some other gentlemen. When he caught sight of her he put down his cue stick and excused himself.

"Come with me." She took his hand. "I want to show you something."

He raised his brows but came with her willingly. Viola led him to the duke's study, quiet and hushed in His Grace's absence. She felt a frisson of nerves just entering the room; normally Mr. Martin came to her when she needed to know something about the duke, to tell the duchess or arrange the calendar. But sometimes she had cause to enter here, as she had earlier today.

"I had to fetch more quills," she said as she closed the door carefully behind them. "Mr. Martin, His Grace's secretary, keeps a supply of the best ones in his desk." She nodded at Mr. Martin's desk in the far corner of the room. "And while I was here, I took the very smallest peek at the shelves. Guess what I discovered?"

Wes's face blanked. "Do you mean—?"

Flushed with eagerness, she nodded. "The Desnos atlas. At least, I believe it is so. It was put away with the other books." She went to the shelves beside Mr. Martin's desk and took out the book she'd seen earlier. "Only you can say for certain." She brought the book to the duke's wide desk and laid it flat.

There was a haunted hunger in Wes's face as he opened the cover. It was not a terribly large book, but it was bound in fine old leather, the titles stamped in gilt. Viola watched his fingers caress the binding, lingering on a small crease near the spine. "It's very like my father's," he murmured. Reverently he opened it, turning a few pages.

"A map of the new world." His finger barely touched the page as he indicated the illustrations. "These were the maps that sent me off to read journals of explorers, and to scalp Anne's doll." He turned another page. "And here—star charts to navigate by! I should have studied these more closely, to be able to discuss them intelligently with you." Viola felt a burst of pleasure at his words. He turned more pages, scrutinizing some in silence and exclaiming over others.

Through it all his enthusiasm for travel shone through. He would pause and relate some story of his travels to India, and to Caribbean islands where pirates roamed. Only when he turned to the end of the book did words fail him. The last two dozen or so pages were covered with close-written notes. Wes's face went still.

"Is it his writing?" Viola ventured.

Silently he nodded, reading.

She slipped her hand into his. It must be bittersweet, to see his father's journal entries in the back of the atlas and know he couldn't have it. This was indeed the atlas the Duke of Wessex had purchased for the duchess.

After several minutes he closed the book, giving the cover one last brush of his hand. "Thank you."

"Perhaps His Grace will be moved by your story," she said.

Wes smiled wryly and shook his head. "Perhaps." He pulled her into his arms. "You found it and gave me a chance to see it again. Thank you."

"I wanted you to see it and know it wasn't lost." She glanced at the atlas in apology. "Even if His Grace won't part with it."

Wes looked at her for a long moment. "You," he said at last, "are extraordinary."

"No," she scoffed. "Very ordinary."

"Not remotely," he whispered, and kissed her. She placed her palms on his chest and went up on her toes, kissing him back. She might not be extraordinary, but *this*—this deep-seated contentment and awe at the way he felt and the way he made her feel—this *love* was the most dazzlingly extraordinary thing she'd ever experienced. Whatever happened later, she would have this moment of true joy and love to remember.

"What the devil?" said a terribly familiar voice. Viola froze, her eyes flying open. Wes raised his head, and as one they turned toward the door.

The Duke of Wessex stood framed in the doorway. As Viola watched, stricken, Mr. Martin peeped around the duke's shoulder before immediately retreating.

Oh dear heavens. She took a step backward and pressed her hands to her burning cheeks. His face as grim as a thundercloud, Wessex strode across the room. "Winterton, I presume."

Wes bowed. "At your serv—"

The duke shoved him backward. "How dare you. Mrs. Cavendish is our cousin."

Wes's eyes flew to Viola, who shook her head mutely. "I meant no offense, sir."

Wessex raised one dark brow. "And yet I find you making love to her in my own private study." Then his gaze fell on the atlas, still on the desk behind them, and his eyes grew dark with anger. "I suppose that is the atlas you wrote to me about."

Wes cleared his throat. "Yes, it happens to be, but—"

"Get out." The duke glared at him.

"Wessex," said Wes, "allow me a moment to explain."

"I see," said the duke with icy finality, "that you have persuaded Mrs. Cavendish to search my personal study to find the book you sought. And I suspect I know how you persuaded her." He looked at Viola for the first time in minutes. "You may go."

Viola wet her lips, but had no words. She never argued with the duke; she barely spoke to him at all. To protest now, when she had violated his trust by invading his study to show her lover one of the duke's private possessions . . . "Sir," she said bravely, "Your Grace . . . If I may . . . It was my fault."

The duke's expression didn't change. "No, ma'am. I wondered at Lord Winterton's persistence in seeking that atlas, but I didn't imagine he would go to this length, corrupting you into helping him."

"Viola? Oh—there are you are." Bridget's bright voice cut through the room. "And Gareth!" With a squeal Bridget launched herself at the duke, who caught her in one arm and kissed the top of her head. "When did you return? Did Helen have the baby? Is everyone well?"

"Just now." The duke smiled briefly at his sister. "I'm busy here, and Cleo will be able to tell you all about Helen, who is very well, as is her new daughter."

"How brilliant! A baby girl! And how wonderful you've come home!" She beamed at him. "We're staging a play tomorrow and now you can see it."

"A play?" Wessex looked at Viola in alarm.

"A farce," Bridget amended. "I wrote it! Everyone is in it except Mama and Aunt Sophronia. It will be the best entertainment at Kingstag in years. I've come to fetch Viola; Lord Gosling is dripping feathers everywhere and no one sews better than she does. Oh, and Lord Winterton must come rehearse his scenes."

Slowly Wessex turned to look at Wes. "He is in your play?"

Bridget nodded. "He plays the king who dies."

The duke's expression darkened. "Very well," he said, still watching Wes. "He'll be down soon. I need a word with him first, Bridget."

"Thank you, Gareth." She bounced up on her toes and kissed his cheek, then hurried out of the room.

"When is the play to be performed?"

"Tomorrow, Your Grace," Viola murmured.

The duke jerked his head. "You may stay until the play is over," he told Wes. "The next morning you leave. I will not have my own cousin's widow seduced under my roof. And if you think to wheedle that atlas from me, I suggest you spare your breath."

Wes's eyes were stormy blue. "If you'll allow me to explain, sir . . ."

"Winterton," said the duke, "I don't care to hear it." This time when he pointed, Viola rushed for the door.

Outside, Geoffrey Martin waited. He was a kind man, and now he simply gave her a sympathetic smile. "Happy Christmas, Mrs. Cavendish."

"Happy Christmas, Mr. Martin," she murmured, feeling as though she would be ill. The duke was not happy. He might be taking it out on Wes at the moment, but eventually he would focus on her part in the debacle. She had dodged being blamed for Alexandra's indiscretion, but now she had done even worse.

The study door opened again and Wes stepped out. He nodded once to Mr. Martin, who slipped obediently inside and closed the door again. Wes looked at Viola.

"I must go," she said in a rush. "See to the rehearsal—the costumes—the play is tomorrow, you know—"

He reached for her hand. "I'll speak to Wessex when his temper cools and tell him you weren't to blame."

She backed up, shaking her head. "No. I—I will explain to him. He's been very kind to me so far, and I hope . . . I hope not to lose my position."

A thin line creased his brow. "About your position—"

"No!" She tried to smile, but failed. "I cannot lose my place here, Wes—Lord Winterton. I cannot. The salary is far above what I could expect anywhere else; I told you the duke has been *very* kind. If I lose this position, my brother will have to leave university, and I don't want that. I won't *allow* that." She took another step backward. "Please don't anger the duke further, if you have any care for me at all."

Grim-faced, he gave a faint nod.

Viola blinked back a tear. She had known it wasn't to be forever between them, but she hadn't thought to lose him so soon. Then again, she'd never thought she'd fall in love with him. "Thank you, my lord."

"Viola," he said in a low urgent voice, but she turned and ran, away from his beautiful hands and beguiling laugh and eyes as blue as the midsummer sky.

$\mathcal{W}$es seethed with frustration.

The duke refused to listen to his explanation. Part of him wanted to punch the fellow in the face and make him listen, and part of him knew the duke was absolutely right. If it had been any other fellow kissing Viola in there, Wes would have thrown that blighter right out into the snow.

The look in her eyes though, when she said she dared not lose her position . . . That look gutted him. She had risked a great deal to show him that atlas, and he was bound and determined that it would not cost her everything.

On the other hand, he didn't like the duke's plan at all. Wessex had told him in no uncertain terms that he was to pack his trunk and be ready to leave early in the morning after the play. It ought to have given him a bit of hope, that the duke was willing to allow him to stay so that Lady Bridget's play wouldn't be spoiled, but all Wes could think of was the second part of the duke's order: never come back.

What are your intentions? echoed his own voice in his head.

He intended to make her happy. He intended to win her favor and make her smile at him again. He intended to get her back into his bed, as often as possible. He intended . . . to make her fall in love with him.

What had he told Justin? *If you don't see yourself marrying her, don't kiss the girl.*

He knew that was the answer. Even more, it was the answer he wanted. When he woke in the dawn to see her dark hair spread across the pillow and her beautiful face soft with sleep right in front of him, Wes had known. He would have been content to stay there in that room with her forever, he who had never felt content in one place for more than a few weeks. He had never felt more at home than with her.

Because he was in love. He'd kissed her, he'd fallen in love, and he wanted to marry her.

And that meant he wasn't about to leave without her, no matter what the Duke of Wessex said.

CHAPTER ELEVEN

𝒯he play was going to be an epic disaster.

It began with Miss Penworth declaring that her music had gone missing. Bridget scowled and stomped around until Withers located the pages, under a tea tray in the parlor. Lord Gosling's costume dropped its feathers again, and it took Viola more than two hours to replace them. Everyone else seemed to have forgotten their lines or lost some part of their costume, and two footmen were required to track down people who had wandered off before their scenes. In addition, the Duke of Frye had arrived at last, and no one knew quite what to say to him now. Only Lady Charlotte Ascot seemed willing to speak to him, while Serena had to restrain Bridget from pushing him out into the snow. Blessedly the duchess resumed her role as hostess, both sparing Viola from the job and preventing the duchess from delivering any sort of remonstrance about Lord Winterton.

There was a sharp little pain in her chest every time she thought about Wes, and how he would depart the next morning. She'd lain in bed all night, wishing he could come to her once more and yet terrified that he would. Was it worse to see him as much as possible and lose even more of her heart to him, or to cut herself off now? She didn't know, and ended up stealing longing glances at him across the room as she sewed feathers.

At long last the production was ready to begin. The dowager duchess sat in the audience beside her daughter-in-law and the duke, who wore a wary expression. Sophronia looked filled with eager expectation, which only deepened Viola's sense of impending disaster. Bridget had directed Viola to sit behind the stage with a copy of the script and remind everyone of their lines before they went on. If women could join the army, she reflected, Bridget would be the most fearsome general of them all.

The script had become utterly ridiculous. Viola had Bridget's own copy, which was covered with crossed out sections and additions in the margins. She did her best to keep up, but when Wes approached to make his entrance, dented crown in place, she faltered and busied herself with adjusting Alexandra's ghostly draperies. He strode past her onto the stage. Just hearing his voice made her flinch, and she accidentally stabbed a pin through the draperies into her finger.

When Alexandra went on stage to issue her prophecy about the death of the king, Viola found herself face to face with Wes.

"Do you know your lines, sir?" she asked formally.

He nodded.

"Very good. I'll go where I'm needed, then—"

"Viola!" He caught her hand before she could retreat.

"Please don't," she whispered in distress. It was gouging out her heart to think that he must leave tomorrow morning and she would probably never see him again.

"Just for a moment. Please." She hesitated, undone by the urgency in his face, and he pulled her back behind the curtain at the back of the stage—which had been borrowed from the billiard room.

"The play," she began.

Wes waved one hand as if to shove the play away. "I've just died by decapitation and had my entrails eaten by wolves. I've done my service to Lady Bridget's play. I need to speak to you before Wessex tosses me out."

He wanted to say good-bye. Another wave of misery rolled over her, but she managed a slight nod. She could do this. She had to.

He took a deep breath. "Marry me."

Viola blinked.

"I came here determined to get the Desnos atlas," Wes went on. "I wanted to retrace my father's last journey with it, see what he saw and experience what he did. I've barely spent six months at a time in England since I was eighteen, and I wanted to be off as soon as I recovered the atlas.

"But you said something about travel the other day, that it was no hardship to stay home when everything dear to you was here. When Wessex told me to get out, I didn't even think at all about my father's atlas—all I could think of was that I didn't want to lose *you*. I don't want to go anywhere without you."

"But . . ."

"I love you," he added softly. "If you could care for me enough to give me a chance—"

A sound escaped her, half laugh, half sob. "I fell in love with you when you took me to see the stars."

"Did you?" His face lit up. "Then I have a chance." He pulled her into his arms, his dented crown slipping to one side. "Will you marry me, my darling Viola? Will you travel the world with me and manage my household perfectly when we're home? Will you have a pack of children with me, who will surely vex us almost as much as Justin and Alexandra?"

"Oh, but—but . . ." Viola blushed. "My brother," she said in despair.

"I should be very proud to sponsor his fees," he said. "He can teach me how to navigate."

She smiled, then she laughed, and then she kissed him. "Yes. Yes, Wes, yes."

"You should always say my name that way."

He kissed her again, long and thoroughly. There was an outburst on the other side of the curtain. Viola ignored it for once. The duke and duchess could intervene in any uproar caused by their guests.

"It sounds like Lady Serena has got over being jilted by the Duke of Frye," Wes murmured against her hair.

Viola pressed her cheek to his chest and smiled. "I know."

His laugh rumbled though her. "Did you really?"

She squeezed him tighter. "Since the Christmas Eve rehearsal. She's in love with someone else. I recognize the look."

"Do you?" He tipped up her face to kiss her. "What does it look like?"

She put her hands on the side of his face and smiled, reveling in the way he looked at her. "Like this."

ABOUT THE AUTHOR

Caroline Linden was born a reader, not a writer. She earned a math degree from Harvard University and wrote computer software before turning to writing fiction. Since then the Boston Red Sox have won the World Series three times, which is not relevant but still worth mentioning. Her books have won the NEC Reader's Choice Award, the Daphne du Maurier Award, the NJRW Golden Leaf Award, and RWA's RITA Award, and have been translated into seventeen languages.

Visit her online at www.carolinelinden.com to join her VIP Readers' list and get a free short story exclusively for members, as well as get notified when her next book is available and get sneak peeks at upcoming books and occasional notice about fantastic deals or contests. You can also follow her on twitter at @Caro_Linden or like her on Facebook.

~ALSO BY CAROLINE LINDEN~

~THE WAGERS OF SIN~
MY ONCE AND FUTURE DUKE
AN EARL LIKE YOU

~THE SCANDALOUS SERIES~
LOVE AND OTHER SCANDALS
IT TAKES A SCANDAL
ALL'S FAIR IN LOVE AND SCANDAL (NOVELLA)
LOVE IN THE TIME OF SCANDAL
A STUDY IN SCANDAL (NOVELLA)
SIX DEGREES OF SCANDAL
THE SECRET OF MY SEDUCTION (NOVELLA)

~THE TRUTH ABOUT THE DUKE~
THE WAY TO A DUKE'S HEART
BLAME IT ON BATH
ONE NIGHT IN LONDON
I LOVE THE EARL (NOVELLA)

~THE BOW STREET AGENTS~
YOU ONLY LOVE ONCE
FOR YOUR ARMS ONLY
A VIEW TO A KISS

~THE REECE FAMILY~
A RAKE'S GUIDE TO SEDUCTION
WHAT A ROGUE DESIRES
WHAT A GENTLEMAN WANTS

WHAT A WOMAN NEEDS

~ANTHOLOGIES~
AT THE DUKE'S WEDDING
AT THE BILLIONAIRE'S WEDDING
DRESSED TO KISS
AT THE CHRISTMAS WEDDING

Hot Rogue on a Cold Night

MAYA RODALE

CHAPTER ONE

In Which Our Hero Arrives.

The most interesting thing that had ever happened to Lady Serena Cavendish was being jilted by Horace Breckenridge Church, the Duke of Frye, to whom she'd been betrothed since birth, practically.

By all accounts, she was an excellent match: a classic English beauty of rank and wealth, exquisitely mannered, a sterling reputation, talented in all the ladylike arts, and essentially born and bred to be a duchess. It was a known fact that ladies of such qualifications got married, not jilted.

But as a jilted woman, Serena now had an aura of tragedy, an air of mystery, and a whiff of scandal. As such, she had finally become interesting.

This was according to one Mr. Greyson Jones, a close personal friend of the Duke of Frye. Mr. Jones was widely reported to have remarked, "If you ask me, Frye dodged a bullet by avoiding a match to Lady Serena. I know, she's a perfect lady, but she's a little too perfect. This will make her more intriguing, now, don't you think?"

Serena longed to point out that no one had asked him, least of all her. For that matter, she had not aspired to be *interesting,* she had aspired to be *married.*

And now she was still unwed and less of an excellent match.

Time passed in which Serena entertained no suitors.

It was between London seasons, and eligible gentlemen were not exactly thick on the ground at Kingstag and its neighboring counties.

Her mother, the dowager Duchess of Wessex, decided that such high-quality bridal potential ought not languish on the metaphorical shelf. Her daughter appeared a touch too pale, as the spark of excitement in the young girl's heart had been extinguished by the duke's shocking end to the betrothal. Something had to be done to restore a blush to Lady Serena's cheeks, a sparkle to her eye.

Something like a suitor.

Something like a romance.

Something like a wedding.

Waiting for the next season to start in a few months' time was too risky, as too much precious time could elapse. Thus, Serena's mother decided a Christmas house party was the perfect occasion upon which to invite some eligible bachelors, along with family and friends who could be counted on to bring spirit and joy to the holidays *and* to Serena.

The guest list also included Horace Breckinridge Church, the jilting Duke of Frye, in the event that he had a change of heart and wished to honor the agreement his father had long ago made with Serena's dearly departed father—a marriage between their children to unite their two families.

Really, they would have made an excellent match.

And yet for some reason an otherwise honorable and upstanding gentleman like Frye broke off the betrothal.

Something had to be done.

And so the house was decorated with boughs of holly and garlands of greenery, the guest rooms were readied, the menus planned and everything was prepared to host a splendid Christmas house party. The fires were roaring, and a soft snow started falling, leaving a light dusting along the fields and drive.

Then Serena's mother had taken ill and her sister-in-law Cleo's secretary, Viola, was left in charge. But it was up to Serena to assume most of the hosting duties and to demonstrate to their guests—their unwed, eligible gentlemen guests—what an excellent wife and hostess she would be.

Guests who, at this moment, were arriving.

Serena sat in the drawing room serenely, waiting.

She heard the crunch of wheels on pea gravel, followed by the sound of the butler opening the door, footmen crossing the foyer to wait in attendance, a hearty hello from a male voice she did not quite recognize.

Eventually, the first guest was shown into the drawing room where she waited, seated elegantly by the fire where it was warm and where the light of the fire cast a flattering warm glow on her complexion.

Serena rose to greet him; her smile faltered when she saw the youngish man with sandy-colored hair, grayish eyes, and wide shoulders, which were lightly dusted in white snowflakes.

The words *good afternoon* died on her lips.

"Oh. It's *you*," she muttered in a rare lapse of manners. She refused to give much thought to the who and why and how this particular person could step into a room and make her forget years of ingrained etiquette. Recovering, she forced a smile and said most graciously, "Good day, Mr. Jones. Welcome to Kingstag. I trust you had a pleasant journey."

"Lady Serena. A pleasure. As always." His voice was low and he spoke as if savoring the words. *Serena. Pleasure. Always.* His eyes had the audacity to sparkle as he spoke.

"Is it *really*, Mr. Jones?"

She was not convinced.

He gave her a wolfish smile.

"Whyever would you think it was not?"

"Oh, just visiting a dull country mouse out at her remote country home doesn't seem like the sort of thing to captivate a dashing man about town such as yourself." Then she added, pointedly, "Although I suppose I am *slightly* more intriguing now."

"I see you are up to date on the London gossip rags."

"Yes, they arrive out here. Surely not at the speed with which you are accustomed, but nevertheless we do manage to keep informed. When we're not dodging bullets, that is."

"As it happens, your gracious mother invited me, along with Frye, when she learned that I hadn't a place to go for Christmas."

This was news to Serena.

Most unpleasant and decidedly unwelcome news.

"She invited the two of you . . ."

Serena knit her brow and pursed her lips. Her mother had casually mentioned that she was inviting Frye—she did have hopes that they might rekindle their courtship and that her daughter would become a duchess after all.

But to invite Mr. Greyson Jones after what he said about her?

Well, she never.

"Yes. As I said, it was very gracious of her, considering . . ." He paused anxiously. She did not let him finish.

"If you'll excuse me a moment."

Serena stormed past him and quit the room.

Upstairs

Serena did not bother with knocking as she burst into the bedchamber of the dowager duchess. She found her mother abed, looking wan and pale as she sat up and took very small sips of tea.

"Mother, how are you feeling?"

"Well enough. What is the matter, dear?"

"I know you intended to invite Frye against my wishes, but to extend an invitation to Mr. Greyson Jones as well? I am shocked. Simply shocked."

"Oh, have they arrived? I do hope everyone arrives shortly. If this snowfall keeps up at this pace, the drive might become impassable. I should hate for our little party to have uneven numbers."

Uneven numbers of ladies and gentlemen was every hostess's nightmare. One was tempted to keep spare cousins lying around in the event a seat needed to be filled.

"Just Mr. Jones has arrived. The Mr. Jones who, if you'll recall, was heard to publicly say that Frye dodged a bullet by avoiding marriage to me and that being jilted was the only thing that made me interesting."

"The gossip rags are always misquoting people, Serena. You mustn't take them as gospel."

"I just don't understand why Frye and Mr. Jones were invited. Especially given how upsetting I find both of them."

No one had ever disliked her or spoken ill of her before this and Serena found the whole business very unsettling. She was not used to feeling unsettled, either, which disturbed her equilibrium further.

"I had already mentioned spending Christmas together before . . ." her mother said, voice trailing off, not wanting to say the words *before he jilted you.* "It seemed rude not to issue the invitation and I confess, dear, that I had hoped that some time together might provide an opportunity for you two to renew your courtship."

"And as for Mr. Jones?"

"When I learned he had nowhere else to go, I simply had to extend an invitation. Besides, uneven numbers, Serena. Uneven numbers."

Her mother coughed.

"What am I to do with him? I have left him in the drawing room, even though I would really like to stuff him back in his carriage and send him off to London."

"You left him in the drawing room?" Her mother gasped, and this set off another round of coughing. "Serena, I raised you better than that. Put him in the blue room in the guest wing and endeavor to be the gracious hostess I taught you to be."

"Fine." She gritted her teeth. She thought he seemed hearty enough to survive a carriage ride back to London in a snowstorm. But she was a (mostly) perfect young lady, so she would banish him to a guest room instead. "But I still cannot fathom why you issued an invitation to him."

"Well, someone has to cast all the other eligible suitors in a better light." Then her mother fell back against the pillows and closed her eyes.

"Now that is a reason that makes sense."

Downstairs

$\mathcal{M}$r. Jones was right where she'd left him: standing near the fire for warmth and appearing to admire some porcelain figurines on the mantel.

Perhaps he was thinking about how she'd been rude to leave him abruptly, without refreshment. It was something no perfect woman would ever do.

Or perhaps he was reconsidering how rude his own words had been and he was mentally penning a retraction to be printed in all the London papers. Which she would read about a week or two after publication.

"Mr. Jones. Please accept my apologies for my brief absence. I had to confer with my mother with regard to which guest bedroom she had intended for you."

"It is no trouble, Lady Serena. I understand perfectly." He smiled devilishly at her. "You had to go have a heated conversation with your mother and to demand an explanation of my presence in your drawing room for a Christmas house party after I reportedly insulted you in the papers when I said you were too perfect, implying that perfection is a defect of your character."

Serena scowled. "That is the right of it."

"How is your mother, by the way? Or shall I say *where* is your mother?"

"She is abed. She has taken ill."

"I wish her a speedy a recovery."

"I as well."

"Though this does afford you the opportunity to act as a supremely gracious hostess, all the better with which to impress the bevy of eligible suitors your mother has undoubtedly invited."

"Precisely. You know the ways of marriage-minded mamas quite well."

"It's how I have managed to stay unwed."

"That's the only reason?" Serena replied coolly.

Mr. Jones gave no indication that her insult had landed. Instead, his lips tipped into a smile.

"You're not doing very well at this whole gracious hostessing business."

"It is ungentlemanly of you to point that out."

"And it is unladylike of you to point out my lapse in manners. You see, I can tell my presence infuriates you, which it logically should, given that I am taking too much fun in needling you and given what I was reported to have said about the untimely demise of your betrothal."

The untimely demise of her betrothal.

If it weren't for that, she wouldn't be stuck in her drawing room, with a fake smile plastered on her face, endeavoring to be a perfectly gracious hostess to a man whom she wished to bash over the head with a porcelain figurine. Then again, Mr. Jones was Frye's best friend, so this moment might have been inevitable after all.

"But you look rather fetching when you are angry," Greyson continued, once again giving her that wolfish smile that was probably all the rage among the ladies in London. She was completely and utterly immune to it.

116

"And you look like you would enjoy some time to rest after your journey." Serena moved quickly toward the drawing room doors and called for the butler, Withers, who was but a few steps away.

"Our butler will show to your room. Withers, take our guest to the blue room in the guest wing, please. Do come down at seven for dinner. Hopefully some others will join us."

By hopefully she meant *dear lord above please* ensure other guests arrived. Serena glanced out the window—the snow was still falling and showed no sign of abating. The last thing she needed was to be stuck alone with the awful Mr. Jones.

CHAPTER TWO

In which our hero becomes ensnared in a plot and a scheme.

*G*iven Lady Serena's reception of him, Grey would not have been surprised if he were shown to a dank room in the basement or sent to bunk with the servants or perhaps even out in the barn with the horses. But no, she was all that was right and good in a lady and he was given a fine guest room with every comfort one might wish for.

Gracious hostess indeed.

In truth, Lady Serena had every right to be cross with him. Or even downright furious. The newspapers far and wide had reported him as saying the following regrettable sentences upon news breaking that Frye had jilted her:

"If you ask me, Frye dodged a bullet by avoiding a match to Serena. I know, she's a perfect lady, but she's too perfect. This will make her more intriguing, now, don't you think?"

He had said that. Exactly. Word for regrettable word.

He could explain.

Grey had always found Lady Serena to be beautiful. Anyone would. The soft pink pout of her lips, the smooth, creamy complexion of her skin, the dark waves of her hair, her large, expressive brown eyes all enchanted him. Every time he saw her, his gaze traveled to the swells of her breasts in the virginal white dresses she so often wore. He imagined her hair unbound, her lips reddened from his kiss, those eyes looking at him with lust.

But one was not supposed to lust after the likes of Lady Serena. No, one was supposed to admire her for blossoming into the perfect example of an Englishwoman. She was unfailingly polite, well-mannered, kind, beautiful, educated in the way ladies were educated.

Born to be a duchess was something everyone said about Lady Serena at one point or another.

Lady Serena was not for the likes of him. Though Greyson had gone to Eton—which is where he'd met and befriended the Duke of Frye—he wasn't wealthy or titled or in any way considered a possible suitor for a woman of her station.

And so Grey nurtured a tortured desire for her, from afar, for years. Loving her and hating that he loved her. Loving her and hating the fact that she was so perfect that no other woman could measure up. Hating that his friend was going to wed her out of some notion of duty to an arrangement made by their fathers years earlier.

But then this business with Frye happened.

The betrothal. The jilting.

Grey looked at Serena more curiously now. What on earth would possess the duke to ditch the perfect future duchess? Frye hadn't given much of a reason. By all accounts she didn't seem that devastated over it, either.

Once he started wondering, he was consumed.

He was intrigued.

He dared to wonder if maybe this secret something he'd silently nurtured for her all these years had a chance.

Given the direction of his life, this Christmas party was his *only* chance to see if there could be something like love between him and Lady Serena.

But of course Serena wouldn't want to hear any of that, ever. She certainly wouldn't want to hear it from him, especially at a Christmas house party she was hosting. He had only secured an invitation because the duchess had ideas about Serena and Frye rekindling their betrothal and when she'd learned from Frye that he hadn't had plans, she extended an invitation to him as well.

As an unwanted guest left to his own devices, Grey considered his options at present: he could enjoy a leisurely afternoon reading in his room—he did need to continue reading *An Englishman in India, Or; One young Lord's journey to the Indian subcontinent and a thorough examination of the culture, customs, geography, languages, and its people.*

Or he could embark on a walk through the grounds before the snow began falling in earnest. He might stroll through the house to see if other guests had arrived or if there were other family members more amenable to his presence.

Or he might find Serena and convince her not to hate him . . .

Was he in the mood for an impossible task, or not?

Grey quit his chamber and strolled through the house. On the ground floor he followed the sound of a commotion until he found the source: a large room in an advanced state of disarray. A stage was half built at one end. Footmen were at work and two women, one young, one old, stood in the thick of it all.

"Pardon me for interrupting," Grey said, backing away from the sense of impending doom and disaster that permeated the room.

"Are you here for the house party?" the young woman wanted to know.

"I am an invited guest, yes." He felt the need to point that out, given that he wasn't exactly a *wanted* guest. "Mr. Greyson Jones, at your service."

The old woman eyed him in a manner that could only be described as *lascivious* and he wanted to laugh. He had never been eyed thusly by a woman who seemed like she had cruised on the ark with Noah.

The young woman stared at him directly and said, "I'm Lady Bridget Cavendish, no relation to the American Cavendishes of London, and this is my Great-Aunt Sophronia."

"Great as in stupendous, magnificent, and extraordinary," Sophronia explained. "Not pertaining to some convoluted family tree nonsense. Probably."

"I would never assume otherwise," Grey murmured.

"Are you looking for Lady Serena?" Lady Bridget inquired.

"Not precisely," Grey said, hesitating. His instincts told him that she was the sort of person who pried information out of people and used it mercilessly and endlessly. If so, she'd be a remarkable asset to the Foreign Office.

"Pray tell, how are you imprecisely looking for Serena?" The Great and Stupendous Aunt Sophronia wanted to know.

"I am wandering around your great house, seeking company and perhaps other guests."

"We're busy here. We're putting on a play. Come to think of it . . ." Bridget looked from him to Sophronia and back again. There was a glimmer in her eye that he didn't care for.

"Yes, I see where you're going, girl, and I quite agree," Sophronia said. The sense of doom increased. "We do yet have some male roles in need of actors."

"He'd be smashing as the Lord Pirate Captain. Those shoulders. That rakish gleam in his eye. The tousled hair. What a dream."

Sophronia nodded her head in agreement. "I couldn't have imagined better casting."

Grey had a feeling he was about to play the role of Lord Pirate Captain, whether he wished to or not.

"I, um, that is to say . . . Where is Lady Serena?"

"I imagine she is greeting our other guests. All the eligible bachelors and whatnot," Bridget said dismissively. "I heard from a maid that two other eligible gentleman arrived. Lords, both of them."

"You needn't bother her now," Sophronia said. "Not when she's in the midst of such important work with her two eligible lords."

"What makes you think that I am not an eligible bachelor?"

"Ah, so you are! Ha! You fell right into my trap!"

Great-Aunt Sophronia beamed. Grey forced a smile. He was an unwed male person in possession of all of his teeth and an income, who had not yet crossed over to the far side of forty. Of course he was an eligible bachelor.

By making a point of it, he had essentially intimated that he was looking for a wife. Which wasn't exactly true. Though it wasn't exactly false. Now wasn't exactly a good time, considering what was ahead in his horizon.

What he was looking for was Serena.

But Lord Help Him if these two lady terriers got wind of that. Best to change the subject then.

"Tell me, what was the role in the play that you had in mind for me? If I am going to be cast, I should like to know more about my role."

Lady Bridget cackled with glee and Great-aunt Sophronia did too, providing a glimpse of what Lady Bridget would be like six or seven decades down the line.

She answered by handing him a dusty black cloak, a tricorn hat, an eye patch, and a script.

Rehearsals commenced immediately.

CHAPTER THREE

In which our heroine finds the perfect man (who is not our hero).

The next day

The drawing room, before dinner

After the unpleasant arrival of Mr. Greyson Jones, the rest of the house party guests—with the notable exception of Frye—descended, somehow managing to complete their travels to Kingstag in spite of the weather.

Serena greeted them as they shook off snowy capes and caps in the foyer and then escorted them all to warm up by the roaring fire in the drawing room.

With the assistance of the duchess's secretary, Mrs. Viola Cavendish, she saw that trays of tea were provided and that esteemed guests were shown to the appropriate chambers.

She oversaw the hanging of mistletoe in doorways, draping of evergreen garlands along the banister, and the lighting of beeswax candles for decoration.

While the purpose of this house party was purportedly to cheer her up, she knew her mother really meant for her to find a suitable husband. Yet how could she when her every waking moment was spent seeing to everyone else's comfort? At least it kept her occupied and out of the way of Greyson Jones, with his penetrating gaze that managed to find her in crowded rooms. She pretended to ignore him.

But then Lord Gosling arrived. A stroke of guest list genius on the part of her lamentably ill mother. All and any thoughts of Greyson Jones left her head.

Lucian, Lord Gosling, was, in a word, perfect.

He was so handsome with his golden hair and his sun-kissed skin (even in winter!) and his perfectly molded features that spoke of generations of noble breeding. He was tall, but not too tall. His frame was lean, but also strong. His manners were exquisite. His conversation was engaging. He really looked a woman in the eye when he spoke to her too.

"And so that is why I insisted that my sisters have the best possible tutors," Lord Gosling told Serena over glasses of champagne in the drawing room prior to supper. "Why should a woman have a lesser education than a man?"

Be still her beating heart! A forward-thinking man!

"I quite admire your forward thinking, Lord Gosling. What subjects did they study?"

"Greek, Latin, mathematics, of course. We also study botany, discuss history, and, as a family, we gather to read poetry aloud after supper."

"That sounds lovely. Perhaps we might do the same here. I daresay you must breathe life into verse when you recite it."

"I would happily share some of my favorite poems if it would please you." His eyes were very blue, and gazing into hers in a way that made her heart pitter-patter. "There is a fellow whose work I am fond of. Wordsworth is not well known now, but I venture that he'll be renowned and taught in all the schools in a hundred years."

"Oh yes," she cooed. Cooed! Had such a warm, breathy, flighty sound actually come from her person?

Serena was slightly embarrassed by such a display of interest in a man; women were to hold themselves above demonstrations of great emotion, lest they appear too forward or terrifying. But Gosling didn't seem to mind. Given the way he smiled at her, blue eyes sparkling, he didn't mind at all.

She smiled back at him, at a loss for words—other than words like *perfect* or *I love you let's get married even though we only just met.*

And then they were interrupted.

By none other than Mr. Greyson Jones. Her smile tightened.

"Good evening, Lady Serena. Lord Gosling, Lady Jane Rutledge was just expressing a keen interest in your charitable endeavors. I think you might be able to persuade her to donate to your fund for war widows and orphans."

Serena gritted her teeth. But still, she smiled.

"Oh, you must go speak to her, Lord Gosling," Serena said. "For the sake of war widows and orphans."

Even though she would much rather stay in conversation with Lord Gosling and not Mr. Greyson Jones, who was clearly up to something nefarious. The man had a knack for ruining everything for her.

$\mathcal{H}$aving dispensed with Lord Gosling, Grey now had Serena all to himself. It was an easy trick to unite Lady Jane with Lord Gosling (and his funds), thus benefitting war widows, orphans, and himself in one fell swoop.

"I don't suppose you've received word from Frye," she said straightaway. She cast an anxious glance at the window—the snow was falling heavily, had been for hours, and drifts were piling up. "I daresay he ought to have arrived by now."

"I haven't heard from him and for that, and his tardiness, I blame the weather. But fear not, Lady Serena, I'm certain that his arrival is imminent."

Actually, Grey wasn't sure of this at all. But he wasn't too distraught about it either. Frye was a supremely competent and hearty fellow; one generally needn't fear for his safety. It was clear to him that he would be competing with Lord Gosling for Serena's attentions. He didn't need the duke in the mix too.

"I do hope so," she said softly, revealing that she might indeed have been fantasizing about a reconciliation. This was intriguing. It meant that perhaps she'd held a tendre for the duke after all, when Grey had just assumed that theirs was a match made only on paper by their fathers, years and years ago, and with little consideration for the hearts involved.

"Although it seems he is already too late. It is only the second day of this house party and already you are enamored."

I see that I am already too late.

"If you can see that, then why did you interrupt?" Serena asked. Her eyes flashed.

Because I want you for myself.

"That is the question, isn't it? Perhaps I think you can do better."

At this, Serena sputtered with rage.

"How is this any of your concern whatsoever?"

Because I have always wanted you for myself.

For as long as he had known her, Grey been infatuated with Lady Serena Cavendish, the Perfect English Lady. She was too perfect and elegant for the likes of him—a mere mister who had hustled his way into society by exploiting every opportunity and connection that came his way. A longtime friendship with the Duke of Frye being most helpful. Betraying his friend by secretly lusting and longing for the man's fiancé was beyond the pale, so his feelings for her were kept tightly under wraps.

And now . . . the timing was still rubbish.

"I suppose it isn't my concern," he said, because what else could he say. But his heart was howling. "But I still wonder if perhaps you might do better."

"Better than Lord Gosling? Who could be better than he? He is amiable, handsome, in possession of a modest fortune. He is kind to the servants and believes in women's rights. This afternoon, he ventured out to feed the birds and squirrels because he didn't want them to go hungry in the storm."

Hang the birds and the squirrels. They had survived worse without the likes of Lord Gosling flinging bits of seed and grain at them on a blustery afternoon.

Grey wanted to ask her how Gosling made her *feel*. Did he make her heart ache as if it might burst from so much wanting? Did the man command her attention like a magnet that she was helpless to resist? Did her every other thought stray to fantasies of kissing him? Not a nice kiss, either, but the sort that left a person dazed and drunk and unsure of the hour or day.

"I shall confirm that it is not in any way at all your concern. And I'll thank you not to scare off another suitor or wreck another betrothal."

Serena's eyes flashed. She was quite fetching when she was angry. She was finally *alive* when he had provoked her into a state of vexation. None of those placid smiles and polite conversations; in their place were flushed cheeks and the slight flare of her nostrils as she breathed heavily, angrily.

There was more to her, she just didn't know it. Grey very badly wanted to be the one to unlock that side of her, and show it to the world. Show it to *her.*

Then again, perhaps Lady Serena Cavendish was just the woman she appeared to be. One who aspired to nothing more than a titled husband with a prosperous estate, with whom she could beget an heir and a spare and hold house parties.

If there was more to her—and a chance for them—time was running out for him to discover it.

CHAPTER FOUR

In which Bridget and Sophronia. That is all.

The following day

A note arrived in Grey's room informing him in no uncertain terms that play rehearsal was to take place immediately after breakfast. There was no requesting his attendance; it was merely understood that he would be present. While the rest of the house party would be enjoying sleigh rides in the fresh fallen snow, he would be assuming the role of Lord Pirate Captain.

Someone really ought to recruit Lady Bridget as a general. The enemy would probably surrender to her before the war could even be fought.

Upon arriving at the appointed time and place, Grey discovered an unfolding disaster. The set was still only half built. There was an explosion of props and costumes. A few actors—presumably they were actors—milled about, looking nervous. Grey recognized a few faces from supper the night before. As for the rest, he had no idea who they were or how they came to be participating in this . . . this.

Whatever it was. *This.*

Grey was leaning against a pillar reading a copy of the script and attempting to learn his lines—and oh, what lines they were—when Serena entered. He was shaking with laughter and she was all business.

"Ah, there you are, Bridget. Sophronia. The guests who have not embarked on the sleigh ride are about to play some parlor games and we are in need of extra players. Do come join us."

"My dear, parlor games are all well and good, but we're in the middle of something grand," Sophronia said. "We are making *art.*"

Serena glanced warily around the room. "Dare I ask?"

"Play rehearsal," Grey said, stepping into the conversation.

Serena looked at him and blinked. Repeatedly. She pursed her lips. Just when he thought she had reached peak disapproval, a giggle escaped her sweet little mouth. Then she laughed. That dulcet laugh.

Shit. His costume. Sophronia had insisted on a white shirt with an excess of white lace ruffles, a cape, a tricorn hat. And the eye patch. One could not forget the eye patch.

"And you are . . .?"

He bowed extravagantly.

"I am Lord Captain, a pirate from Shropshire."

"But Shropshire is inland," she pointed out.

His gaze locked with Serena's. And he could tell she sized up the situation in an instant—Bridget had a ridiculous notion, and he was going along with it, and something in her heart was pointing out that this was a sweet thing for him to do even though she did not wish to recognize it. He knew, because he saw the line of her mouth soften, and he saw the laughter in her eyes, even if she wasn't laughing out loud.

"How astute of you," he murmured.

"It's not astute. It's basic geography." She turned to her sister. "Which someone who had excellent tutors should know." She turned to Sophronia. "Or someone who has spent over eighty years in England should know."

"I'm not a day over forty-five," Sophronia replied.

"Be that as it may," Bridget began. "We need someone to read lines with the Lord Captain, inland pirate of Shropshire."

"Don't look at me. I have a parlor full of guests ready to play games, and a luncheon to oversee. To say nothing of approving tonight's menu and finding music to play after supper. I must also check on Mother, who is still quite ill."

"Never mind all that boring nonsense," Sophronia said bluntly. "Your mother will be fine. Leave the tedious house party business to Viola. The duchess asked her to help manage it all, so you have some free time to . . . you know . . ." Serena's cheeks reddened. "Enjoy the company of eligible gentlemen."

"Which I would like to do. In the parlor. With the other guests." Serena tried to control her impatience. "What about the two of you? Why can't either of you read lines with him?"

"I am directing," Bridget said haughtily.

"And I am stage managing," Sophronia added.

And I am eternally grateful for this excuse to be with Serena. Not that Grey would say that. Instead, he handed her the script.

Their fingers brushed.

He felt it everywhere. Shocks and sparks. Wanting.

She seemed oblivious.

"What is my role?"

"Lonely Spinster."

"Bridget!"

And with Bridget's impish, unapologetic grin, play rehearsal began. They were ushered to the makeshift stage, Serena grumbling all the way.

Grey felt ridiculous, but also . . . happy.

He suspected the duchess had invited him out of pity—he was Frye's friend, the one with no family with whom to spend the holidays. He was probably just there to even out the numbers. He was the last person Serena would have invited.

But now he was about to see what it was like when Serena Cavendish *liked* him. Granted it would be in their roles as Lonely Spinster and Lord Pirate Captain, but he would take it.

At Bridget's direction, he began halfway through the scene. No, he did not know why they didn't start at the top.

"Arrgh, my lady."

"This just says that I faint," Serena said, annoyed. "I don't even have a line."

"So faint," Bridget said.

"But I shall fall."

Grey pointed to a line three-quarters of the way down the page. "No, it says I am to catch you in my strong, muscular arms."

"It does not say that."

"It does. See."

She leaned in so she might get a closer look. He ought to have been looking at the words too, but instead he was breathing her in, a lovely scent of lavender and woman.

"It does not," she murmured. And she was right. It only said, *Lord Pirate Captain catches her.*

"Try again!" Bridget declared.

"Argh, my lady!"

Serena pretended to swoon. Greyson caught her easily. Again and again they practiced swooning and catching. Each time he might have held her for a second longer than necessary because this was probably the only chance he would ever have to hold her thusly. She didn't seem to notice that extra second, precisely as long as one extra excited heartbeat, that she was in his arms.

But she did notice when Lord Gosling arrived.

"What is this?"

"Oh, it's just play rehearsal," Serena said, hastily returning to her feet and smoothing out her hair and skirts. "A silly performance . . . my younger sister . . . keep her busy . . . out of trouble . . ."

She was so anxious to please him that she couldn't complete a sentence.

"I have been known to enjoy a bit of playacting," Gosling said, being perfect. "Is there a role for me?"

Grey did a quick scan of the page. No, he did not see a part for romantic interloper. If said role did exist, his inland pirate would probably murder him by the end of the first act.

"My stage manager and I shall have to confer," Bridget informed him. After a moment of a heated, whispered conversation in which Grey overheard his name, Serena's name and the words *suitor, elephant,* and *homicide,* Bridget was ready to make her pronouncement.

"You may play the role of the lovesick swan."

"You mean swain," Lord Gosling said.

"No. I mean swan."

The group took a moment to process this. What the devil was a lovesick swan doing in a play about an inland pirate from Shropshire and a lonely spinster?

Then again, why wouldn't such a play include exactly that cast of characters?

But Gosling, being perfect, took it all in stride. "Very well, I shall be the most gallant, lovesick swan ever to grace the stage. With whom am I in love?"

Grey cursed the man's agreeableness.

"Serena, of course," Sophronia barked.

Serena beamed. She had no idea what that smile did to him. What all her smiles for other men had done to him. Once, just once, he'd get her to smile like that at him.

He had a week left at the house party to accomplish this. Just seven days before he forever lost his chance. As long as she didn't fall too hard for Gosling in that time, or pin all her hopes and dreams on Frye arriving, it could happen.

Maybe. A man could dream.

"She's playing the role of Lonely Spinster," Bridget added. Serena scowled.

"It might be funnier if the Lovesick Swan were in love with Lord Pirate Captain," Sophronia mused.

"It would," Grey agreed, seizing an opportunity to thwart their budding romance between the lonely spinster and lovesick swan.

"Oh, now you're being ridiculous," Serena replied.

"I think that ship sailed some time ago," Grey said. No one disagreed.

"It doesn't matter anyway, because Serena will fall in love with the pirate," Bridget said.

Serena gazed at him warily. "Is that so?"

He and Sophronia said, "Yes."

"Well, you can't fall in love with a swan now, can you?" Sophronia replied. "Now *that* would be ridiculous."

"I'm sure I could," Serena said, now holding Gosling's gaze. Bridget made a gagging sound. Privately, Grey concurred.

"Love isn't something you *could* do," he said. "It's something that happens to you. It is something that you are helpless to stop. Something you don't even want to end. If you're lucky it happens to you and you hold on to it for as long as you possibly can."

Serena looked at him and blinked. "I wouldn't have thought that you know so much about love, Grey."

He held her gaze. "More than you know, Serena. More than you know."

CHAPTER FIVE

In which our heroine's curiosity is piqued.

The next afternoon

Serena kept busy from morning until night with the house party.

While she did have the assistance of Viola, the maddeningly essential task of keeping an eye on Great-Aunt Sophronia and Bridget had fallen to Serena. As an actor in their play, it made sense that she should keep an eye on them. This was a demanding endeavor.

Especially when one was also endeavoring to snare Lord Gosling as a husband and to stop thinking about what Greyson Jones had said about love.

Who knew *he* would speak so authoritatively on love?

But she did not have *time* to consider matters of love.

There were seating arrangements and menus that needed her immediate attention. The snowstorm necessitated concocting indoor entertainments to keep the guests happy and occupied—at this point, everyone had had enough of sleigh rides. The sheet music for all the carols had gone missing—Serena suspected they had been appropriated as props for Bridget's play. The household staff was kept busy keeping the guests comfortable and Serena was busy managing the household.

Though Serena had been trained for this from a young age—with the assumption that she would one day grow up to be the Duchess of Frye with her own house parties to throw—she was finding that the reality was not quite the same as the actual practice.

Serena did not know what to do with that discovery.

She had been raised to be a lady!

A perfect lady and gracious hostess!

Smile!

She had taken to stealing moments in the butler's pantry where she might be alone to breath deeply and have a moment's respite and not smile.

Those stolen moments were hardly calming though. New, even more troubling thoughts intruded. If this life she had prepared for was truly exhausting and unfulfilling, what did she wish for instead? What alternatives were there for a lady who had been raised to be a duchess or, at the very least, a countess?

What she wished for was to ask Greyson why he kept staring at her with those inquisitive eyes of his, to demand that he explain what he knew about love, and perhaps apologize to her for what he'd said in the newspaper.

How ridiculous.

Foolish.

Impossible.

Instead, Serena went to visit her mother in her bedchamber.

The duchess was still abed, looking very pale and wan. "How fares everything with the house party?"

"Very well." *If one did not mention Sophronia and Bridget and the absent duke and Greyson Jones's gaze.*

"Has the Duke of Frye arrived yet?"

"No, he hasn't. He hasn't sent word either."

"Pity, that. I hope he is well. But 'tis his loss I suppose." The duchess was holding more of a torch for the duke than Serena. Especially now that she wasn't sure that she fancied being a duchess with a ducal-sized household to manage. "Are there any other interesting suitors?"

"Mother! At least try to be subtle about it."

"Why? I'm a mother speaking to my daughter and I might be on my deathbed."

"You are not on your deathbed. If I didn't have a physician's report and Viola telling me otherwise, I might even suspect that you are deliberately malingering to avoid the house party."

"Why would I wish to avoid a house party that I have arranged? Especially when my maternal guidance is needed. We do need to find you a husband, Serena. Planning a wedding should cheer you up."

"Well, I do hope you recover soon," Serena said. "There is a perfect suitor here for me, but I am distracted by Bridget and Sophronia's shenanigans."

"What are they doing now?"

"Putting on a play. An utterly ridiculous play." Serena couldn't even bring herself to mention the lovesick swan and the pirate from Shropshire. And those were only her scenes. As for the rest of the play, the less said about it the better.

"I should think that's for the best," her mother said.

"Oh?"

"It keeps them occupied in a predetermined, confined location. Do you really want them running wild, interfering with the menus, concocting entertainments, conversing freely with our guests?"

"You do have a point."

"Of course I do. Mothers always know best. Now what were you saying about a perfect suitor?"

"Lord Gosling has much to recommend him . . ." Serena began. As she listed his many fine qualities, her thoughts kept straying to Greyson. What did he know of love? What did *she*? And what had he done to make his arms so strong and muscular? Inquiring, swooning girls wished to know.

In the hothouse

𝓘t was unbelievable but true: even a monstrous residence like Kingstag Castle could feel too small when too many guests were cooped up inside for days on end. The snowstorm had by now limited the outdoor activities—one could hardly skate on the frozen pond when it was covered in two feet of snow. Many guests passed the hours in the drawing room, playing games and gossiping. Bridget and Sophronia wrangled many more into their theatrical production.

Serena was delighted to be showing the hothouse to Lord Gosling.

Alone.

Just the two of them.

He had approached her in the foyer—she'd just been returning to the guests after one of her moments of respite in the butler's pantry. Lud, but he was resplendent in his perfection. Why, he managed to seem golden even in the faint winter light, like a ray of sunshine on a snowy day.

"Lady Serena! I heard there was a hothouse here at Kingstag and I was wondering if I might entice you to walk through it with me."

"I would love to, Lord Gosling."

Linking arms, she led the way. The room was a fair size, made of glass, incredibly warm, and stuffed with a variety of plants from specimens gathered all over the world.

Falling snowflakes melted as soon as they hit the glass ceiling.

"Our gardener keeps the fires burning, which helps keep the plants warm enough to grow and thrive, even in the depths of winter. It's how we are able to grow oranges, which our cook likes to use."

Oh blast. She had to speak to the cook about dessert. There had been a problem with the cakes.

As they strolled through the small, hot space, Gosling admired the plant life and Serena admired him.

She could certainly look at a face like his over the breakfast table every day. They probably did make an attractive couple—she would have to engineer a walk past a mirror so she could be certain. She imagined family portraits of him, her, and their future son and daughter. She imagined how they might look together as they made an entrance at a London ball.

"What a wonderful orchid," he said, pausing to examine one in particular. "I've never seen this variety in real life, only illustrations. As you must know, they are difficult to cultivate in this climate. Not every flower is meant to flourish in an English country house."

"You must study botany," she said.

"I study things of beauty," he murmured.

Their gazes locked.

A blush crept upon her cheeks.

What a perfect thing to say.

"I must also compliment you on the house party thus far. Everything has been exquisitely planned and managed, all the guests are enjoying themselves and praising their time at Kingstag. I think I speak for all the guests when I say what a perfect hostess you are. A perfect specimen of womanhood."

Serena replied automatically, "What a lovely compliment. Thank you."

She tried to smile, but found herself faltering.

Because receiving this compliment was not as wonderful as she had always anticipated. Who wished to be considered a perfect specimen? She was beginning to wonder if she was like that orchid: not meant to flourish in an English country house.

Perhaps she *and* Frye had dodged a bullet.

Damn it, Greyson Jones!

Of course, these were not thoughts one would ever intimate to someone like Lord Gosling, whom she of course still considered a prime specimen of husband material. One did not throw off years of training and expectation overnight.

"I do look forward to hosting gatherings of friends at one of my country estates, when I am married. I shall need a wife who would enjoy assisting me in such hospitality."

Lord Gosling gazed at her.

Gah, he was perfect. She wanted to take a ruler to his features and confirm that they were indeed as symmetrical as they appeared. He would probably laugh about it, and offer some humble statement because he was so perfect. But he wasn't insufferable. And he wasn't vague, like some men. In fact, he'd just made his intentions quite plain.

Serena waited for her heart to start fluttering and pounding because Lord Gosling intimated that they might be a perfect couple.

But lud if there wasn't a little voice inside of her whispering *but don't you want more?*

She was spared from responding by the intrusion of other voices—one low, one lilting.

"It looks like we have company," Gosling remarked.

"Indeed." It was Greyson, with a woman on his arm. It was Mrs. Carlyle, a married woman whose husband was on a diplomatic mission. She was invited because she shouldn't spend Christmas alone and also because she would help even out the numbers without competing with Serena for any beau.

Not in the matrimonial sense, anyway.

Serena experienced a surge of irritation upon seeing them. How dare *he* interrupt her perfect moment with Gosling, which might have led to a proposal or a kiss.

"What a luxury, isn't it? A hothouse in the dead of winter," Greyson remarked as they joined them. Mrs. Carlyle clung to his arm, quite like one of the vines twining itself around the trunk of a citrus tree.

"I believe January is the dead of winter and we are only in December," Serena pointed out.

"Are you calling one of your guests a liar, Lady Serena?" Greyson teased. "That doesn't seem like something a gracious hostess such as yourself would do."

"Oh, I beg your pardon, I would never," she replied sweetly, while wishing she could silence him with the power of her furious gaze alone.

"Well, by January, I shall be en route to a hot climate where plants like these grow wild, year-round, unstoppably."

Serena snapped to attention. This was news to her.

"Where are you going?" she asked. She'd never imagined him leaving. Not that she cared. Of course she didn't care. It hardly signified to her.

"India. I have a diplomatic assignment. Orders from the King, et cetera, et cetera."

"I was not aware you were involved in politics," Gosling remarked.

"Foreign Office. Discreet sort of stuff. Probably shouldn't mention it, but it does impress the ladies." Greyson grinned.

Mrs. Carlyle laughed and fluttered her lashes. "Does this mean that you are a spy? Here I thought you were merely a diplomat."

"I couldn't tell you if I was a spy, now could I?" Grey winked.

"Oh, you could trust me to keep a secret," she replied. Cooed, really. Serena experienced an urge to inflict violence upon the woman. Flirting like that when she was married!

Or was it that she was flirting with Grey?

"How kind of you to take time to visit us when you have such important work abroad," Serena said politely. But then the mask fell. "When do you leave?"

"After the holiday. There's nothing like Christmas in England, now, is there? I couldn't miss that." Greyson gazed deeply at her; she had the feeling he wasn't talking about Christmas at all. *What, then?* And *now* her heart started to flutter and beat in an irregular rhythm, at the prospect of Greyson leaving, of all things.

"Of course. There is nothing like an English Christmas," she replied. But her curiosity was piqued. How had she never known this about him? Frye had never mentioned it . . . Did he even know?

Where was the duke, anyway?

And why had she not thought about him at all?

Serena waited patiently for joy to bloom in her heart at the news that this man with the cruel words printed in all the newspapers would be gone, possibly forevermore. Instead, there was something like yearning and curiosity and a mad desire to get him alone and demand satisfaction. By satisfaction, she meant answers to all her questions, naturally.

CHAPTER SIX

In which there is more play practice.

The next afternoon

$\mathcal{A}$s Grey made his way from luncheon to play practice, he found himself actually looking forward to it. Which isn't to say he hadn't enjoyed the other entertainments offered at the house party so far—sleigh rides through the magical woods around Kingstag castle before the snow had become too deep, card games and musicales, fine feasting, caroling, and, his favorite, watching Lady Serena bustle about while pretending to be enjoying herself, but in fact sneaking off to quietly take panicked deep breaths in the butler's pantry.

She didn't realize it yet, but this life might not be for her.

She probably didn't realize there were other options.

His blood-pumping organ gave an extra hard squeeze because there was another option: *him.*

Grey had always loved her, but never expected anything to come of it. A woman like Lady Serena was to wed a man like His Grace, the Duke of Frye. But if that was no longer the life she wished for *and* she was no longer betrothed . . .

That blood-pumping organ clenched again.

This was really Grey's one and only and last chance to win her heart.

Hence his enthusiastic acceptance of the invitation to the house party.

But Serena hadn't exactly given him a warm and encouraging reception.

Hence his enjoyment of play practice. Where she had to at least *pretend* to like him.

Today they all wore fragments and scraps of their costumes as the full costumes were not yet ready. Grey wore his eye-patch and the cape; his perfectly good tricorn hat had been deemed "in need of improvements and flair" and had disappeared.

The trio of Grey, Serena, and (argh) Gosling stood on the makeshift stage.

Gosling, wearing a snowy white jacket, uttered his one line: "Quack, my love! Quack, my love!"

Serena couldn't hold back her giggles and burst into laughter. Her lovely lilting laugh was one thing, but what was really enchanting was seeing her let down her guard.

Bridget frowned. "Serena, your character isn't supposed to laugh."

"But it's funny."

"Not to your lovesick swan. His story is a tragedy and it won't do to have you mocking his pain."

Gosling made an appropriately sad face.

"Carry on!" Sophronia shouted. That was Grey's cue.

He stepped into center stage with a dramatic swish of giant cape and delivered his line: "Argh, my lady."

Serena placed her hand on his forearm and declared, "I swoon" as she sort of collapsed in his general direction. He lunged forward to catch her and held her close for oh, two or three blessed seconds longer than necessary.

"I'm not convinced by your swoon, Serena," Bridget said.

Sophronia concurred. "It appears more like you've been conked on the head with a blunt object rather than overcome with lust and desire for our Lord Pirate Captain. Who, I might add, was cast precisely for his abilities to inspire a woman to be overcome with lust and desire."

Then Sophronia winked at him.

Grey, being a flirt, winked back.

"Apologies that I haven't spent much time practicing my . . . swooning," she said tensely.

"Isn't it one of the things perfect Englishwomen do?" Grey teased. "Arrange flowers, play the pianoforte, paint watercolors, and swoon?"

"It so happens that swooning is not one of the critical life skills included in a young English lady's education. But do remind me to show you my watercolors."

"Carry on," Sophronia barked. "And remember you are in love. Madly in love!"

Love. Serena caught his eye. His heartbeat slowed, then stopped, then started again. She didn't immediately look away. And he couldn't imagine a better Christmas gift than that: hope that he might have a chance.

"Wake up my lady," he said, resuming the lines. "There is danger and adventure out yonder." He gestured to the rest of the room, but really, he meant the whole world. Or, say, India. "You don't want to miss it."

"Oh, danger!? Adventure!? Where?!"

"Well, not here, in Shropshire, naturally. We must get to my ship!"

He reached out for her hand, to lead her to his imaginary horse, which would take them on a perilous journey across imaginary England to whatever great adventures lay beyond.

Rather than recite her next line, Serena looked up from the script. "Bridget, this is ridiculous."

"Actually," Bridget said, "the line is 'But we shall be besieged by my lovesick swan.'"

"Quack, my love! Quack, my love!"

Serena sighed.

"Very well, my Lord Pirate Captain, let us go at once to your ship."

Despite the lack of drama in her delivery, Grey swept her into his arms. His heart thudded. They had never been this close before, and now they had an audience for an embrace he'd much rather enjoy in private.

"It shall be a dangerous journey, but I vow to protect you."

She awkwardly clasped the lapels of his jacket as the cape he wore fell in folds all around them. This was really a dangerous amount of fabric.

"I need you, as I am prone to swooning at the slightest provocation. One wonders how a lovely spinster with such a delicate constitution has managed to even survive into adulthood. How lucky I have been not to have fallen and hit my head on a rock and suffered an untimely demise, given all this swooning I do."

"That's not the line!" Sophronia shouted.

Serena rolled her eyes. "Oh, Captain, I shall cling to you forevermore with my delicate lady arms."

"I wish to be clung to by your delicate lady arms."

Gad, these lines were ridiculous. He felt absurd saying them, even if they were the God's honest truth.

"Halt!" Bridget shouted. She regarded them thoughtfully, while tapping a pencil against her lips. "I'm just not feeling the passion between you two."

And that was enough, *enough* for Serena. She disentangled herself from his embrace and the voluminous cape and stepped aside. Facing the director and stage manager, with arms akimbo, she really gave it to them.

"This is absurd! There are no pirates in Shropshire or lovesick swans! And why is my character such a ninny? And now you want passion? You are eighteen years of age. What do you even know of passion?"

"This is only act one, Serena," Sophronia said with a cackle.

"But I haven't time for acts two and three. I have things to do. Important things to do."

Sophronia wasn't having it. "No time to fall in love! Hummph."

CHAPTER SEVEN

In which our hero and heroine conspire to avoid an international incident.

Later that afternoon

Serena was a bit surprised when Greyson sought her out that afternoon. He had said that awful thing about being jilted making her interesting and she'd been cold and rude upon his arrival. She had assumed that they would bide their time, feigning politeness until Christmas came and went, the house party concluded, and she would wed Lord Gosling and Grey would go off to India.

India! Oh, what that must be like! She couldn't even imagine all the dramatic sights, bright colors, exotic scents that one might encounter there. She'd heard about Goddesses with a thousand arms, wild tigers, an overwhelming heat, and fabrics in colors like saffron and crimson.

She knew, deep in her bones, that it would be a richer, more exciting experience than she would ever have here in England, where the best travel she might hope for as a Noble Lady would be a trip to Bath, or perhaps a visit to Paris. Her gowns would be in demure, pastel shades. There would be no tigers.

Suddenly, her world seemed rather small.

So when Greyson tugged her aside and said, "I am wondering if you would like to help me avoid an international incident," she replied, "For the good of England, I suppose I cannot say no to that."

"Excellent. Join me in the duke's study in a quarter of an hour," he murmured.

Since when did Greyson Jones murmur things to her? Since when did she like it?

"But I have to—" There was an issue with the tea sandwiches Cook wished to speak to her about. And the housekeeper urgently needed to discuss the linens. But Viola could deal with all that. "Oh bother. Never mind all my hostessing duties. It's rather dull anyway. I shall meet you there."

"The safety of England depends on it, my lady."

She didn't believe him of course. But she was intrigued.

A quarter of an hour later, in the duke's study

Serena mostly closed the door behind her—leaving it a few inches open for the sake of propriety. Though the whole purpose of this house party was to land her a husband, being caught in a compromising position with Greyson Jones in her brother's study was not how she wanted to go about it.

She probably ought to have a chaperone, but she rather thought one might get in the way of thwarting an international incident.

Greyson didn't seem to notice her slip into the room, and she took a minute to look at him, really look at him. He was slightly taller than average, with broad shoulders and a lean, strong body cloaked in simple, but well-tailored, clothes. His sandy-colored hair was cropped short. His lips were full. His eyes were gray, like his name, and they sparkled when he noticed her.

"Excellent. How good of you to meet me." He crossed the room, as did she, and they met in the middle. "Here—papers of the utmost secrecy."

She took the offered pages and glanced at them. Her face fell.

"These are lines from Bridget's play."

"And I daresay that if we do not have them memorized by practice this afternoon, I fear violent retaliation from Lady Bridget. I wouldn't put it past her to spark an international incident."

Her first thought: what a silly ruse! But the man did have a point. It was never a good idea to underestimate Bridget's capacity for creating mayhem.

"Especially with Sophronia on her side. Are you really a spy?"

"Diplomat and ambassador. I recently returned from an extended stay in Bavaria and shall soon go abroad to represent England's interests, while working to establish good relationships with the locals in foreign countries. Namely, India."

"That didn't answer the question."

"Would you like me more if I were a spy? Because then I shall write directly to the Foreign Office, demanding a position."

"Don't be ridiculous," she scoffed, while thinking *yes*.

"Speaking of ridiculous . . ."

"Yes. These lines. Let's learn them. I have a million things to do. Problems with linens and tea sandwiches and one of the guests keeps moving all the mistletoe, though that might be Bridget and Sophronia."

"Do you like all this?" Grey asked earnestly, waving his hand to indicate something, or everything.

"What is all this?" She mimicked him.

"Hostessing, entertaining, keeping house. Dealing with crises involving tea sandwiches and linens and unruly relatives. Bustling about, trying to be the Perfect English Lady because that's how everyone will judge you."

Her breath caught for a moment. How astute of him to read right into the contents of her heart and head. Especially when no one else seemed to.

"It is what I was raised to do. And I'm not certain there are other options for a woman of my station."

Grey took a step closer.

"But do you like it?"

"I . . . I . . . never thought about it," she stammered. But this was a lie. Those traitorous little thoughts had been crossing her mind more and more frequently. Just a moment ago, she was sad that she would likely never see India or wear a saffron-colored dress.

Serena gazed up at Grey. He seemed disappointed that she wasn't *more:* that she wasn't unhappy being a gently-bred lady of quality, that she didn't seem to want more to occupy her time than household matters, that she would be content with a supposedly stultifying existence of marriage and babies and managing servants and not much else. But she didn't have the words to tell him that she didn't know of any alternatives enough to really long for them.

But India, though . . .

That tempted her.

"Shall we do the lines?"

Grey nodded and adopted his stance as Lord Pirate Captain.

"Argh, my lady."

"I swoon . . ."

Serena swooned, trying to fall softly, languidly, like the fall was an elegant movement from a dance, and like she knew he would catch her. And he did. Strong arms enclosed her, keeping her warm and secure. But not safe, no. There was something slightly dangerous and thrilling about Mr. Greyson Jones, agent of the throne, and about being held in his arms for one, two, three seconds longer than necessary or proper.

It was something she wanted to explore.

"Wake up, my lady," he said softly, words only for her to hear. "There is danger and adventure out there. You don't want to miss it."

I don't want to miss it.

"Oh, danger? Adventure? Where?" This time she didn't sound scared. She sounded curious.

"Well, not here, in Shropshire, of course," he murmured, a hint of amusement infusing his voice. "We must get to my ship."

"But we shall be besieged by my lovesick swan."

They paused for a moment of silence where Gosling would utter his ridiculous line of "Quack, my love. Quack, my love."

"Very well, my Lord Pirate Captain, let us go at once to your ship," she whispered. And oh, it felt like weight was lifting from her chest, even though it was just pretend.

"It shall be a dangerous journey, but I vow to protect you."

"Oh, Lord Pirate Captain, I shall cling to you with my delicate lady arms."

"I wish to be clung to by your delicate lady arms." His voice was low, and rough, like he meant it. Really meant it.

It was then that Serena realized he was still holding her—she had never quite recovered from swooning into his arms, never quite disentangled herself and put distance between them.

That realization was followed by another: that she liked it here, in his arms. She liked the way he looked at her with such fierce, unabashed longing that it took her breath away.

When had that happened?

How had she never noticed?

Her heart started to pound, slowly and steadily, but insistently. And she knew, just knew, what was about to happen. Mr. Greyson Jones was going to kiss her.

And she wanted him to.

In an instant his lips were on hers. The moment between before and after was over so quickly she didn't have time to think about it. One second they were at odds, as always, and the next, his lips were firm upon hers and she was yielding.

With this kiss, her senses began to awaken. To the soft pressure of his lips, the warmth of his body, the way her heartbeat drummed up its intensity, the way his hair felt as she slid her fingers through the soft strands, the way her core tightened with something like wanting.

From yielding to yearning within the space of a kiss.

"Serena . . ." There was no teasing in his voice now, just a low urgent growl. It thrilled her, that.

All of the sudden she felt positively giddy. Sparkly. Alive. She had done a wicked thing, kissing a man in the study, a man whom she hated, and she had liked it.

More than liked it.

She smiled at him, pressed one more kiss upon his lips, and said, "Well, that is the second most interesting thing that has ever happened to me."

CHAPTER EIGHT

In which there is dancing. And it is romantic.

Later that evening

Serena and Viola had arranged for dancing and music in the great hall as that evening's entertainment. The guests took turns performing on the pianoforte, as the local musicians who would have comprised the orchestra were all stranded by the snowstorm.

The room was dominated by the large evergreen tree, which had been embellished with candles and other decorations the ladies had made while gossiping and drinking tea all afternoon. Garlands of holly and other greenery decorated the windows. Mistletoe hung in the doorways.

Footmen milled about with spiced mulled wine and crisp, cold champagne. The guests were all merry and starry-eyed and singing and indulging in biscuits and mince pies. The younger guests— Bridget, Alexandra, and the young Viscount Newton—were making mischief under the mistletoe and sneaking sips of wine.

Grey paused, taking it all in, remembering when he had been one of those young 'uns. There was *nothing* like an English Christmas. He was deeply glad, down in his heart and soul, to be here enjoying it in such splendor, especially since he didn't know when he'd be back to do so again.

But as wonderful as it all was, none of it compared with the softness and desire in Serena's eyes after he had kissed her.

He had kissed her.

He had kissed the lovely and perfect Lady Serena.

He had hoped and dreamed of that moment for years. Even when his best friend was engaged to her, he dreamed of her. And especially when Frye revealed he'd broken the betrothal, Grey had hoped and dreamed. He had carried a torch for her that whole while.

If he hadn't been leaving England, Grey didn't know if he would have taken the chance. As it was, he hadn't known how she would react—would she slap him? Or kiss him back? He just knew that he couldn't live with himself if he didn't try.

And when he thought she would give him a chance . . . well . . . there was only one thing to do.

Kiss the girl.

Every second had been better than the fantasy. The softness of her lips, the way she surprised him by yielding at first and then matching his passion, the way her fingers threaded through his hair, the breathy sigh of something like sweetness and contentment after.

And then she had gazed him with softness and desire, instead of her usual stormy and flinty gaze.

It was clear that she was almost as undone as he.

He wanted to get undone with her again.

Grey also badly wanted to know what she meant by "that is the second most interesting thing to have ever happened to me."

The good thing about being snowed-in together in a castle was that he had a good chance of being able to find her and ask her.

He found her easily; unfortunately, she was dancing with Gosling, the lovesick swan who was currently proving to be quite the rival. Well.

Grey strode determinedly across the room, through the dancers.

"May I cut in." It was not phrased as a question.

Gosling was startled by Grey's impoliteness, but then took advantage of the opportunity to demonstrate his gentlemanliness and chivalry. Or maybe he didn't fancy a fight. He acquiesced.

"I shall look forward to another dance with you later, Lady Serena." He kissed her palm.

Grey took over.

"I hope you don't mind."

"No," she said softly. "I don't mind."

They began to dance.

Of course, Serena was an excellent dancer. The result of the finest instructors, hours of practice, her innate grace. She was made for ballrooms.

"I've been dying to see you all evening," he told her.

"We have spent the better portion of the day together."

"There's something I've been dying to ask you."

"Dying, Mr. Jones? You seem to be in perfectly fine health to me."

She was teasing him. Maybe even flirting with him. This was all the encouragement he needed.

"You said our kiss was the second most interesting thing to have happened to you. What was the first?"

"I would think you, Mr. Jones, should know."

"Relieve my poor male brain of the struggle of figuring it out."

"Being jilted, of course," she said, with a rueful smile and his heart sank and he remembered what he'd said. "Nothing like being thrown over by a duke to give a girl an air of mystery and tragedy."

"Ah. Right."

Words he would never, ever live down. Words she would never, ever let him forget.

"Speaking of dukes, where is Frye? I am worried that he hasn't arrived yet, especially in this weather. I confess I did imagine at least a dozen horrible things happening to him after he jilted me, but none involved him freezing to death in a blizzard, which I am beginning to worry about."

"He's a strong and resourceful man; I'm sure he has no need of our worry. Tell me more about the kind and lovely Lady Serena and her violent fantasies for her former betrothed."

"Are you surprised? Just because I am well-mannered and demure, you think that I am not imagining all sorts of wicked things?"

"Please, *please* tell me more about your wicked thoughts."

Grey tried to give her a charming, wicked grin and didn't quite manage it. He and Lady Serena were conversing about something real, she was revealing another side of herself, one that she didn't show at all, if ever, and he was the lucky man who got to hold her and waltz with her while it happened. His grasp on her tightened.

"When Frye jilted me, it was the first time the world did not conform to my expectations. It was an eye-opening experience, to say the least. But now I often wonder what else might not go according to plan. I cannot quite imagine another life for myself, other than wife, mother, and Lady of the Manor, but still . . . I wonder. The possibilities are endless."

"And the kiss?"

"Of course you would ask about the kiss. I suppose you want to know if it turned my world upside down, made my heart burst, sparked a deep longing within . . . all that romantic stuff."

"Yes," he whispered.

"What does it matter to you? A rake, man about town, about to leave for foreign lands perhaps never to return . . . What does one little kiss matter to you?"

He nearly stumbled.

What did one little kiss matter to him?

To start, it was hardly one little kiss. It was only something he'd fantasized about for years. He could have made some flippant remark about collecting kisses from English lasses before setting sail for foreign lands. But this was his moment to give her an idea of how much he had longed to kiss her and of what it meant to him when their lips touched.

Finally.

"It matters to me. And it wasn't a little kiss," he said, his voice low but firm. "A little kiss is quick, fleeting. A brief caress of lips, if that. It's almost perfunctory, being so quick, because a real kiss makes you want to linger. Our kiss lingered. I don't know about you, but time stopped when I kissed you. It could have been moments, or hours, or days, I know not, just that something so soul-consuming can't have been *little*. What I do know is this: I've wanted to kiss you since forever. If it pleased you, I could kiss you forever."

He had watched as a blush crept into her cheeks as he spoke. Was he embarrassing her? Or was that the flush of desire? Grey didn't know. He hadn't been able to stop himself from saying all those things. So much for his training as a diplomat—there he was, laying all his cards on the table, leaving his heart open to a crushing attack.

"I . . . I don't know what to say."

"You could say that you feel the same way," he said, because this was no time to retreat. Grey continued. "You could say that when our lips touched you felt the whole world spark to life. That time stopped as it did for me. That when it was over you felt like life might never be the same."

"Until yesterday I despised you."

"I know," he said, with a faint sigh. "I deserved it. And today? Tonight?"

"I am confused."

Confused. He would take confused. It was better than being despised, and a step in the direction toward love. He had less than a week before the conclusion of the house party to maybe make her love him.

"That, my dear, is the power of a kiss. It might make you fall in love with me."

CHAPTER NINE

In which prospects are discussed.

The dowager duchess's chamber

Serena stole away from the party to visit with her mother. Her kiss with Greyson and their conversation was weighing heavily on her mind, inspiring questions about the rest of her life that she didn't know how to answer.

Namely, why did the thought of Greyson leaving England cause an odd pang in the region of her heart?

Why had she spent more time imagining what India might be like than how she might redecorate Hartley Hall, one of Gosling's residences? Imagining herself as Lady Gosling, on a redecorating mission, should have made her downright giddy.

Her mother. She needed to talk to her mother.

"How fares the party?" the dowager duchess asked. She was propped up against a pile of pillows and attempting to sip some tea.

"More importantly, how are you faring, Mother? I should have thought you'd be on the mend by now."

"I'm at least not getting worse, though I am a bit bored, lying here while the whole house makes merry. Tell me, how are things going with your suitors? I hear Lord Gosling has been *most* attentive."

"How have you heard that if you have not attended the party and I have not told you?"

"You are not my only caller. Perhaps I have spies." Her mother managed a faint smile.

Spies only made her think of Greyson. But her mother was probably thinking of Viola or Bridget.

"Well, how is he?"

"He is constantly attentive. He has been nothing but a perfect gentleman. He has spoken to me extensively about his various residences, his ideal marriage, the names for his future children, all sorts of things that have led me to believe that he will propose by Twelfth Night."

What Serena didn't mention was that he was . . . too perfect. And that made time with him a little boring, if she was being honest. She knew that he would always say the correct thing: a compliment on her dress, a comment that demonstrated what a kind and amenable husband he would be, a question that would show someone to the best advantage.

There was no risk that he would shock or anger or inflame or inspire.

Serena gasped, then and there, as it dawned on her.

He was just like *her*.

Perfect. Predictable. Perfectly predictable.

She understood, now, what Greyson had said so inelegantly: "If you ask me, Frye dodged a bullet by avoiding a match to Lady Serena. I know, she's a perfect lady, but she's a little too perfect. This will make her more intriguing, now, don't you think?"

Gah! Greyson Jones was right!

Talk about a Christmas Miracle.

Her mother hadn't realized that Serena's understanding of the world had just transformed.

"Oh, Serena, you might be betrothed before Christmas and wed to Gosling within a month!"

"Mother, wait—"

But what if she didn't wish to marry Gosling? What if he were so right that he was wrong?

Her mother carried on, oblivious: "Then everyone will forget about that business with Frye. Gosling isn't a duke, but that's really his only drawback. He's as rich as one, certainly, even if he only is a viscount."

"Mother, wait. Is that really the best reason to marry someone? So that everyone will forget that I was once jilted?"

154

"Of course not. You know I didn't mean that. You must have many other reasons for marrying Gosling. You have said yourself that he is exceedingly handsome, well-mannered, and thinks highly of women. He has a fine estate, excellent connections, and that highly respected title . . . Plus, he is demonstrating an interest in you."

But Serena could now think of other reasons to wed, like kisses that did indeed make time stop, sparked a fire within, and made her feel well and truly alive for the first time in her life.

She thought of an adventure with her husband; instead of trips to town or to Bath, they might travel to India together or even further abroad.

She thought of life with a man who maddened her, confused her, and, as such, challenged her. It wouldn't be perfect, but she wouldn't be bored, and that seemed just right.

"I know, but—"

"How is the theater production getting on? It does seem to be keeping Sophronia and Bridget too busy to make mischief, for which I am forever grateful."

The play? It was a disaster. It was wonderful. It was ridiculous. It led to kisses with a man to whom she was not betrothed, which was inspiring crazy notions, like ditching her perfect lovesick swan and running off to India with a man who might not even like her.

"You don't even want to know, Mother."

CHAPTER TEN

In which our heroine receives a curious Christmas gift.

Christmas morning

The day dawned bright, with sunshine reflecting brightly off all the snow. Heaps and heaps of snow covered nearly everything outside. The world seemed cold, still, and quiet, while inside the house was warm, glowing, and bustling with activity.

Grey was happy to be here.

Something else was warming up his heart, though, and it hadn't anything to do with Christmas, unless it was some sort of Christmas miracle. That something was Serena.

She no longer avoided his gaze. In fact, more than once he'd caught her dark eyes fixed on him at mealtimes. She didn't look away, either, when their eyes met.

And now, while they were in the foyer, having just returned from church services with all the guests, he would have sworn that she was lingering. For him.

Which was perfect, because he needed to steal her away for a private moment.

Grey caught up with her near the doorway to one of the smaller, private drawing rooms.

"I have a gift for you," he murmured.

"Oh?"

"But first . . . oh look." He glanced up. "It seems we are standing under some mistletoe."

She looked up and saw that yes, indeed, a sprig of mistletoe hung above them. Her lips twisted into an adorably peevish smile.

"Are *you* the one who keeps moving it? I thought it was Bridget."

"Moving mistletoe so one might strategically engineer a kiss is clearly the work of a juvenile male who feels he must resort to tricks in order to get kisses from pretty girls." Grey paused. "I absolutely did it and I will not apologize for it."

"You . . ."

Grey could see all the thoughts racing through her head—admonishments, protestations—before she decided it wasn't really that important.

She stepped into the parlor; he followed and closed the door behind them.

"Well, then kiss me, so your work wasn't for naught."

"Is that the reason?"

"The only reason."

He didn't believe her for a second. Fancy that: Lady Serena lying! Lady Serena stealing into parlors to kiss him!

Grey kissed her before the moment was lost forever.

This kiss started sweetly and tentatively, with a soft fumbling press of her lips against his, or his against hers. It was only a moment before they both gave up the pretense. Grey's mouth claimed hers.

He was wild with lust for her. Oh, he'd always been, but now there was no point in pretending anymore. Not when she wanted him too.

Serena grabbed fistfuls of his jacket and pulled him close as Grey wrapped his arms around her and kissed her deeply. She kissed him right back, matching his passion.

Grey stumbled.

This was happening. Really happening.

She smiled. "Am I making you weak in the knees?"

"Something like that," he murmured before kissing her again. He'd never tire of kissing her. Or touching her—he badly wanted to touch her. Everywhere.

He pressed kisses along her neck, eliciting moans from her parted lips. That sweet sound made him hard. God, he wanted this woman.

Wanted to lose himself in her. Wanted to bring her to dizzying heights of pleasure. Wanted to love her. Forever.

Which reminded him . . .

"I have a gift for you."

He held out the poorly wrapped present and she took it.

"You didn't need to get me anything."

But I did.

"Go on, open it."

Serena sat on a nearby settee and proceeded to open the present in the exact manner that one would expect Lady Serena Cavendish to do so: she opened it slowly and carefully, as if to preserve the wrapping for reuse, which was silly since she was so rich, or as if to prevent making a mess, which was just as silly, given the number of servants at Kingstag Castle.

Finally, she held the leather volume in her hand and turned it over so she could read the very long title: *An Englishman in India, Or; One young Lord's journey to the Indian subcontinent and a thorough examination of the culture, customs, geography, languages, and its people.*

Serena peered up at him. "What does this mean?"

It means that I want to show you the world. To know of things beyond dukes, weddings and house parties.

It means that I would be utterly lost in India without that book. I won't be able to perform my duties to the crown without reading it. But I'd already be wrecked if you don't come with me.

It means that I want you to come to India with me.

As my bride.

He was too nervous to say all these things. He was not yet sure of her response, and he feared it would not good for him. After all, they'd only just kissed the other day and now he was asking her to consider leaving the life she'd planned behind and sailing halfway around the world with him.

"It's a book about India, which I'm certain you gathered from the title. It's a book one would do well to read if they were going to India. Or one might like to peruse it before their friend sets sail for that foreign land, so they might still feel close while they are actually quite far apart."

"Mr. Jones . . ."

"You might as well call me Greyson now. I've kissed you twice and messed up your hair."

To her credit, she only grinned and didn't check on the state of her coiffure.

"This is surely the most interesting gift I've ever received. I look forward to reading this, Greyson." She gazed at him with those unfathomable and unreadable dark eyes of hers. "Thank you."

CHAPTER ELEVEN

In which there is a stunning turn of events.

The next evening

Serena had stayed up late reading the book. She snuck off throughout the day to read it too. After all, Grey would be departing for India soon and he absolutely could not set sail without this volume in his possession—he would need it to aid in his diplomatic endeavors. Why, otherwise he might inadvertently cause an international incident! She would read it quickly and return it to him.

That wasn't the whole truth, though. Serena found it fascinating: she learned about all the various regions, customs, languages, and the like. It was all so different from England and what she was used to.

And yet, it was precisely what she excelled in: learning a new set of rules so she might understand how to blend in and put others at ease.

Serena entertained thoughts—utterly insane and completely scandalous thoughts—of traveling to India and assisting Grey in his diplomatic missions.

Not just because she could be helpful.

Those kisses hadn't escaped her attention.

What had escaped her attention: matters concerning the house party. Her lines for the play. And Lord Gosling, her lovesick swan. Her dear friend, Lady Charlotte Ascot, had arrived that morning after years abroad and even their reunion couldn't completely distract

Serena from thoughts of Grey and what he'd meant by giving her that book.

She certainly hadn't thought of Horace Breckenridge Church, the Duke of Frye, and wayward house party guest.

Who arrived unexpectedly after dinner.

The gentlemen were in the dining room, drinking port, smoking cheroots, and discussing improper subjects while the ladies were in the library, sipping tea and discussing indelicate topics.

A commotion in the foyer captured everyone's attentions.

Port glasses and teacups were set down. People stood and made their way toward the foyer to assuage their curiosity. They were greeted with the sight of the Duke of Frye arriving.

What? Now?

"Hello everyone," the duke said cheerfully. "You may have noticed there was a bit of a snowstorm out there, which made the roads fiendishly difficult to pass through. I hope better late than never isn't just a saying, but a sentiment."

What? No!

The duke scanned the crowd until he spotted Serena. He bowed deeply and gave her a very, very apologetic look.

"Lady Serena. My apologies for my late arrival."

"Frye. How good of you to join us."

She bit back the word "finally!" because that would be unnecessarily rude.

"I hope I haven't thrown off your numbers."

He smiled at her. She couldn't help but smile back. Sweet, shy, sorry smiles. He was a duke. She'd been raised to be a duchess. Circumstances had conspired to throw them apart, but now . . . he was here. Fretting about her numbers, which she had completely forgotten to worry about these past few days.

Her heart started to thud hard in her chest.

Why had Frye come at all? Given the delay from the snowstorm, he would have a perfectly fine reason to keep away and send his regrets later. Unless he had a reason for coming to this house party that was at once a Christmas celebration and also a mini-marriage mart for her.

There could only be one reason.

Serena turned and fled.

$\mathcal{A}$ short while later, Grey found her sitting on a settee before the fire in the private parlor where she had unwrapped the book. She now understood it hadn't just been a gift, but a proposal. He sat next to her without asking for permission; she was glad to have him near and glad that they had achieved such an intimacy that he didn't feel the need to ask.

"Lady Serena, are you alright?"

"I am perfectly well. Why do you ask?"

"Because you were confronted with the sight of your former betrothed arriving unexpectedly. And then you fled."

"It's not what you think. Besides, I didn't run. Ladies don't run. They don't pick up their skirts and flee to the nearest room where they might have some privacy to be alone with their thoughts."

It was not a hint and he didn't take it as such.

"What else don't ladies do?" Grey asked.

"They don't find themselves alone with handsome men to whom they are not married."

"Why is that?"

"They might do wicked things. Things that ladies don't do," she murmured as she turned to look at him.

"Such as . . ."

"Kissing." Her voice was but a whisper. The sound didn't need to travel far, for their heads were bowed together and the distance between their lips was slowly drawing to a close. Lips touched lips. Softly, sweetly, achingly.

This meant something, this kiss.

And so did what came next.

Greyson couldn't keep his hands off her. One minute he sank his fingers into her hair, undoubtably making a mess of it, and he held her, just kissing her, as if it were all he wanted for Christmas, his birthday, and Easter too. But then he needed to feel more of her.

Especially when she needed to feel more him. Serena smoothed her palms across his chest, feeling the firm muscles underneath the fine fabric of his jacket, and waistcoat and shirt and . . . She wanted to growl in frustration at all the layers that separated her bare palms from the bare skin of his chest.

"A proper lady would never request that a gentleman disrobe so that she might gaze upon his naked body," she murmured. "And feel it, too, with her delicate lady hands."

This made Greyson laugh, but not before he was locking the door, shrugging out of his jacket and fumbling with the buttons on his waistcoat. One by one, the layers hit the floor.

Serena gazed upon him: the smooth skin, strong limbs, the evidence of his arousal for her and how proud he seemed to stand there while she drank in the sight of him.

He kissed her again while she embraced him. His hands started exploring her, feeling her, learning her while layers of her gown were tugged down or pushed up and her stays were undone and soon he was able to touch her too.

His palms closed around her breasts, his fingers teased the pink centers until she threw her head back and sighed. He tugged her down to the settee and pushed her skirts up while he sank to his knees. Grey kissed her again—this time in that sacred place between her legs. This time she moaned. Every hot, slow, teasing circle of his tongue made her writhe in pleasure.

He teased and taunted until she couldn't restrain herself any longer. Serena cried out in pleasure.

And that was only the beginning.

She felt Grey's warmth and weight on her.

"Serena . . ."

"Yes . . ." she whispered. "Yes."

She wanted this. Wanted to feel him. Wanted to be connected with him. She knew this would change everything.

She said "yes" once more.

She gasped as he eased his hot, hard length into her. The wickedly wonderful pressure began to build inside her again as he moved within her, slow and steady and relentless. The world beyond them ceased to exist. There was only his warmth, his touch, his low groans of desire. Nothing mattered except the feeling of his hands in her hair, his mouth on her body, the way he felt inside her.

Just him.

And her.

And this pressure and pleasure building and building and building. Until she cried out once more. And he gave a shout, and one hard and deep final thrust. And then, stillness and silence, wrapped in each other's arms.

They stayed like that for a while, all tangled up in each other.

Serena nestled into Grey's embrace and her racing heart finally started to slow. She felt at peace.

"What were you really running from, Serena?"

She turned to face him, her hair falling around her face, lips reddened from his kiss and her cheeks pink from pleasure.

"Becoming a duchess."

CHAPTER TWELVE

In which the play is performed.

The final day of the house party

A few days later

$\mathcal{J}$t was hard to believe that the house party was coming to a close. Throughout the house, ladies' maids and valets were busy packing up trunks.

In one particular trunk, a copy of *An Englishman in India, Or; One young Lord's journey to the Indian subcontinent and a thorough examination of the culture, customs, geography, languages, and its people,* was also packed away, ready for the journey ahead.

Meanwhile, Grey and Serena were to be found upstairs in the corridor, closing the door to the dowager duchess's bedchamber behind them. Her Grace was thankfully on the mend and eager for news from the house party, visits from some guests, and hints about what to expect from Sophronia and Bridget's production, which would be that evening's entertainment.

Grey turned to Serena with a question. "Shall we mention anything to Bridget?"

"Oh no."

"But don't you think she'll be mad when she finds out that we've meddled in her production?"

Serena grinned. "Oh yes."

"Ah, that is not a bad thing. You *want* to make her mad."

"Sisters," Serena explained. "Also it's the least she deserves for casting me as the Lonely Spinster."

The play

𝒥ortunately, the dowager duchess was well enough to dress and leave her chambers for the final evening of the house party. She was granted a prime seat in the front row.

When Serena and Grey took the stage, dressed as a Lonely Spinster and Lord Pirate Captain, they delivered a performance that brought Bridget's absurd play to life, for now there was an undercurrent of romantic tension surging beneath all those silly lines. There was palpable passion when she swooned into his arms. Sparks flew between them as they bantered their dialogue, each line more ridiculous than the last.

Serena had also, to her great embarrassment, practiced swooning. But only in the privacy of her bedchamber, of course. She did, after all, have a reputation for perfection to maintain.

Finally, they entered the third act, when their storyline was drawing to a close.

"I shall now vanquish your lovesick swan, who has managed to pursue you all the way from Shropshire to the great English coast where my pirate ship awaits!"

Grey dramatically unsheathed his sword.

There were gasps in the audience.

"Quack, my love! Quack, my love!"

Gosling, being perfect, managed to play the role of Lovesick Swan with humor and grace, neither making a laughingstock of himself or the character.

"No! Do not hurt him!" Serena cried. "I spy another swan with whom he might fall in love when the memory of me fades from his swan brain."

Indeed, another swan made her way upon the stage. She shook her tail feathers in an effort to catch Gosling's attention. She succeeded.

"Quack, my love!"

And with that, Serena's Lovesick Swan was lovesick for her no more.

"Whatever my lady wishes," Grey said, pulling Serena into a dramatic embrace. "And now, let us sail off into the sunset, on our way to happily ever after!"

The audience erupted in applause, led by Bridget and Sophronia, who were under the impression, along with the audience, that the play had concluded. After all, this is where the script stopped.

"But wait!" Serena cried out. "It is most improper for a lonely spinster such as myself to be alone with a gentleman, especially in the close and confining quarters of a pirate ship. I daresay pirate ships are not adequately stocked with chaperones."

A murmur rippled through the audience.

"What is this?" Bridget was heard to ask loudly. Sophronia shushed her.

"What is this talk of a *lonely* spinster?" Grey boomed. "I think you mean a *lovely* spinster."

"I swoon!"

And she did. Serena swooned elegantly into Grey's awaiting arms. He caught her effortlessly. Not only did he hold her for one, two, three, four seconds longer than necessary, he also pressed a kiss upon her lips.

"But you shall be a spinster no more. Marry me, Serena. Make me the happiest man in the world."

"Oh yes, my Lord Pirate Captain, yes!"

"As I am a captain I could marry us at sea. But as we are not at sea, we require a vicar."

"Did someone say a vicar?"

It was none other than Bertram, the local vicar.

The audience erupted in gasps and a smattering of applause as it dawned on them what they were witnessing. A wedding. A Christmas wedding.

"Look! It's a vicar and he just happens to be holding a special license!" Grey declared. In truth, Frye had just happened to call in a favor with the archbishop so that Grey and Serena could wed. It was the least he could do.

"It is as if this union were meant to be," Serena said. "As if it were blessed."

The couple ducked their heads for another kiss, but were thwarted before their lips could touch.

"Ahem," the vicar coughed. "Might I remind you that you are yet unwed."

"Let us remedy that. For I should like to take my bride to bed!"

Grey grinned wolfishly. Serena blushed demurely.

And with that, the bride and groom were wed.

It was, to say the least, not the wedding Serena had ever dreamt of or expected, but in its own way it was perfect. It was, so far, the third most interesting thing that had ever happened to her.

And that was only the beginning.

ABOUT THE AUTHOR

Maya Rodale began reading romance novels in college at her mother's insistence. She is now the bestselling and award winning author of numerous smart and sassy romance novels. A champion of the genre and its readers, she is also the author of the non-fiction book *Dangerous Books For Girls: The Bad Reputation Of Romance Novels, Explained* and has written for The Huffington Post, NPR, Bustle.com and more. Maya lives in New York City with her darling dog and a rogue of her own. Visit her online at www.mayarodale.com or follow her on Twitter @MayaRodale.

~ALSO BY MAYA RODALE~
~KEEPING UP WITH THE CAVENDISHES~
LADY BRIDGET'S DIARY
CHASING LADY AMELIA
LADY CLAIRE IS ALL THAT
IT'S HARD OUT HERE FOR A DUKE

~BAD BOYS AND WALLFLOWERS~
THE WICKED WALLFLOWER
THE BAD BOY BILLIONAIRE'S WICKED ARRANGEMENT
WALLFLOWER GONE WILD
THE BAD BOY BILLIONAIRE'S GIRL GONE WILD
WHAT A WALLFLOWER WANTS
THE BAD BOY BILLIONAIRE: WHAT A GIRL WANTS

~THE WRITING GIRLS~
A GROOM OF ONE'S OWN
A TALE OF TWO LOVERS
THE TATTOOED DUKE
SEDUCING MR. KNIGHTLY
THREE SCHEMES AND A SCANDAL

Snowy Night with a Duke

KATHARINE ASHE

CHAPTER ONE

Three days before Christmas, 1816

The Fiddler's Roost Inn

Somewhere off the main road, near Dorchester

*W*hen the Mail Coach from London skidded into the yard to disgorge its frozen contents before the tiny inn, its team was lathered and the poor souls atop laden with snow. Yet not all passengers immediately disembarked. Two lingered within.

During the slog through the thickening snow, as the other passengers had grown increasingly alarmed by the icy road, these two young men had alternately snored, yawned, and traded an engraved flask between them. By their fine coats, shiny boots, and thorough disregard for proper public coach decorum, it was clear to everybody that they were town rowdies.

Why they had stooped to travel on the coach, one passenger guessed: the sprigs of high society must be pockets-to-let and fleeing costly London for the less costly delights of Christmas in the countryside. The other passengers simply wished all of high society to the devil, and especially this unimpressive example and his obviously French friend.

But when the last of the respectable passengers had climbed down from the coach, the change that came over the two young sots was extraordinary. Slumped shoulders squared, slack jaws grew taut, and eyes that had been hazy with drink gleamed with sharp determination.

"Right, then," the Englishman said in a baritone of such smooth, confident resonance that the Prince Regent had given its owner a fond nickname: Church Bell.

"As planned," his companion replied, his voice inflected by the cadence of speech of his native island. For he was not, after all, French, rather Haitian. "Then we part ways, my friend, you to return to—"

"No."

"Mon ami." The Haitian leaned back against the worn squabs, folding arms thick with muscle. "You cannot—"

"No," the Englishman said calmly, his breath frosting in the chilly air. "That is over and done with. The best thing I can do now is to leave her be."

"Scoundrel."

"Undoubtedly," the Englishman concurred.

The Haitian's scowl looked more like a half-grin. The two had known each other since age ten and were like brothers.

"Now, to our present concern." The Englishman extended his right hand and the Haitian grasped it hard, sinews and bones meeting exactly as they had for fifteen years, since their school days, every time they embarked upon another such mission. In those days, their missions had been minor: return the Headmaster's stolen wig without detection, hide spiders in the Head Boy's bed linens, and the like.

Now they did missions on behalf of the crown, and they were deadly serious.

"Solve the mystery," the Englishman said, the words a sacred ritual.

"Fight the battle." The Haitian's eyes glimmered with pleasure.

The Englishman cocked a grin. "Save the girl."

Then they were opening the door and—shoulders slumping and strides intentionally unsteady—they tromped through the snow toward the inn that glowed with warm welcome.

CHAPTER TWO

An hour later

The Fiddler's Roost Inn: the taproom and yard

Sometimes it was not in a lady's best interests to follow any dictates but those of her own heart. Because Lady Charlotte Ascot, daughter of the Earl of Ware, had discovered this at a young age— eight, to be precise, during a footrace against boys with considerably longer legs than she—when faced with a challenge to her courage at the age of twenty-one, she did not hesitate to set out from London alone for Kingstag Castle, where all of her friends were gathering for a holiday party.

For in fact the gathering was not *really* a holiday party. It was an emergency. Charlotte's dear friend Lady Serena Cavendish had recently been jilted by her longtime betrothed, the Duke of Frye, mere months from the wedding. It had shocked the ton. According to a letter from Serena's sister Alexandra, it had sent Serena into a spiral of distress.

Serena needed all of her dear friends around her now, and Charlotte was one of them. It mattered nothing that Charlotte had only just returned from a two-and-a-half-year trip abroad; friendships cemented in childhood and matured in young womanhood could never be undone, even across an ocean. Also, Charlotte and the Cavendish sisters had written letters to each other constantly since she had left England.

None of those letters had ever hinted that the wedding of Serena and the Duke of Frye had been in jeopardy. Betrothed to Serena since childhood, the duke had always been gorgeously attentive to Serena, everything that a lifelong fiancé should be. Despite the fact that he was the only person in the world whom Charlotte had literally climbed a tree to avoid, she had always particularly admired that about him.

The jilting was as much of a surprise to her as to anybody.

So when the invitation to Kingstag arrived in London, Charlotte did not wait before instructing her family's coachman Fields to ready the team for travel or her maid to pack her clothes. That was how Charlotte found herself running through a curtain of snow from the carriage and into a little roadside inn in the midst of a blizzard.

And it was how, shortly afterward, she was sipping hot tea in the taproom—for the inn was so small there were no private parlors—and becoming acquainted with a pair of modest gentlewomen who had arrived on the Mail Coach.

"How do you come to be traveling alone, my lady?" Miss Mapplethorpe inquired. At least sixty, with pale eyes and an air of fragility, she smiled gently. Maiden aunt to the orphaned Miss Calliope Jameson, she was accompanying her niece to a distant relative's home for the holidays.

"Lady Charlotte is not precisely alone, Aunt." A shy, sweet girl of seventeen, Calliope Jameson shared the same pale eyes and slender frame as her aunt, but to great advantage. She was a beauty. "For she has come with her maid."

"Oh, yes, of course," her aunt said. "Dear Niece, you are so much cleverer than I."

"Most of my family are still at my family's home in Devon," Charlotte explained, letting the heat of her teacup burrow into her palms. "They planned to join me in London for Christmas, but I suspect they have been delayed from that anyway." And a good thing that was. While she missed them dreadfully, her father's last letter to her in Philadelphia had made clear his intentions: she must return to England and marry. Since she had taken up her aunt's invitation and fled to America two and a half years ago to avoid marrying, she was hardly eager to see her father anyway.

"My younger brother, Henry, is staying at a house quite nearby," she added. "Although I don't suppose the snow will allow me to see him this holiday either."

"Oh dear, my lady," Miss Mapplethorpe said with a shake of her head. "How dreadful to be far from family at Christmastime."

"Perhaps not so dreadful," Charlotte replied with a smile at both of them. "I shall have you two as company, after all."

It was at that moment that they were roused from their cozy tea by a ruckus just outside. Miss Mapplethorpe went to the window to investigate.

"Good heavens," she said. "I believe there is a brawl taking place in the yard."

Calliope leaped up and went to her side. "It is those young men from the coach!"

The other guests were streaming out into the snow.

"Who can resist a brawl between two toffs?" one of them said excitedly.

Miss Mapplethorpe and Calliope hurried in that direction. Possessed of a natural curiosity, Charlotte followed.

And so it was that in the snow that still fell in thick curtains, Charlotte discovered the jilting Duke of Frye engaged in a flagrant bout of fisticuffs only moments before his opponent got the best of him.

Horace Chesterfield Breckinridge Church, the eleventh Duke of Frye, was not a Gargantua. He never had trouble finding boots that fit, and neither his tailor nor his valet ever bemoaned the width of his shoulders or thickness of his thighs. Rather, those inestimable persons praised said shoulders for the muscle that made buckram padding unnecessary, not to mention his flat, narrow waist. And they often exclaimed in glee over his marvelously well-toned legs, which made their labors so satisfying.

But Frye was not a particularly small man, either. He was, in fact, of average-to-tall height and average-to-wide shoulder breadth, and under normal circumstances he had no difficulty matching punches with Freddie, who was his same size (in truth an inch taller, but Frye never admitted it, at least not aloud).

Under normal circumstances was when Frye was not throwing a fight.

Barreling toward him at perfectly timed speed, Freddie's fist made an arc meant to appear haphazard to the crowd that was streaming into the inn's rear yard to watch, despite the snow.

As planned.

The speed of Freddie's punch allowed Frye precisely the seconds he required to dodge to the side. The knuckles only grazed his jaw before he pitched onto his elbow in the snow.

"Cur!" He allowed the epithet to roll over his loose tongue in a tone suitably garbled to sound drunken. "I'll ge'sshu now!"

"*Cochon,*" Freddie replied soberly. Freddie was, after all, the hero in this make-believe scenario. "A gentleman never allows an insult to a lady to pass unpunished," he said in English better than the King's. Lord Frédéric Alexandre Fortier had, after all, received higher marks than Frye in the study of Rhetoric and both English and French Literature—although only a bit higher, Frye occasionally reminded his old friend.

"Was only flirting," Frye slurred, swinging a loose left at Freddie's shoulder, which his friend nimbly sidestepped. "She didn't mind."

"The next time, *chien,*" Freddie said, his eyes narrowing with stalwart menace—for Freddie always played stalwart menace particularly well—"flirt with your words, not your hands." Boots braced in a foot of snow, which their pugilistic theatricals were swiftly packing into ice, Freddie jabbed at him again.

Tilting madly, arms windmilling, Frye hurled himself to the ground.

It was shameful.

But they had played this scene to excellent effect many times before: Freddie accused a drunken Frye of insulting a lady, they fought, Frye got banished belowstairs or to a stable, and was then able to ask manservants or coachmen all sorts of questions they would never answer to a duke or to even a proper mister. Meanwhile, the dashingly heroic and intriguingly foreign Freddie would be inside encouraging polite company to raise toasts to honor integrity and good manners. Lots of toasts.

Violence and spirits both tended to loosen men's tongues.

Now the group of coach passengers and others huddled in the inn's doorway were casting Freddie looks of guarded admiration. He was obviously defending a woman's virtue from his drunken friend.

In fact, Frye had not drunk a drop in years, though he'd splashed a bit of whiskey on his cravat to lend to his general aroma of dissoluteness.

On the other hand, there *was* in fact an insulted woman: Serena Cavendish.

But Frye had excellent justification for that.

Freddie, however, still thought fences required mending with Lady Serena. The punches he was throwing now, and the taunts, were not entirely make-believe.

"Someday you will meet a woman whose good opinion you will want," Freddie said, the snow falling all about them. He swung again.

Frye dodged the blow, intentionally stumbling over his own boots.

"An' you know all there's to know about women, I s'pose?" he mumbled, landing a weak left on his friend's shoulder.

"I know a fine woman when she stands before me." Freddie jabbed, pulling the punch just enough to make it look like a near miss. "What is your problem, friend?" His narrowed gaze slipped sideways for an instant.

"You're my problem, *friend*." He threw a sloppy right.

"You're blind, man!"

Blind?

What was Freddie telling him?

There. At the doorway. That man must be their quarry. He fit the description perfectly: fifty or so, narrow cheeks, pale gray hair, and a complacent smile that masked a mind bent on nefarious gain.

Then he saw her.

Framed in snow and haloed in firelight from inside: a woman.

The woman.

Full pink lips. Pale cheeks stained with pink from the cold. Dark curls tumbling over her brow. And gray eyes fixed on him, snapping with vexation.

The world abruptly glittered all about. Then tilted.

Charlotte Ascot.

Here.

Everything slowed—the snowfall, Frye's heartbeats, Freddie's voice coming to him as though through a tunnel.

Oh, no.

No, no, no.

Not here. Not now. Not when he had a job to do. Not in front of so many people.

Not in front of *her*.

But he felt no pressure in his chest, no numbness in his hands, and there was no light glowing across his vision, only the aura of bemusement caused by a pair of snapping gray eyes.

"Do you need to be hit over the head with it?" Freddie exclaimed.

Then Freddie's fist slammed into his jaw.

Frye was sitting in the snow, shaking his head, and blinking hard when his friend grasped his hand.

"*Mon Dieu*," Freddie whispered as he hauled him off his arse, his dark brow pleated and eyes full of worry. "What in the devil?"

Stumbling to his feet, Frye snatched his hand away and managed to mumble, "Damned slippery— Think you've broken my jaw, ol' friend." He tested it back and forth and cut a glance toward the doorway.

The man was gone.

But she still stood there. And the daggers her smoky eyes were throwing hit him like little jolts of lightning straight to his groin, with predictable effect.

Then again, Charlotte Ascot had always been able to make every part of him lose control.

"Sir," the innkeeper said to Freddie as he came toward them from the doorway. "This is unacceptable."

"A friendly disagreement, my good man," Freddie said pleasantly. He offered the innkeeper an easy smile, grasping Frye's shoulder.

Frye obligingly staggered anew.

"S'a friendly bout," he muttered, struggling not to look toward the doorway. Toward her.

Blast, his jaw hurt.

"Bring us a pot of your strongest coffee," Freddie said, pushing Frye toward the door.

"Begging your pardon, Mr. Fortier," the innkeeper said. "My missus and I run a respectable establishment. There are women and children within, you see. This gentleman," he said with a frown. "Well, Mr. Church here isn't welcome inside till he's fit for decent company."

"Sir!" Frye let his mouth hang open a moment, then lifted his fisted hands up before him. "I'll beg *your* pardon with my fives here!"

"Enough, *mon ami*. You have made your bed. Now you must sleep in it—a straw bed," Freddie said with a chuckle and a placating smile for all. "Monsieur Innkeeper, point my friend to your stable where he can sleep away this unseemly inebriation."

Which is how Frye came to be stumbling toward the stable, where he would seek out their quarry's coachman and commence the next stage of their mission, and stumbling away from the lady with the smoky gray eyes whom he had once thought never to see again.

CHAPTER THREE

An hour later

The taproom and stable

𝒥n the taproom, Monsieur Fortier was charming everybody. It was hardly to be wondered at. He was handsome, expensively dressed, delightfully amusing, and telling tales of heroic deeds of war against Napoleon's army. A gentleman of obvious wealth and education, he was not in fact French but Haitian, and had fought in the war of rebellion in which his young country had thrown off the "yoke of French tyranny," along with the entirely non-metaphorical shackles of slavery.

With the end of England's war with France only a year and a half earlier, everybody was happy to join in the toasts celebrating the sound trouncing of that wretched little Corsican.

Under normal circumstances, Charlotte would have raised toasts to Napoleon's defeat too. But Monsieur Fortier had, only an hour earlier, beaten the Duke of Frye quite literally into the ground. That the duke had apparently deserved it—he had gravely insulted a woman, everybody whispered—and that the two seemed to be bosom friends—and that the duke had been obviously intoxicated— were factors to seriously consider.

But it was Christmas. At Christmastime especially, everybody deserved compassion. Also, as her mother had told her long ago, a true lady was measured not by the blood in her veins but by the courage in her heart.

As much as she dreaded speaking with him, Charlotte had no choice now.

Gathering from the kitchen a pitcher of warm water, a washbowl, soft linens, and a little jar of salve from her luggage, Charlotte went outside into the thickly falling snow and followed the short path to the stable. Within, all was quiet: the only sounds were horses snuffling in their stalls and somebody piping a little tune on a flute at the stable's other end.

Male laughter tumbled along the stable corridor. *His* laughter. She would recognize Horace Church's deep, wonderful laughter from her grave.

Pitcher and basin clutched in her damp mittens, she went forward.

From the cozy warmth of the taproom, she had imagined a much worse scene than that which she came upon now. Lit in the glow of a lantern, four men lounged about the neat little tack room on benches, sharing a bottle.

Holding a slab of meat against the side of his face with one hand and lifting a glass of spirits to his mouth with the other, the man she had seen pummeled to the snow an hour earlier was smiling. Every one of his beautifully straight white teeth was showing.

All four men turned their eyes toward her.

Her family's coachman Fields, the ostler, and the other coachman came to their feet at once.

"Milady," Fields said. "How may I be helping you?"

"Not at all, thank you, Fields," she said. "It seems, *Mr. Church,* that you do not need nursing after all."

The duke stared at her. Then, shaking his head once, sharply, he dropped the slab of beef and stood up.

"My lady," he said.

He had tanned skin, dark hair cut short to suit fashion, the most intensely blue eyes, and high cheekbones, to one of which now clung several filaments of raw meat and a quantity of beef blood. Beneath the filaments, the skin was split and a bruise was forming on his gorgeously firm jaw.

She set down her burden and stripped off her mittens.

"You must allow me to tend to that wound," she said, pouring water into the basin and soaking a square of linen in it. "If you do not, it will fester, and then where will those handsome good looks be?"

He blinked. "I beg your pardon?"

"Best allow milady to do as she wishes," Fields said with respectful affection. He had, after all, taught her to ride when she had barely even learned to walk, and to drive when she was still shorter than the gig. "Takes after her sainted mum, she does."

"Thank you, Fields. I suspect nobody here is interested in that inaccurate account of my virtues. Now sir, will you sit down voluntarily so that I can reach that wound, or must I level you as your friend did earlier?"

He reseated himself on the bench, not removing that brilliant blue gaze from her and saying nothing. Which was for the best. His voice did things to her insides. Hot, inappropriate things that had precipitated her flight to America two and a half years earlier.

The ostler and the other coachman departed and finally the duke's gaze shifted away from her. It looked as though he was sorry to see the other men go.

"Fields," she said, "don't let my presence keep you from your work. I am certain Mr. Church here would not think of giving insult to a lady."

"That's not what that other gentleman was saying, milady," Fields said.

"Well, that must have been a mistake. Wasn't it, Mr. Church?"

"Upon my oath," the Duke of Frye said quite sincerely. He had a beautiful voice, rich and sonorous and deep, as though created for oratory or song.

"Call if you need me, milady," Fields said. Then her coachman was gone and she lifted the damp linen to the duke's jaw and found herself looking down into his striking blue eyes now filled with pleasure.

"'Upon my oath'?" she said, hand hovering over his face. "And what is that oath worth, *Mr.* Church? A ha-penny, I daresay?"

"Why didn't you tell them?" he said without preamble, as though they had last seen each other perhaps yesterday at a ball and not two and a half years ago in the park in the rain.

"Why didn't I tell them that you are not humble Mr. Church? Oh, I don't know. Perhaps because I wish you were mere Mr.

Church, then you would not have recently broken the heart of one of my best friends."

"It was unpardonable of me," he admitted. "But her heart is not broken."

"That is not true. Alexandra wrote to me only two days ago that Serena is miserable."

"Misery and heartbreak are not necessarily one and the same."

There was something in the tone of his beautiful voice that suggested he had experienced both misery and heartbreak. That gave her some consolation.

She tried very hard to focus entirely on his wound and not his lips that put her in mind of kisses. Long, slow kisses. Deep, passionate kisses. She had never had either. But her American sister-in-law had told her about such kisses. After that, fantasizing about those sorts of kisses from the Duke of Frye had become something of a habit.

Thus her flight overseas.

"Why are you traveling incognito?" she said, chancing another glance at his eyes as she dabbed at his jaw. They were smiling and, she realized, they were clear. She jerked back. "You are not intoxicated, are you?"

"Which question would you like me to answer first?" he said, the corner of his tempting lips curved upward.

"I suspect they lead to the same answer." She recommenced her ministrations. In the charitable work she and her Aunt Imogene had done in America, she had occasionally nursed wounded sailors. None of that had made her heartbeats pound violently. But she had not been this close to the Duke of Frye in many years. She had ensured that again and again. "Now tell me, Your Grace: what shenanigans are you and your friend engaged in? Are you both pockets-to-let, as Mr. Clayton guessed?"

"Who is Mr. Clayton?"

"One of our fellow guests at this inn. Very starchy and righteous. His wife and son as well. As we all watched your friend pound you into the snow, Mr. Clayton suggested that you must be on a repairing lease from town, having spent all of your money on gaming and women."

"Risqué talk for a starchy fellow, wouldn't you say?" he murmured upon a half-smile.

"I should have instead said that he is *my* fellow guest, not yours— yours being Fields's team and the other horses. Oh, and a cat." She lifted a brow.

"No shenanigans."

"No?" she said skeptically.

His hand came around her wrist, big and warm and strong.

"Will you tell them?" he said very seriously.

"Will I tell the innkeeper that he has banished a duke to the stables?" She pried her arm free and dipped a corner of clean linen into the salve. "I am surprised Fields did not recognize you. But I suppose he hasn't seen you since we were children. My mother was still alive when we last visited Kentwood. Now, hold still."

"You haven't answered me."

"Is it so important that I keep your secret?"

"It is."

"As important as your broken vow to Serena?"

"Yes."

She backed away. "Horace Church, you are a cad."

"Charlotte," he said, coming to his feet and taking the single step that brought him within inches of her. This time he grasped both of her wrists. "I beg of you, do not reveal me."

His voice was very deep and her heartbeats were very fast. Her tongue was dry too. In all of the years that she had known him, he had been a duke. As a boy he had behaved according to his rank: when other boys had scrapped and threw fisticuffs in the dirt, he had negotiated truces. As a man, he had worn the mantle of his responsibility with grace and sobriety. Even when his friends took mistresses, according to Charlotte's brother Trent, the Duke of Frye had not. He had always honored his long-time betrothal to Serena.

Charlotte had never thought to see him again before his wedding. Of all the forbidden fantasies she had had about her friend's fiancé, she had never imagined *this* moment: a moment when he was no longer betrothed.

"H—How is your mother?" she heard tumble from her lips—her lips at which he was now staring.

His gaze shifted up to her eyes as though it cost him effort.

"My mother?" he said a bit hoarsely.

"Your—Yes, your mother. I understand she took on your responsibilities at Kentwood when you went abroad with Mr. Jones."

"You know I went abroad?"

"Word gets around."

"How? You were in America."

"Boats sail there. Boats with people on them. And letters."

When his perfect teeth glimmered between his curving lips, it made Charlotte dreadfully warm inside. *Hot.*

That, of course, had been the principal reason she had sailed on one of those boats for America. A lady was not supposed to have lascivious thoughts about her dear friend's betrothed. A lady was not supposed to have lascivious thoughts at all.

Horace Church, therefore, was the devil.

"I thought you had moved there," he said. "Permanently." His hands about her wrists were loose, but warm and large and strong. It felt *wonderful.*

She extracted herself from his grasp yet again and stepped back.

"I really don't see how my travel has anything to do with your subterfuge here. Didn't you imagine anybody would recognize you?"

"No one has until you," he said, and then blinked, as though his own words surprised him.

She frowned, and the dart of displeasure between her feathered brows was as pretty as the rest of her. Frye had fantasized about being alone with Charlotte Ascot again. Now here they were, yet his tongue would not function. Nor his brain.

No one has until you.

For pity's sake, he might as well come right out and tell her that he and Freddie regularly did tasks for the government.

"Fortier and I are on holiday," he managed to say. "Taking a breather before he's got to return home." *Not far from the truth.* "Thought we'd relax, enjoy the journey, don't you know? And bachelorhood, finally," he added upon a lazy grin. "Easiest to do that if nobody's sending tales back to my mother, of course." He hated himself. But the fewer people who knew his and Freddie's purpose at this inn, the better.

The disappointment in her eyes was the color of the rain the last time he had seen her in that park in London.

"Then Mr. Clayton, it seems, was correct," she said. "You are a pair of heedless rowdies with only pleasure in mind." She raked him with a troubled gaze. "You have changed, Horace Church, and not for the better. I admit that I am sorry to discover it." Taking up her bandages and ointments, she went to the door.

Frye's ribs cinched about his heart.

"Since I received Alexandra's letter," she said, looking over her shoulder, "I have felt poorly for Serena. Now I think she has had a fortunate escape. Good evening."

When she was gone he sank down onto the bench, dropped his head into his palms, and tried not to think of her expressive eyes and beguiling smile, and failed. But he didn't berate himself too harshly for it. He had already been failing at that task for years.

CHAPTER FOUR

Two days before Christmas

The taproom

$\mathcal{D}$awn came the following morning all gray and white, the sun covered entirely by clouds, and those clouds continuing to disgorge quantities of snow upon the countryside.

Descending to the taproom, Charlotte found the other guests all taking breakfast as the innkeeper and the serving girl moved in and out of the room with dishes and pots of tea.

Only the Duke of Frye and his friend were absent.

Finding Miss Mapplethorpe and her niece in the corner closest to the kitchen door, she went to them.

"May I join you?"

"Oh, good gracious, my lady, would you not rather break your fast with Mr. Clayton's family?"

From across the room, the starchy Mrs. Clayton lifted her nose from her teacup, perused Charlotte's gown, and offered her a condescending nod.

Charlotte turned back to Miss Mapplethorpe.

"I so enjoyed our conversation last night." She offered Miss Jameson a warm smile and sat beside her. Calliope wore a yellow muslin gown that, while simple and thoroughly out of season, showed her youthful beauty off to remarkable advantage this morning.

Charlotte frowned. If the rowdy Duke of Frye and his companion were intent on enjoying *bachelorhood* on this journey, Miss

189

Calliope Jameson would need more than her timorous aunt to protect her.

Mr. Fortier finally arrived at breakfast, followed by the duke. Charlotte had always thought Horace Church handsome. With rumpled hair, his jaw shadowed with whiskers, and the bandage she had fashioned for him the night before stretched over his cheek and jaw, he was somehow even *handsomer*.

His gaze came directly to her. Swiftly it shifted to Miss Mapplethorpe, then Miss Jameson. It lingered on the pretty girl before returning to her aunt.

The barmaid, Nancy, passed his table. He turned a wide smile up at her, said something Charlotte couldn't hear, and the serving girl's giggle bubbled across the room. When Nancy walked away, her round hips swaying, his gaze followed her. Then it returned to Calliope and her aunt.

Charlotte's hackles rose.

She might have nursed an impossible tendre for the Duke of Frye since she was a girl. She might have anguished in her diary for years that he was intended for her friend Serena—sweet, affectionate, generous, beautiful, quietly funny yet always proper Serena, who deserved a happy marriage and would be an excellent duchess. She might have battened down that anguish for years until making the decision that she required an ocean between them to put away her wrongful infatuation. She might have *almost* grabbed him that rainy day in the park and then for two and a half years wondered what would have happened if she had . . .

But if Horace Chesterfield Breckenridge Church imagined now that she would stand by and watch him make sport with an innocent girl, within only months of having jilted his sweet, affectionate, generous, beautiful, funny, and proper betrothed, then he was bound for disappointment.

*W*hen she left the taproom, it was as though she carried all the air away with her.

"*Mon ami*, you are staring."

Frye swiveled his attention to Freddie. "What?"

Freddie lifted a brow. "You were staring at the lady. Just as yesterday when you failed to dodge my fist."

"She thinks I'm a lout." He had already told Freddie about the fair Lady Charlotte, and how, although obviously displeased with him, she seemed unlikely to reveal them. "It is what it must be."

His friend shrugged. "You could tell her the truth."

The truth.

Charlotte was furious with him for breaking it off with her friend Serena Cavendish. Neither she nor anyone knew that he had done it because it was the most honorable thing to do—that in his heart he had had no choice. A man could not commence married life in good conscience knowing what he knew about himself, no matter how long the betrothal had gone on.

That worry had kept him up so many nights since Serena's introduction to society that he had come to dread the wedding that their now-deceased fathers had planned eighteen years earlier. Still, he had done nothing about those worries, not hastening the wedding along but not breaking it off with Serena either—not until an enlightening conversation the previous summer with his other best friend, Greyson Jones.

"If you ask me, Frye," Greyson had commented casually one evening, "Lady Serena Cavendish is almost a little *too* perfect. Don't you think?"

"Is she?" he had replied, noting the peculiar tone of Greyson's voice and the odd evasion in his eyes. Greyson Jones was one of the most upstanding men Frye had ever known. Evasion simply was not in Greyson's character. Nor was speaking poorly of a lady.

Frye had long suspected his friend admired Serena. But that was the moment he had known for certain that Greyson loved her.

After that, he'd had no hesitation in calling off the wedding.

He had told Serena the truth—a version of it, at least: that he wanted more for her than the fond friendship they shared. She was too exceptional a woman to settle for mediocrity in marriage. She deserved more. It was only fair to release her from their betrothal.

She had accepted it with her customary grace.

He had told his best friends, Greyson and Freddie, an invented story: he was having far too much fun to settle down to marriage already. At the behest of a friend at the Foreign Office, he'd spent the last six months in Bavaria with Greyson. Next it might be

Bulgaria! Or Bengal! He was only twenty-five, for pity's sake. Grand adventure was still to be had!

Neither believed him, but both were too decent to say so.

He had told his mother mostly the truth: he could not curse Serena with early widowhood. His father's sudden premature death had rocked the whole family and devastated her. Frye could not condemn a young woman to that fate too, not given his own excellent chances of perishing early.

His mother had tried to dissuade him, but he had held firm. His younger brother would be a fine duke someday.

He had told no one the *entire* truth, though. That remained his secret.

"Until we've the villain in manacles," he said now, "it's best to share our purpose with no one."

Freddie lifted his pint. "Solve the mystery."

Frye lifted his too. "Fight the battle."

Freddie glanced at the elderly lady across the room. "Save the girl."

Frye leaned back in his chair, surveying the room full of stranded travelers.

They were a motley assortment: a jowly fellow, his harried young wife, and their five small children who, full of tea and marmalade, were now running about the place like a pack of unruly puppies; the Claytons, the starchy, well-to-do Yorkshire couple and their starchy son that Charlotte had mentioned; and two modestly impoverished gentlewomen with whom the daughter of an earl had just breakfasted.

Frye had known Charlotte Ascot since he was a boy and had always found her fascinating. Every girl he met had treated him to smiles, curtsies, dimples, and compliments. But whenever he'd seen little Charlotte Ascot, she had always screwed up her nose and asked him ridiculous questions, such as: *how did he like her brother's new punting boat,* or *how far had he ridden that morning,* or *had he been to the top of that hill yet because she had.* Just a girl, and she hadn't a pretty word to say to a duke four years her elder.

It had irritated him to no end.

At some point along the way, that childish irritation had turned to preoccupation.

Later, when her figure had sprouted, preoccupation had turned to admiration.

Soon after that, admiration had turned to hunger.

That was when he had accepted the Home Secretary's invitation to perform some light espionage—for the crown—as men of wealth and rank could do without detection during war.

The war had been over for more than a year. Yet villains remained aplenty in England.

Mr. Sheridan had not come to breakfast. During his stable sojourn, Frye had learned from the ostler that the weasel-faced fellow was alone and traveling north. If he were in fact the man suspected of duping softhearted elderly women travelers out of their fortunes, Frye would unmask him.

The elderly woman, Miss Mapplethorpe, and her niece went into the foyer.

"Sir?" Miss Mapplethorpe said to the innkeeper, a tremble in her reedy voice. "My niece and I had a terrible night. The chimney in our bedchamber smokes wretchedly. We could hardly breathe."

"I'm terrible sorry, ma'am," the innkeeper said. "A mason was to come yesterday to patch up that crack. Suspect the storm kept him."

"Oh, I see. Well, may my niece and I have another room?"

"Trouble is, we're all filled up."

"Oh, dear. But I mustn't complain. For I'm sure others are in more dire straits than we are now. And of course our Lord and Savior's own parents were obliged to sleep in a stable." She offered a game smile. "My niece and I will make do."

"Forgive me for intruding." The voice came first, and then Sheridan moved into sight. "The chimney in my chamber pulls splendidly. It is a delightful room, madam. You would make me the happiest of men to allow me to vacate it for you." He bowed deeply, his pockmarked face a portrait of gratified humility.

"Oh, sir," the woman said, "you are too kind. But it would not be proper to impose upon you."

"It will not be an imposition. Rather, my honor, Mrs. . . . ?"

"Miss Mapplethorpe," she said, her cheeks turning pink.

"Robert Sheridan at your service, madam." He bowed again.

"Aunt Margaret," the girl said. "He has offered so kindly. Please allow it."

"It would be my honor," Sheridan said, all graciousness. As slick as a well-greased clock.

"Oh, well, then, yes, if you wish it, dear Calliope."

Frye got a sour flavor on his tongue. But here it was: the set up, the ingratiation. Next would come the winning her over. Then the fleecing. And with it, the proof Frye needed to haul the villain to a magistrate.

The bedchamber exchange settled, the trio and the innkeeper departed to make it so.

"Whist or dice?" Freddie said, reading his thoughts. While Freddie was occupying Sheridan with game, Frye would slip into Sheridan's bedchamber and search his belongings.

"Cards," he said. Best to keep appearances aboveboard. That he did not relish the idea of Charlotte Ascot believing him a dice-throwing cad, he hadn't time to ponder now.

CHAPTER FIVE

An hour later

The foyer, the corridor, a bedchamber and another bedchamber

Charlotte was stomping the snow from her boots and shaking out her cloak when Miss Mapplethorpe and her niece came down the stairs, arms linked.

"Have you been to the stable, my lady?" the aunt said.

"Yes! My coachman says that no one will be traveling today, or perhaps even tomorrow." Delaying her yet longer from joining her friends at Kingstag Castle, where they were gathering for Christmas and to lift Serena's spirits after the cruel jilting by her long-time fiancé.

The jilter was playing cards with Mr. Fortier and two other gentlemen. Charlotte could hear the sound of his delicious voice in the taproom, rising in laughter.

"The storm is here to stay, it seems," she said.

"Dear me," Miss Mapplethorpe said, "it will be wretchedly cold for those poor coachmen, not to mention the horses! They must all be chilled to the bone."

"It is remarkably cozy in the stable, in fact," she said, depositing her cloak on a peg. Cozy enough to make a handsome young duke's eyes shine as he had looked pleadingly at her the night before. "Is luncheon served yet?"

"Our hosts have just announced it, my lady," the duke said from the taproom doorway.

Charlotte could not fathom why the simple words should send her stomach to her toes and her heart into her throat. But everything the Duke of Frye had ever said to her had made her sillier than a widgeon. Even with a bruise coloring his handsome jaw and a thin line of plaster along the bone where the skin had broken, he was outrageously handsome.

She tipped her chin upward. "Thank you, *sir*."

He had the gall to smile with every one of his white teeth. With a quick bow, he passed her by and went up the steps two at a time.

"I will join you for luncheon," she said to Miss Mapplethorpe and her niece, "but first I must change out of these soaked stockings."

Ascending, her foot was on the landing when the sight ahead made her gasp: Horace Church slipping into Miss Mapplethorpe and Calliope Jameson's bedchamber and stealthily closing the door behind him.

Charlotte's mind whirled. Only one explanation suggested itself.

The inn mistress appeared in the corridor. Rosy-cheeked and cheerful, she suited her pleasant little establishment.

"Good day, ma'am," she said as she moved past, then paused at the top of the stairs. "Oh, my lady?"

Charlotte turned to her.

"Seeing as it's Christmas Eve tomorrow, and the snow not looking to let up, I thought we'd have a party. For the little ones' amusement."

"That sounds delightful," Charlotte said. "May my maid and I help with preparations? Sally is very clever with garland and I can tie quite a respectable bow."

"That's kind of you to offer. Tomorrow'll be time enough."

When the inn mistress had disappeared downstairs, Charlotte hurried forward, looked both ways, and entered Miss Mapplethorpe and Calliope's room.

It was empty. No handsome duke reclined invitingly on the bed. No jilting scion of high society lounged attractively in the chair before the hearth. He must have slipped out when she had her back turned, speaking with the inn mistress.

She would find him and confront him. He could have no good reason for his subterfuge.

It struck her that he could much more easily seduce innocent maidens as a duke than as a mere mister. But Horace Church's smile was enough to weaken her knees to jelly, so she supposed his game of playing the commoner served him well enough.

Scoundrel.

As she reached for the door handle, footsteps in the corridor halted on the other side of the panel.

"Good day, sir," said a man's crisp voice.

"Good day, Mr. Clayton," Mr. Sheridan's voice replied, its oily obsequiousness clear even through the door.

"I understand that you gave up your chamber for Miss Mapplethorpe," Mr. Clayton said.

"I did, indeed," Mr. Sheridan replied.

Charlotte swallowed a yelp.

"A lady should not be obliged to suffer when a gentleman can come to her rescue," Mr. Clayton said, which Charlotte thought was easy for him when another man had done the rescuing.

The door handle turned.

Charlotte cast her gaze about desperately. *Nowhere to hide.*

Dropping to the floor as the door creaked open, she propelled herself under the bed.

And came face-to-face with the Duke of Frye.

Before she could even gasp, he clamped a big hand over her mouth and shook his head.

Caught between a rock and a hard place, she most certainly was. But the devil one knew was always safer than the devil one did not.

She nodded.

He released her just as the door clicked shut. Then Mr. Sheridan's feet appeared beside the bed. A moment later, he removed his boots. Then both feet left the ground, the underside of the bed sagged into Charlotte's behind, and Mr. Sheridan released another long sigh.

Only then did she again turn her gaze to the man prone beside her.

A crease marred his noble brow.

She frowned.

He frowned back, the plaster twisting over his wound.

She pursed her lips.

His gaze went directly to them. And remained there.

She discovered the urgent need to moisten her lips with her tongue. Every etiquette book in the world was clear on the subject of lip licking: it was not recommended, and never in public.

But this was not public; it was the dusty floor beneath a bed in an inn. Also, Horace Church was the devil, and she fully suspected it was his diabolical gaze that was making her mouth dry as bone.

Darting her tongue between her lips, she licked them.

His face lost all expression.

Oh. Of course. *He* could play at being a commoner, but when *she* made one tiny indiscretion he acted all righteously displeased.

Typical man.

She rolled her eyes.

But when his gaze rose to meet hers, it was not displeasure she saw there. Rather, the opposite. The blue was positively fevered. *Blazing.*

Every kind of explosion went off inside Charlotte. A gasp escaped her throat.

His Adam's apple rose and fell sharply. Then he looked at her lips again.

Their shoulders were nearly touching. She could practically hear her heartbeats pounding against the floor.

Atop the bed, with a rumbling snort and grunt, Mr. Sheridan began snoring. At first it was soft and rhythmic. Within minutes it was a cacophony.

Charlotte nodded and jerked her chin forward.

Ever so slightly, the duke shook his head.

She nodded more emphatically. Dust stirred up by her hair brushing the bedframe's slats cascaded down in a cloud.

The duke shook his head again.

Mr. Sheridan's snoring scaled the heights.

Charlotte nodded yet again.

The duke scowled—silently. That he was outrageously handsome even while scowling was surely her punishment for wanting to close the inches between them and lick his lips too.

Bridling the wanton within her, instead she shinnied out from beneath the bed, turned the door handle, and slipped out into the corridor.

Within moments he followed, shutting the door quietly to the sound of Mr. Sheridan's roaring snore, grabbing her hand, and drawing her along the corridor. He pulled her through a doorway at its far end, closed the door, and dropped her hand.

Charlotte, who had managed to avoid holding the Duke of Frye's hand for nearly a decade, found her throat entirely clogged.

"You could have woken him," he said. His eyes were gorgeously intense.

"Is this your bedchamber?"

"Why did you go in there?"

"I have never been in a man's bedchamber before," she said a bit dazedly, staring at his shaving gear on the dressing table and feeling a remarkable tingling in her belly.

"You were in a man's bedchamber thirty seconds ago," he said, which proved that their little sojourn under the bed had not muddled his brains too. "Why did you go into Sheridan's room? You might have been hurt."

Her muddled brain abruptly cleared.

"I was following you! I thought you had gone into Miss Mapplethorpe and Miss Jameson's room."

"Why would I have done that?"

"Why would you have gone into *Mr. Sheridan's*? You did not intend to steal from him, did you?"

He looked at her like she was daft. "Of course not."

"Well, you are engaged in subterfuge. It's not so ludicrous a notion."

"Charlotte, I own a castle of no fewer than sixty rooms. And five thousand acres of land. And six hundred sheep. And a house on Grosvenor Square. And another house in Bristol. And a coronet, not to mention any number of priceless—"

"All right. I take your point. You know, it strikes me that it is peculiar—him napping in the middle of the day."

"Does it?" Abruptly his eyes were sparkling. She had always loved that sparkle. She had liked to imagine it was especially for her, even though she knew it was not.

"Yes, of course," she said. "He cannot be over fifty. Isn't that a bit young to take to napping in the afternoon?"

"He was up late last night playing cards. Until nearly dawn."

"How would you know that? I thought you slept in the stable."

"Fortier told me."

"And that is another thing: if you are in fact not common Mr. Church, who is common Mr. Fortier?"

"Heir to the duke of Le Cap."

"Heir to a duke! Where is Le Cap?"

"Haiti. But he was educated here. We've been friends forever. Capital fellow. Wonderfully honorable. Nothing like me, of course." He smiled.

More little explosions went off in her belly.

"Now, of course, you must tell me exactly what *this* is," she said.

"I cannot." He looked entirely implacable.

Having grown up surrounded by men, and having spent a successful season in London before traveling to America, and then two years in society in Philadelphia, Charlotte knew how the masculine brain functioned. And not only the brain.

She moved closer to him and tilted her face up. "Are you quite certain?"

He drew a hard breath that lifted his chest.

"Yes," he said rather deeply. "And, just so you know, Charlotte Ascot, you needn't bat your lashes like that to make my brain go to porridge."

Her mouth fell open. Pink and lush-lipped and glistening and inviting.

So he kissed it.

CHAPTER SIX

That very moment

The duke's bedchamber

ⓑending forward, Frye brushed his lips across the lips he had dreamed about in both waking and sleeping, for too many years, each time telling himself he must not, and shutting out the fantasy as soon as it began.

This time he needn't.

When a little gasp of surprised pleasure escaped between the perfectly parted lips, he kissed them again.

The caress of her lips was everything he had dreamed, and more. Generous. Damp. Soft. *Willing.*

He tasted first her lower lip, then the upper, and she tasted like heaven, like lavender and some subtle spice he couldn't place, but it was like the smoke in her eyes: familiar yet mysterious with ineffable, feminine magic. Her breaths were short and shallow, and she did not move except to encourage him with gentle pressure.

He wanted to wrap his hands around her and pull her close. He'd wanted it forever.

He felt the lightest pressure on his chest. Her hand. *On him.* And within an instant he was imagining her hands all over him, everywhere he needed them.

He stepped back.

Her lashes fluttered, her hand dropped to her side, and her lovely features were full of astonishment.

"What was that?" she uttered.

"That," he said, drawing a thick breath, "was a kiss."

"I *know*. I meant—you—that is—you did it without my permission," she said in a bit of a rush.

"May I ask it now, retroactively?"

"*No*. You are—"

"A lout, I know. Charlotte—"

"Why did you kiss me?"

"Because, Charlotte Ascot, you are just so kissable."

"Kissable?"

He nodded.

"But what about Miss Jameson!"

"Who?"

"Miss Calliope Jameson, the innocent, unprotected maiden whose room you just crept stealthily into in order to seduce her."

"I did no such thing."

"Yes, you did."

"No, I didn't."

"You did. Last night you said you were traveling the countryside enjoying bachelorhood. Well, I will have you know, Horace Church, that while that innocent girl may appear unprotected she is not. Not while I am residing in this establishment. And if you attempt one more maneuver, you will find me a formidable guard dog standing in your path."

"I adore the way your nose scrunches up when you're vexed."

Her jaw dropped open a second time.

He moved close again and grasped her hands. Her fingers were slender and soft, yet strong. When they tightened for a moment around his, it required all of his self-control not to drag her into his arms.

"I have no intention of seducing Miss Jameson," he said. "Quite the contrary."

"Then why did you sneak into her room like that?"

"I snuck into *Sheridan's* room. They traded this morning." His thumbs were making a slow, agonizingly delectable exploration of her wrists.

Charlotte snatched her hands away and stepped back from the temptation of him.

"You *are* engaged in subterfuge," she stated. "Real subterfuge. Aren't you?"

"Yes."

"Concerning what?"

"I can tell you nothing more."

"You will tell me everything."

"I cannot. Truly."

"Then I will ask Lord Fortier."

"You must not expose us." He looked unusually severe.

"I wasn't about to," she protested.

"You were."

"I was not."

He smiled.

She could not resist smiling too. "We quarrel like children."

"We never quarreled when we were children," he said.

"Of course we didn't. That would have required you noticing me, which you did not." Even that once, when she had come upon him in the woods, unconscious and sprawled as though he had fallen, and then, afterward, he had pretended it had not happened.

"I noticed you," he said quietly now.

"You did not."

"I did. That summer holiday at Fellsbourne when you won the footrace to the woods."

A frisson of pleasure stole through her, dislodging the other, horrible memory.

"You remember that?"

"Of course I do." His tempting lips curved into a smile. "You beat me. And every other boy there. I was twelve. To be beaten by a little girl was disgraceful."

"I was not a little girl."

"You were a very little girl. And you were fast."

"You were disgusted."

"I was impressed."

"Wait just a moment!" she exclaimed. "You have changed the subject to distract me from demanding to know more about your subterfuge."

"Actually, you changed the subject."

"You did."

"No. But I do insist that you stay out of this. It is a dangerous business—"

"*Dangerous?*"

203

"Anything could happen," he said with a sober nod. "Now." He opened his bedchamber door and peeked out into the corridor. "The way is clear. You must go. But, Charlotte, if you see or hear me do anything that seems unlike me, know that is it for a good purpose."

"Hm," she said, then slipped through the crack. She looked over her shoulder. "Speaking of things that are unlike you, obviously neither of us will ever speak of that kiss again."

"Agreed," he said, stroking a single finger along her soft cheek. "I much prefer action to words."

Dampening down the burst of hot excitement his touch roused inside her, she drew back and hurried down the corridor.

Throughout the remainder of the day as the snow continued to fall without, inside the inn Charlotte played with the Andersons' five little children and watched her fellow guests carefully. While she would not put it entirely past the Duke of Frye to use his charms to entice a woman into minor indiscretions—*like abruptly kissing her in his bedchamber*—she really didn't believe it was in his character to entice two women at the same time. She had known him forever and to her knowledge nobody had ever accused him of being a libertine.

Therefore, she determined, he and Lord Fortier must be pursuing a nefarious villain. Who that could be among this modest collection of hapless travelers, she could not imagine. She knew exactly nothing about intrigue and villainy.

So she watched everybody.

It was better, after all, than watching the duke flirt outrageously with the barmaid. He, charming Lord Fortier, oily Mr. Sheridan, and jovial Mr. Anderson (father of the five little children) had established a continuing low-stakes card game at a corner table in the taproom. As the barmaid Nancy brought them pint after pint of ale, then dinner, and following that whiskey, Nancy increasingly teased handsome Mr. Church and, on each visit to the table, leaned farther into his lap than the time before.

Finally she actually fell into his lap. After a cascade of giggles, and after tilting her bosom precariously close to his face, she extricated herself. If the duke had not then immediately cast Charlotte a swift Meaningful Glance, she would have claimed a complaint of the stomach and departed for her bedchamber forthwith. It was making her nauseous.

The stiff Mr. and Mrs. Clayton had taken up a table near the warm hearth. Their son, young George Clayton, stole longing glances alternately at the men playing cards and at Calliope.

Above the rim of her teacup, Calliope bashfully returned his glances. Miss Mapplethorpe poured tea, oblivious to her charge's silent flirtation with the young sprig of manhood.

And finally, Mrs. Anderson looked about as beleaguered as a young woman could. She held an infant in one arm while feeding another child and casting worried glances at her three older children, who had taken to speeding about the place, up and down the stairs, racing under the inn mistress's feet, knocking over chairs, and generally making a ruckus.

Charlotte did her best to entertain them, playing Jack Straws and fashioning little dolls out of broom straws and her own hair ribbons.

"It is delightful to have children among us at Christmastime, isn't it?" Miss Mapplethorpe said with soft eyes upon the little monsters.

"It is," Charlotte agreed. "You have a kind heart, Miss Mapplethorpe."

"'Suffer the children to come to me,'" she said, quoting scripture.

Charlotte wanted children. Lots of children. But children required a husband. And although her father had bid her return to England and finally accept an offer from a suitor of her choice, finally, she knew now that she could not consider that until she had once and for all quashed her foolish infatuation with the Duke of Frye.

The inn mistress entered the taproom in a busy whirl and came toward them, bringing with her the scent of frying bacon. Stirring honey into her tea, Charlotte drew the scents into her nostrils. There was something so sensual about the scent of frying bacon crossed with honey—salty and sweet at once.

Like that kiss.

That kiss.

Horace Church had kissed her. Her toes and lips and everything in between were still tingling.

He thought her *kissable.*

Now he was flirting with a barmaid.

"My lady, I've settled on a menu for tomorrow's festivities," the inn mistress said. "But I'd be obliged to consult with you on the entertainments."

"I will be delighted. I hope Miss Mapplethorpe and Miss Jameson will assist us."

"Will we have dancing, Lady Charlotte?" Calliope asked, and darted another glance at George Clayton.

"That would be grand. And plenty of games for you," she said to the two eldest Anderson offspring. They cheered.

"What fun we shall have tomorrow," she said.

She would distract herself from the handsome duke by helping the inn mistress prepare for the party.

Nancy set another pint of ale before him, he smiled up at her, and Nancy giggled yet again.

Charlotte rolled her eyes away. The snow was bound to cease falling soon, and then she would be off to Kingstag, where she would comfort her dear friend Serena, who had made a very lucky escape indeed.

CHAPTER SEVEN

Christmas Eve morning

The carriage house

$\mathcal{A}$s dawn began to glow behind the heavy clouds that augured more snow, from his bedchamber window Frye watched a man approaching across the pasture toward the carriage house at a remarkable clip. Slipping only once in the knee-deep snow, he recovered swiftly. Slender, and barely protected from the cold in a thin coat and breeches, he was not one of the travelers trapped at this inn. Perhaps he had come from a nearby farm.

Then the fellow lifted his attention toward the inn, revealing beneath the brim of his cap the face Frye liked above all others.

Charlotte Ascot. Wearing men's clothing. Returning at dawn from . . . *where?*

He grabbed his coat and hurried down the stairs and into the yard.

As he neared the stable he glimpsed her slipping into the carriage house. He followed.

He made no attempt at silence or stealth, but he didn't need to. She was humming loudly enough that the carriages vibrated with the tune. Her voice, though not particularly good, was full of happiness, and his chest filled with warmth and that old awful ache that, before she'd gone off to America, he had gotten used to feeling every time he saw her.

He rounded the mail coach and was met with a sight that made him stagger to a halt: the woman of his dreams, cheeks flushed, hair curling in damp tendrils all about her face and neck, eyes alight, and lips smiling as she hummed.

And only half dressed.

The sound that came out of his mouth was more groan than gasp.

Her head snapped up, eyes flying wide open, and her fingers arrested on the laces of her shift.

There was a moment of taut silence in which Frye swiftly memorized every gorgeous curve concealed by only the thinnest layer of linen, and in which crimson rushed into her entire face and spread down her neck and over the exquisite mounds of the tops of her breasts.

She snatched up her coat and pressed it to her front.

"What are you doing here?" she said breathlessly.

"I think I've better reason to ask you the same." His voice was thoroughly husky. *He was a dog.*

"You do not. Go away."

Tearing his gaze from the vision, he turned his back to her.

"Do finish dressing," he said. "I'll wait."

"I said, go."

"You did not use the magic word."

"Please go away."

"No."

"Yes."

"And leave you unprotected for some other man to happen by? Not on your life." He folded his arms.

Rustling sounded behind him and he imagined her hastily pulling on the remainder of her clothes.

"You are outrageous," she said.

"I did not just return from a walk across the pasture in two feet of snow wearing another person's clothes. So of the two of us, really, I don't think I am the outrageous one."

"They aren't another person's clothes," she said.

"No?"

"They are mine."

"Interesting."

"It is easier to move in the snow when wearing breeches."

"Is that so?" He was enjoying this beyond reason. He would never forget the vision of her in that chemise. Ever.

"You would know that if you had ever tried running through snow wearing skirts."

"I suppose I would. But as I am neither an Eastern prince nor a Catholic priest, I haven't any experience wear—"

Then she was beside him and he was looking through the murky dimness into her beautiful stormy eyes.

"You won't tell anyone, will you?" she said.

"That you enjoy dressing as a man?"

"It isn't that I enjoy it," she said, her brows dipping together at the bridge of her perfectly pert nose. She wore an unexceptionable wool gown that covered every inch of her arms and neck and made him wish the entire species of sheep—not to mention weavers and seamstresses—to the devil.

"It is that I . . ." She halted her own words.

He waited.

Her cheeks were still dark pink, her lips nearly red, and he needed to taste them again. Urgently. He wanted to kiss her and touch her and strip her to her undergarments and haul her onto one of these carriage seats and do things to her he'd dreamed about doing to her. *With her.*

"I was running," she said.

His heartbeats stumbled. "From whom?" *He would murder the villain.*

"From no one. Just—I just ran."

"You ran?"

Her shoulders seemed to settle. "I find it invigorating to run places. That is, not really to run to *places*, rather to run fast, any place that I can without notice."

Memory of the footrace that she had won when she was a girl of eight came back to him.

As though she knew the direction of his thoughts, she nodded.

"I never outgrew it," she said. "I have always enjoyed riding and, of course, walking in the park. But then I must always be with a footman or maid, moving slowly and decorously. Early in the mornings like this, when Sally is still abed and I am able to run alone, I feel . . ." Her words petered out.

"What do you feel when you run, Charlotte?"

She bit her sweet lips. "I have never spoken of this before to anybody. I don't know why I am telling you."

"In fact, you have told me almost nothing as yet," he said with a slight smile.

She frowned.

"And you have done the same." Moving around him, she took up her men's clothing, wrapped them in a little ball, and headed for the door. "I will see you at breakfast, Your G—"

He reached for her arm. She turned in his grasp and she was so close he could see every dark lash curling from the damp, and feel the heat radiating from her body.

"You can tell me," he said. "You can always tell me."

"Why did you go into Mr. Sheridan's room yesterday morning?"

He said nothing.

"Come now. You have seen me in my shift. The least you can do now is to share this mystery."

Which was true.

"Fortier and I occasionally do odd jobs for the government. We are now on the trail of a thief who has been cozening defenseless women into giving over their money to a noble cause, and then pocketing it all instead."

Her perfect lips fell open. He wanted them beneath his. Then the rest of her beneath the rest of him too.

"The *government*?" she said. "Are you *spies*?"

"No. I have plenty to see to at Kentwood, with my mother trying to run the place like it's a charitable foundation and my sisters getting into endless scrapes. And Fortier is not even English, of course. We are merely helping out a bit, doing tasks it's easy to do under cover of roguish foolery."

"You have done this *before*? How many times?"

"A handful." Dozens. "During the war it was mostly passing messages between actual spies at social gatherings. That sort of thing. Nothing spectacular."

"Actual spies?" She was still gaping and it took every mote of self-restraint in him not to cover those lips with his. "Horace Church, you are a hero! You and Lord Fortier."

"Nothing so grand. Only doing my duty to the kingdom."

"I daresay you do that well enough in Parliament." Pink was stealing into her cheeks again.

"You are blushing," he said, his voice rumbling over Charlotte's tingling nerves like hot chocolate slipping over one's tongue. He smiled slightly. "I wonder why."

"I am not," she said, lifting her hand over a fiery cheek.

His fingers wrapped around it, his fingertips caressing her skin tenderly, *decadently*.

"Don't cover it," he said, drawing her hand downward. "This is wholly intriguing. I don't think I have ever seen you blush before."

He would have seen her blush if he had bothered to look at her even once that sennight of the party at Cheriot Manor, after she had found him insensible and bleeding in the wood. Only thirteen, she had already loved him, and she had been out of her mind with panic when he would not rouse to her voice. When he finally had, awakening with a start, he had said nothing to her. *Nothing*. Without a word, he had extracted his hand from hers, wiped the blood from his face, climbed to his knees in silence, then his feet, and, stumbling at first, walked away. He had not looked back.

And then he had not looked at her again the entire duration of the house party.

Shame over that dismissal—and terrible hurt—had kept her cheeks ruddy that whole sennight. Even her father had asked if she was ill.

Not ill. Only foolish—foolish to fall in love with a boy who never looked at her and who was promised to another girl—a girl who would *never* for *any* reason be found on her knees in the bracken in the woods, dripping with sweat from having just run miles, her hair in a tight tail to keep it away from her face, and wearing her maid's cast-off homespun instead of delicate muslin.

Yet her infatuation had persisted, because only that once had he treated her poorly. Once in all the years they had known each other. At all other times he had been perfect: kind, generous, funny, intelligent, fair, just, and good.

It had been very easy to love him.

She extracted her hand from his now.

"You suspect Mr. Sheridan is the man cheating women out of their money?" she said.

He nodded. "Fortier and I believe Miss Mapplethorpe is his intended victim this time."

"Oh, no! She is a darling. I will stay close to her."

"Not too close."

"Why not?"

"We cannot apprehend Sheridan without proof. Unfortunately, Miss Mapplethorpe must be taken in by him before we expose him."

"I see. All right."

"You will not confront Sheridan," he said.

The tingling returned, this time beneath her ribs. He was not telling her to stay out of the intrigue entirely. He trusted her.

"I will not," she said. "What shall I do if I learn anything of use?"

"Find me. Tell me."

"You are Mr. Church," she said, wanting to smile. "While Lady Charlotte Ascot might seek conversation with the Duke of Frye without censure under these circumstances, she cannot very well do so with a strange *mister,* under any circumstances, now can she?"

"Find me," he said again, his gaze dropping to her lips.

With a nod, she hurried out of the carriage house. They had achieved a friendly armistice. But she still did not trust him. Not entirely. Not until she had spoken with her friends at Kingstag and learned the entire story of the dissolution of the eighteen-year-long betrothal between the Duke of Frye and Lady Serena Cavendish.

CHAPTER EIGHT

Christmas Eve

The taproom and kitchen

The ground floor of the Fiddler's Roost had been fitted out for Christmas. Evergreen boughs decorated with ribbons hung from each lintel, candles glowed cheerily, and the innkeeper had mixed up a bowl of punch. A space had even been cleared for dancing after the feast.

Frye knew he ought to be following Sheridan's every move now, especially as everybody was relaxed and this would be the ideal time for the blackguard to ingratiate himself further with Miss Mapplethorpe. But Freddie, again pretending to imbibe with Anderson, the innkeeper, and now the coachmen, was covertly watching their quarry too.

And Frye simply could not manage to look away from Charlotte.

Nearly all evening she had been playing with the children, running about with them, tossing rings and making paper chains to hang on the boughs, singing carols and laughing with them like a girl herself.

He wanted that. Every day. *Her.* Playing with children. His children. Their children. The longing was wedged beneath his ribs like a heated brick: heavy and searing.

He was only twenty-five. He did not know another man his age in his social set who would admit to longing for children. Perhaps none of them knew that they could never have children, that they could never give themselves to a woman like he ached to give himself to Charlotte Ascot. Perhaps if they did, they would feel this awful pressure of hopelessness in their chests too. This loneliness.

When he had finally told his mother he intended to break it off with Serena Cavendish, she attempted to convince him otherwise. Lovingly she had insisted he could have a family and be happy. He had seen the tears spring up behind her eyes, the tears she had been unable to withhold when his father died at the age of thirty-six. She had begged him to reconsider.

But she did not know how he felt about Charlotte.

The final children's game wrapped up with a rain of confetti and a flurry of laughter and exhausted little bodies strewn across the floor.

"Now, dancing!" the innkeeper announced, lodging a fiddle betwixt chin and shoulder, and struck up a tune.

Frye went directly to Charlotte.

"My lady, may I have this dance?"

Urging the last of the children toward their mother on the stairs, she looked at his extended hand, then into his eyes—and the whole world seemed brighter, life more precious than Frye had ever thought it could be. She was shining, pink with exertion and joy. An earl's daughter, yet she had donned no jewels or costly ball gown. She wore a simple dress the color of roses and ribbons in her hair that tumbled now halfway down her back in soft curls.

"Thank you, Mr. Church." She placed her fingers on his palm and he nearly fell over.

Eight years and five months: a lifetime since she had last willingly taken his hand with her strong fingers that day in the wood. He had been so ashamed that she had seen him helpless like that, he hadn't been able to speak to her, even to look at her, for the remainder of that sennight at Cheriot Manor. Yet she had said nothing, not to him and not to anyone, about what she had seen. To his knowledge, she never had.

It was their secret.

Now she offered him a small smile and entered the pattern with him. It separated them soon enough, but he was not to be deterred.

"What did you do while you were in America, Lady Charlotte?" he said when he again had the sublime pleasure of her hand in his.

"Do?" she asked with a lifted brow. "Oh, well, each day I dined on pheasant and chocolates decorated with gold leaf, and each evening dashing gentlemen showered me with poetry and posies."

He smiled. "I have no doubt of the latter."

"Don't try to flatter me, sir," she said with a flick of her fan. "I have seen you practice flatteries on others and am not impressed."

"Tell me truly, Charlotte," he said. "How did you pass thirty months away from England?"

"My Aunt Imogene is an eccentric. Consequently, I had a lot of adventures."

"Climbing mountains, sailing up rivers, and riding in hot air balloons? Those sorts of rugged American adventures?" He could imagine her embracing every one of them.

"Rather, nursing poor sailors, reading stories to orphan children, and serving food to starving war veterans. I told you she is an eccentric. But in truth, it was a grand time. I met many interesting people," she said. "Oh, don't look at me like that."

"Like what?"

"As though I have grown horns atop my head."

"I am not looking at you as though you have grown horns atop your head."

"You are."

"I am not. You are an extraordinary woman."

"I am a lady," she corrected him, arching her brows.

She had never flirted with him before. Of course.

This was a good sign.

"An extraordinary lady," he said with bow.

"When I was very young," she said seriously, "my mother told me that I must always care for those in need. She said not wealth or beauty or blood, but compassion was what truly made a lady. I have never forgotten those words. At least, my aunt made certain I would not."

He drew her close, closer than the dance required, and they halted in the middle of the room. Nobody noticed. The fiddling and dancing and clapping swirled around them.

He simply had to touch her. More than the gorgeous touch of her hand on his palm. More and more and more, and damn every fear within him telling him he mustn't, that the more he had of her now the harder it would be when he had none of her.

He led her from the dance floor and into the foyer.

"Where are we going?" she said, glancing back, but not resisting as he drew her into the kitchen. The room was empty, everybody making merry in the taproom.

She looked into his eyes. "Shouldn't we—" Then the kitchen door was closing and they were immersed in the scents of Christmas cooking and entirely alone.

He wrapped his hand around the back of her neck. Her hair was silky and heavy over his knuckles, *beautiful,* and her skin warm and so damn soft.

"You should kiss me," he said above her lips.

His lips on hers were soft, commanding, intoxicating. Charlotte didn't know quite how it happened, but within seconds she was leaning back against the doorjamb and parting her lips to let him kiss her more deeply. Then his other hand was on her waist, his body brushing hers—barely—her knees then her thighs, then the tips of her breasts that were agonizingly tender.

"Touch me, Charlotte," he said roughly. "Put your hands on me."

She did, her fingers curving around his elbows and shifting to his arms. Beneath the fine fabric of his coat he was all unyielding muscle. A rumbling sound came from deep in his chest.

"Yes," he whispered against her lips.

"Yes?"

"A thousand times yes." He sounded entirely unsteady. Her heartbeats were unbridled, wild, her body thoroughly hot and aching. She wanted to lick his lips that were kissing hers so beautifully. She wanted to delve completely inside him and devour him.

Darting the tip of her tongue out between her teeth, she stroked his.

Instantly he drew back from her mouth. His eyes were fevered, his breathing fast.

Then his arm was wrapping around her waist, and he was pulling her against him entirely and capturing her mouth beneath his.

It was more than a kiss. It was lips seeking, tasting, getting as close as possible, inseparable, and tongues laving, feeding, ravenous for more. Everywhere he touched her she was wild for more, wild to press against him more tightly, to feel every gloriously hard inch of him with her own body. She was wholly wanton and she didn't care.

His hands holding her were strong, certain, his lips a maiden's fantasy.

Then both of his hands were in her hair and he was bearing her up against the wall and she was frantic from need racing through her, in her tongue that he stroked as though he would consume her, and in her hands that wanted to feel every taut inch of his arms and chest. The sensation of the contours of his body beneath her palms set off heavy blooms of heat and pleasure between her legs. She wanted to feel the skin over that taut muscle, to feel the hard surface of his bare belly against hers, their thighs together without layers of fabric, and the cruelly tight peaks of her breasts against any part of him. She had wanted to touch him for so long, helplessly, hopelessly. Now she needed to touch all of him at once.

Sweeping his hands over her shoulders and down her back, he held her hips hard against his and his lips served her—her tongue and teeth and the corners of her mouth, then her throat.

Her tiny cap sleeve was slipping over her shoulder, then lower, his fingers tugging it, his lips following where her skin was laid bare. She moaned, loving his mouth on her, the heat of his breath and his tongue.

"Not enough," she heard him utter so deeply she thought it might be her imagination. "This is not enough." His words were exactly what her heart was shouting. "Beautiful woman. We *must* cease this." He sounded breathless. Bewildered. *Desperate.*

Cease?

Cease.

She dragged herself away and fell against the opposite counter. His cravat was destroyed, his shirt pulled halfway out of his trousers from where her hands had sought him, and his perfect lips damp and parted. He was everything she had always wanted. *Always.* She could not even remember what it was like not to love him.

"We cannot do this," he said. His eyes upon her lips looked dark and full of confusion.

"We cannot?" she panted.

His fevered gaze went to her exposed shoulder. "No."

"Here? Oh, of course." She pulled her sleeve back up. "You should not undress me here."

"I *must* not undress you *anywhere.*"

She tried to think, but the *feeling* part of her seemed thoroughly in control.

"Two months ago you were betrothed to my friend," she said, reminding herself of the reason she should in fact not be kissing him now, not until she was able to speak with Serena.

After a moment's pause, he nodded. "Yes."

Yet he had kissed her anyway. Unpleasant feelings smothered the pleasure.

"Did you kiss Nancy like that last night?"

"Nancy." His brow crinkled, then his eyes snapped wide. "Nancy, at this inn? The *barmaid?*"

"Yes."

Anger sparked in the blue. "No."

"Well, you needn't take offense."

"For pity's sake, Charlotte," he said, raking his fingers through his hair. His eyes were afire. "Is that what you think of me?"

"I don't know what to think of you! You just kissed me and then said we cannot."

"I was flirting with her to learn what she knows of Sheridan."

"Why would she know anything of Mr. Sheridan?"

"Because she spent two hours in his bedchamber last night."

"*Oh.* I see."

"I am sorry I had to tell you that."

"I forced you to."

He cast her a dark look. "A man of honor does not tarry with maidservants."

"A man of honor does not break off an engagement of eighteen years' duration, either."

"He does if he must," he said grimly. Then he turned away from her, only halfway, and she saw the hard rise and fall of his shoulders. He ran his hand through his hair again, then over his face and she wanted to *be* his hands, to feel the angles and textures of his features. She wanted to feel every inch of him. "You are impressively loyal to your friend," he said.

"Of course I am."

He turned to her and there was warmth in his eyes, and something else. Admiration.

"If I could inspire that sort of devotion in you," he said, "it would make me the happiest man on earth."

"You are a tease, Horace Church," she said with a little break in her voice that made her furious.

"Only honest." *Finally.* And it felt fantastically good. To no satisfying end, of course. He could never actually court her. But it felt incredible saying this aloud to her. And kissing her . . . There she stood, her hair undone by his hands, her lips soft and reddened by his kiss, and her cheeks as rosy as her gown. "It is not true—the reason I gave yesterday for kissing you."

The lashes fanned about her storm cloud eyes. "You do not think I am kissable after all?"

"God, yes. Obviously. More than kissable. Much more," he said without perfect control of his voice, or that other part of him that wanted the *much more* now, immediately.

"I don't understand," she said.

"The truth is, I have wanted to kiss you for years."

"Years?" she said in little more than a whisper.

"Years." Every sinew and muscle in his body was tight and hard and wanting her. "But Charlotte . . ."

She looked abruptly wary.

Good.

"What?"

He had to make himself say it. "I have no intention of marrying. Ever."

"Ever?"

He nodded.

For a moment she said nothing.

"But you are a *duke.* You . . . There are *expectations.*"

"I already have an heir. My brother is an exceptional person, intelligent, moral, dedicated to the people of Frye, to our family, and to England." And his younger brother Preston did not fear falling from his horse suddenly, or losing control of his carriage in traffic, or the world believing he was possessed by the devil at worst and insane at best, *every day of his life.* "I needn't marry."

"I don't know what to say," she said in a peculiar voice.

"Say what I deserve. That I am a scoundrel. A cad. A low, wretched cur."

Two of her fingertips touched the lips he now knew tasted like heaven.

"You are a scoundrel, a cad, and a low, wretched cur," she said.

"Finally we agree on something," he said.

She looked fixedly at the floor. "I should return to the party and Miss Mapplethorpe," she said in short syllables, her hands sweeping over her skirts to smooth them and then her hair.

"Charlotte."

She met his gaze.

"Kissing you was better than I even dreamed," he said. "Far better."

"Then I guess we have both learned something tonight." Eyes very bright, with quick steps she passed him by and went out of the room.

CHAPTER NINE

Christmas morning

Various places in the inn

Christmas day dawned bright and shining, all blue sky and white earth and brilliantly golden sun. Pinning his attention to the floor, Frye drew his bedchamber draperies closed as Freddie entered.

"The Mail will shortly venture forth," Freddie said. "When the coach departs, Sheridan intends to follow."

"He could have closed the deal here. We gave him ample opportunity last night, and she is a softhearted soul. Why didn't he?"

"Because he is not our villain." Freddie spoke Frye's thoughts. "But in the event that we are mistaken in this, I will ride with him now."

Frye would remain at this inn, at least until sundown. The brilliant snow and sparkling sunshine were a disaster in the making for him. They rendered the inn his prison.

"Send word if there is any to send," Frye said.

Freddie clapped him on the shoulder. "Solve the mystery."

But Frye could not respond according to their ritual.

"After this," he said, "I will return to Kentwood permanently."

Freddie remained unsmiling. He had never shown Frye pity and he had never told him how to live his life. He had always been the best and most honorable of friends, just as Greyson Jones was. Their trusted companionship had allowed him a measure of safety away from his estate. In return he would do anything for them.

He knew that at least part of Freddie's wish to see him married and settled was Freddie's own desire to return home to his country where turmoil was brewing anew.

"I will be well, my friend," he said.

"I know you will, *mon ami*." Freddie gripped his shoulder tightly for a moment then released it. "In the meantime, there is a beautiful girl who has not yet left this place. Give yourself a gift. For Christmas." He winked.

Then he was gone, and Frye closed the door to his bedchamber and shut out the voice in his head telling him that Charlotte also deserved a goodbye. But he had already seen her before the sun rose: across the field, breeches soaked to her knees, hair flopping on her back in a queue, running as swiftly through the snowfall as she had run as a child.

She did not need a goodbye from him. The best thing he could do now was to stay far away from her.

Best for her, even if not for him.

"My lady?" The soft scratch came at her bedchamber door.

Charlotte laid the last of her clothes in the traveling trunk and went to the door. Sally was in the kitchen packing a snack for the road. Kingstag Castle was not far, but with the snow and ice on the roads, the journey could be slow.

"Good morning, Miss Mapplethorpe. Happy Christmas! Wasn't that a marvelous party last night?" All except the part where she danced with the Duke of Frye and then he kissed her senseless. Or perhaps especially those parts. She was undecided.

"Oh, yes, a delightful party." Miss Mapplethorpe's fingers were twisting agitatedly before her. "But, oh, dear me, my lady, I am afraid something awful has occurred."

"Oh, no." Charlotte grasped her hands. "Do tell me."

"My niece is *gone*."

"Gone? Has the Mail Coach left without you?"

"Oh, not at all. Calliope departed at dawn, it seems, with Mr. George Clayton."

"Departed with him? *Alone?*"

Miss Mapplethorpe nodded and now tears crested the rims of her eyes.

"Good heavens. But why would she— Well, I suppose I understand why." *Intimately.* Sometimes, after all, a lady did not act on what she knew to be in her best interests. "What of his parents?"

"Young George went without their knowledge too. He left a letter for them, just as she left this letter for me." With trembling hands she offered a sheet of paper.

Charlotte read it swiftly. "It is a proper elopement, it seems, against the wishes of his parents. And your wishes, I assume?"

"Oh, dear me, I would have been glad to allow him to court Calliope. He seems a fine young man. But to steal her away from me . . ." She looked paler than usual.

Charlotte took her arm. "Mr. Church and Mr. Fortier will be able to help us."

"What delightful young men," she said miserably. "But I am really not certain, dear Lady Charlotte, how they could possibly—oh, ohh—" She wavered a bit.

"You are very pale, Miss Mapplethorpe. Before you say another word you must calm yourself." She led the frail woman into her own bedchamber and sat her down by the hearth, and tucked a blanket around her. "Sally will bring you tea and look after you while I get help. Please don't fret. We will find her, I am certain of it."

Running downstairs, she looked in the taproom. It was empty. After poking her head into the kitchen to bid Sally wait on Miss Mapplethorpe, she threw her cloak over her shoulders and went outside. The Mail Coach stood in the yard, its team chomping to be off after their long rest. The Andersons were all climbing into it. Neither the Duke of Frye nor Lord Fortier were aboard.

She ran through the brilliantly glittering yard to the stable.

The ostler informed her that Mr. Fortier had hired the inn's only saddle horse, and had departed with Mr. Sheridan. He had not seen Mr. Church that morning.

Was he waiting for her? Perhaps intending to ride to Kingstag with her?

No. Not after what he had said. *I have no intention of marrying. Ever.*

But that kiss.

That *kiss*. She was thoroughly confused. He had kissed her, admitted wanting to kiss her for years, and then told her they mustn't.

He was tangling her up inside and she adamantly did not want that. For two and a half years she had practiced tackling challenges directly. She had gotten so proficient at it that, when her father demanded she return home, she had felt certain she could tackle the challenge of watching her friend marry the man she loved.

She would not hide from this now. Never again.

"Fields," she said, running past him. "I shan't need the carriage yet."

She ran into the inn and, shaking off the snow clinging to her hem, up to the duke's bedchamber.

He answered her knock.

"You are still here!"

"Charlotte." It sounded as though he hadn't spoken in hours. "Are you departing now?"

"Calliope has eloped with George Clayton. She left a message informing her aunt. They departed at dawn and they must have gone on foot. Did Lord Fortier leave with Mr. Sheridan this morning?"

"Yes. He is traveling with him on a pretext, to remain close in the event that Sheridan tries his wiles upon Miss Mapplethorpe at the next stop." His brow dipped. "But she will not board the coach if her niece is missing."

"No. She is enormously distressed, of course. I've just calmed her down, but—"

"But you want me to go after Miss Jameson and return her here."

She nodded. "Yes, of course."

He drew a deep breath. "I am sorry, Charlotte. I cannot go with you."

"Horace, I heard you say that you will never marry. In asking you to chase after them I am not asking *you* to elope with *me*. Obviously. You needn't worry on that score. For heaven's sake, do you imagine I am the sort of woman who would want to entrap a man into marriage?"

His eyes sparkled and it seemed as though he were biting back a smile. "I think I am starting to wish you were."

"I don't know how to interpret that. But I don't have time to now anyway. For while you are making cryptic comments, Miss

Jameson is running farther and farther away from her aunt, with a virtual stranger."

He came into the corridor. "I will speak with Clayton and his wife. But I need you to stay at a distance from me. All right?"

"You are ridiculous."

"I am not."

"And a scoundrel," she added.

"That, however, is true."

"You are standing within six inches of me and telling me that I must stay away from you."

"Contrary to my well-deserved reputation for discipline, when you are near I feel entirely out of control."

"That is not my problem."

He smiled. "Also true. But it would help if you said you understood."

"Of course I don't understand." She could not cease looking at his lips. "And I would like to kiss you again. But I don't suppose we have time for that."

"We have already had far too much time for that." He started down the corridor and she knew she should be entirely focused on the missing girl. But his shoulders were so perfectly broad and rigid and she had touched them last night, *clung to them,* as he had made her feel extraordinary things in every secret and even not-so-secret part of her body.

Now she imagined wrapping her arms around his waist and pressing up against his back and kissing the nape of his neck, and she got dizzy.

At the Claytons' bedchamber door, with his knock the door swung inward slowly. The room was empty.

"They've gone," he said.

"I was just in the stable and the yard. They were not there." Now she was twisting her hands together too. "But the ostler said nothing of their departure."

"Perhaps he was occupied by the Mail Coach's departure. I will speak with Miss Mapplethorpe." He stepped close to her and took her hands between his own. His were large and strong and being held by him filled her with peace and a delicious agitation, both at once. "You mustn't worry. We will find her."

"You are touching me."

"I am."

"You are a horrid hypocrite."

"I told you," he said in a low voice. "Out of control."

Reluctantly she drew away and they went to Miss Mapplethorpe's room.

Within minutes the gentlewoman was telling the man practiced in subterfuge what she had not admitted to Charlotte: that early that morning when she and the Claytons discovered their young ones missing, Mr. and Mrs. Clayton had said they knew a Bow Street Runner in the neighborhood who could help them find Calliope and George, but his price was far too high for them to pay alone. Miss Mapplethorpe had promptly handed over every shilling in her purse. The Claytons had then gotten into their carriage and driven off.

When Miss Mapplethorpe had finished, and was sobbing into a kerchief monogrammed with the ducal crest, the duke asked Sally to attend her and drew Charlotte into the corridor.

"There is no Bow Street Runner, is there?" she said.

"Not this far from London or at this time of year."

"Mr. Clayton is the thief for whom you and Lord Fortier are searching. Not Mr. Sheridan."

"It seems so. I will go after them." He looked unusually fierce and determined.

"George must know where his parents have gone. I will come with you."

"No."

"Of course I will," she said, moving to the stairs. "He will not have taken her by the main road. His parents easily could have found them that way. And there is another, smaller route I've run along that wends away from the inn too. There are only my family's carriage horses in the stable now. If only we had discovered this before Lord Fortier and Mr. Sheridan departed! Still, Mr. Clayton cannot have taken her far yet. Calliope hasn't proper footwear for swift walking."

He grasped her arm and she halted and looked over her shoulder at him.

"You will not come with me," he said.

"It occurs to me that becoming a duke at age ten is probably not very good preparation for a man to accept the wishes and desires of other people."

"You are probably right about that."

"Of course I am." She dislodged her arm from his grip. "Come along, Your Grace. Time is of the essence."

He smiled. "I'll fetch my hat."

𝒥ields offered to drive, but the duke agreed with Charlotte on the runaways' likely route, a path too narrow for the carriage. One of the carriage horses, however, could be ridden, and a saddle and bridle were borrowed. The duke insisted that Charlotte ride, declining her invitation to ride double with a single lifted brow and an inscrutable, "Thank you, no."

Instead, he donned a shabby cloak and pulled its voluminous hood over his head and around his face.

"What on earth is that?" she said. "Part of your commoner disguise?"

"I borrowed it from the ostler. It seems my hat has gone astray." He laid his hand on the horse's neck and walked beside her like that the entire way.

Along the byway that wended away from the inn, within a hundred yards Charlotte discovered the couple's tracks in the snow. Barely a mile from that they found the elopers themselves, tucked in the corner of an old mill, wrapped in each other's arms, and oblivious to the rest of the world.

Given their tangled limbs, Charlotte thought it lucky they were actually still clothed, although the building was chilly and perhaps Miss Jameson was less of a natural wanton than Charlotte had recently discovered herself to be in the arms of a duke.

The duke's boots crunched on the ground strewn with frost and bits of grain, and abruptly the couple broke into two pieces.

"Lady Charlotte!" Calliope exclaimed. "Mr. Church! Why ever are you here?"

"We have come looking for you, of course," Charlotte said. "Your parents, Mr. Clayton, have stolen Miss Mapplethorpe's money and have disappeared."

The youth grabbed the girl's hands.

"I begged them not to do it, darling! I tell you, I begged."

Calliope turned fraught eyes to the duke. "Is my aunt all right?"

"In fact she is worried to the point of illness," Charlotte said. "Now do come with me outside while Mr. Church speaks to Mr. Clayton about his parents' villainy."

"My lady," George said stiffly, "forgive me, but I can't see how my parents' business is any of either of yours."

"You have put both Miss Jameson and her aunt in jeopardy, whelp." The duke did not raise his voice, but it resonated throughout the cavernous space like a bell in a tower. Charlotte got goose bumps all up and down her body. "It is any gentleman's business to take you to task for it," he said. "But my first purpose is to find your parents and apprehend them."

"Miss Jameson, Mr. Clayton," Charlotte said, "I present to you His Grace, the Duke of Frye."

"Duke?" George exclaimed and leaped to his feet. His neck constricted in a gulp. "Your Grace, I beg your pardon!" He bowed.

"The duke and his companion, Lord Fortier, tracked your parents to the Fiddler's Roost, Mr. Clayton. They would have apprehended them there if not for this excursion of yours."

"I had to protect Calliope," George said stoutly. "Father and Mother said that if I told anyone of their plans they would abduct her and send her to someplace horrid. I had to keep her safe."

"You might have asked someone at the inn for assistance," the duke said. "A mill in the frigid cold is no place to bring a lady, Mr. Clayton."

"Yes, Your Grace! But it wasn't to be for long. We only needed to hide today, so that they would give up searching before they must leave."

"Leave?" Charlotte said. "Leave the inn?"

"Leave England. They've tickets for the packet to Cork departing tonight."

"Cork?" She turned to the duke. "Miss Mapplethorpe's entire savings are as good as gone, not to mention the poor women they will surely hoodwink in Ireland."

"Mr. Clayton," he said. "Return now to the inn with Miss Jameson and wait there until I instruct you otherwise. And know that if you disobey me, I will hunt you down and see you jailed on the charge of abduction. Do you understand?"

The youth nodded swiftly.

The duke turned his summer-blue eyes on the maiden. "Miss Jameson?"

"I understand, Your Grace," she said in a very small voice.

"All right then. There is a horse outside. Take it. Lady Charlotte and I will follow on foot. Now be off with you."

Holding hands, the pair scurried toward the door, pulled it wide, and sunlight unfurled across the floor and glittered brilliantly on the snow without, the wind sweeping powder from the roof into shimmering whorls of white and silver, like angels dancing.

The scent of metal was all around.

Dread collared Frye, sucking and hot and prickling.

He stumbled and lost his footing.

"What a gloriously beautiful Christmas day it has turned out to be," he heard Charlotte say as though through a tunnel.

Then the explosion came in his chest.

"The Claytons cannot have not gone far. As soon as we return to the inn, I will bid Fields harness the—Horace?"

He was on the ground. He fought it.

"Horace!"

Pain crowded him everywhere.

Then he lost control.

CHAPTER TEN

Minutes later

The mill

$\mathcal{G}$rowing up mostly without a mother and surrounded by men, Charlotte had never quite learned how to weep modestly like a woman, or really to weep at all.

Now sitting on the ground, cradling his head in her lap, she could hardly see for the torrent of tears pouring from her eyes and streaming down her cheeks to dribble onto his brow to mingle with the sweat there. She tugged up a corner of her cloak and used it to clean his beautiful face—his face that for a horrifying interval she had hardly recognized—all the while whispering through shallow breaths, "Wake up. Wake up. Wake up. Please wake up."

His cheek turned against her palm. She gasped and choked back tears.

"Horace," she whispered, smoothing her hand along the side of his face and willing his eyes to open.

They did, hooded. They were blue, bright blue as they should be, not the filmy white they had been for a million terrible seconds.

His breaths were shallow, his features still slack. But his eyes remained partially open and his chest was beginning to move in a regular rhythm.

His lips moved.

"D—" His eyes clamped shut.

She stroked her fingertips over his temple and brow. "Yes?" she whispered, swallowing back tears of relief. "I am here. I am listening."

"Disgrace," he said thickly and she saw blood between his lips. "Disgrace myself?"

Dabbing at his lips again with the soft velvet of her cloak, she shook her head.

"You are my hero, Horace Church," she said.

His brow creased. "Ch—Char—" His eyes tightened shut.

"No," she forced out. "You did not disgrace yourself. You are still in one very handsome piece, albeit lying on the floor of a mill, so I suspect your overcoat might suffer for it. I have some experience tending wounds, but I haven't ever—that is, I don't know what to do for you now. Give me instruction, please."

"Claytons," he said. "Go."

"I will not leave you. Give me a different instruction."

"No—time to—waste." His hand came heavily around hers that was curved about his cheek. "Charlotte."

"All right." She grasped his hand, choking back the fear clogging her throat. "I will go. Only promise me you will not die while I am gone."

He barely moved his head, but his features seemed to relax, and his lips to curve ever so slightly.

"Worst is over," he said still thickly, as though he were very, very weary. But it was more clearly actual speech. "Dreadful headache, though."

Unclasping her cloak she folded it into a pillow and tucked it beneath his head.

"I would kiss you now," she said, "but I think you've bitten your tongue and I do not want to hurt you."

"You could never hurt me." He did not open his eyes. "Now, run."

"I don't—"

"*Run.*"

Her skirts were awkward, but she hitched them up between her legs and without the cloak she was light. She ran faster than she ever had before.

$\mathcal{L}$ord Fortier returned to the inn just as she was pouring her story into the innkeeper's ears. They had been wrong about Sheridan. Along the road the tradesman had stopped at a farmhouse and, upon entry, introduced Lord Fortier to his sweet elderly mother and three orphaned nieces and nephews, whom he was visiting for the holiday. Despite his low appearance, it seemed he was not a cozener of unprotected women, after all, rather simply a friendly gentleman. Lord Fortier had turned back immediately.

Now he asked her pointed questions about the duke's state. Then, after speaking with George, he departed in pursuit of the Claytons.

With her guidance, Fields and the innkeeper retrieved the duke from the mill and discreetly assisted him to his bedchamber.

"T'ain't right, my lady: His Grace lying to everybody like that," her coachman said afterward with a shake of his hoary head.

"It was for a noble purpose, Fields."

This was proven when Lord Fortier returned again as the sun fell, with the announcement that Mr. and Mrs. Clayton were now languishing in the magistrate's jail two counties away. They had confessed to their crimes, which Mr. Clayton typically perpetrated alone, but, as it was the holiday season, he preferred to be with his family.

Justice had been done.

But Charlotte could not be still. Miss Mapplethorpe and the inn mistress plied her with delicacies all evening, but her stomach was too tight to admit food. She was pacing the corridor when Lord Fortier emerged from the duke's room.

She ran to him. "How is he?"

"He sleeps," he said. "The headache is fierce for many hours afterward. Sleep relieves it."

"You have seen this before, been through this with him, at other times?"

"I have known him since we were boys," he said with a gentle smile.

"That was not an answer."

"*Oui*. It has happened enough times so I know that by morning he will again be his arrogant self."

"Is he ill?"

"Not any more so than he was fifteen years ago. Better, in fact. It has been some time since the last."

"How much time?"

"Years."

"What is it?"

"That is an unsettled mystery. The priests in my country will tell you he has been possessed."

"By the *devil?*"

He shook his head. "Nothing so unkind. In my people's religion, the gods are many. Occasionally they enjoy speaking through the living."

"Please," she said. "Give me an explanation that I can understand—that I can reconcile with the man I know."

"It is a trouble of the brain. A discomfort and an inconvenience, particularly when snow or water makes sunlight bright and inconstant."

"That is why he wore that cloak and held onto the horse as we walked! He was trying to avoid seeing the sunlight reflecting off the snow. Wasn't he?"

"He has learned methods of avoiding the dangers. But sometimes the danger comes when he cannot anticipate it. Mostly it is a frustration. This time, I suspect, his pride will be the greatest casualty."

Because she had witnessed it.

She nodded.

"If you would like to see him . . ." he said, eyes glimmering with playfulness now. He gestured toward the duke's bedchamber door. "I will tell no one, not even him if you wish it."

Gulping a big breath, she went into the bedchamber. The draperies were closed and the man on the bed was very still, his breaths shallow. As the door clicked shut, he did not wake.

Standing beside the bed, she studied the noble line of his brow, the delectable cut of his jaw now shadowed with whiskers that obscured the fading bruise, his strong hands that had held her with such passion, and his lips. Her throat was so thick she could hardly breathe.

"I do not entirely understand what happened to you," she whispered. "But it is clear to me that you bear a burden, two burdens, both this—this *thing* and the burden of keeping it a secret from everybody. How you have done so for so many years, I cannot fathom."

There had been blood too, that day she had found him on that path in the wood at Cheriot Manor. She had thought he must have fallen from his horse and been knocked unconscious. That would have been sufficient cause for a boy of seventeen to feel shame enough to ignore her afterward. Perhaps he had fallen from his horse on that occasion.

So many years of hiding his secret.

Everything inside her was tight and hot and anguished. Her heartbeats would not slow. Yet he slept so deeply; he showed no sign of waking.

Sliding her feet out of her slippers, she crawled onto the bed and turned onto her side to face him. Tracing the familiar, beloved silhouette of his features with her gaze, she swallowed back yet more tears.

"Today I thought you were dying," she whispered. "Until you opened your beautiful eyes, I thought . . ." Her throat clenched. "So, here is the situation, Horace Church: you mustn't die. You see I have learned how to live quite happily without you, that is, with the certainty that you will never be mine. But I do not think I could learn how to be happy if you were no longer in the world. I think then that I would want to die too. So, there you have it. You are forbidden to die."

A fresh tear leaked out of her eye and dripped onto her hands folded beneath her face. She wiped it away.

His chest rose on an abrupt breath, and his lips parted. Before Charlotte could leap off the bed, he turned his head.

"Charlotte Ascot," he said slowly, enunciating each syllable. His eyes shone brilliantly blue. "You are in my bed."

"I . . . That is . . . I . . ." She pushed herself up.

In one fluid movement he turned and rose above her, entrapping her on the bed between his hands to either side and the magnificent wall of his chest that hovered just above hers. Where his hip and thigh leaned against hers, explosions were happening inside her, and glorious heat. A lock of his hair tumbled over his brow and his gaze was all over her face. She couldn't breathe.

"Best Christmas gift ever," he murmured huskily, then bent his head and captured her lips beneath his.

CHAPTER ELEVEN

No one's paying attention to the time

The Duke of Frye's bed

$\mathcal{I}$t required no urging for Charlotte to sink her hands into his hair and accept his kisses with total wanton abandon.

He gave her more than kisses. It began on her face, trailing to her throat, then her neck, his hands and lips creating a havoc of sensations inside her and all across her skin. The tender, maddening rasp of his tongue felt especially good, so good that she found her hands reaching for his shoulders and then his chest, then the tail of his shirt and pulling it up so that she could feel his skin beneath the linen. Taut, hot, smooth. *Perfect.*

When her hands spread on his waist, the rumble that came from his chest made her even hungrier to feel him. Sweeping her palms up, she moaned as she touched his chest, the contoured muscle there. His breaths hitched.

"Don't stop," he whispered against her throat with a raw, urgent sound.

"I won't."

Then he was kneeling above her, drawing off his shirt, and she could hear her own panting. The firelight cut shadows across male muscle and ribs and the dusting of dark hair and brown nipples.

There was not enough air in the room. *In the world.*

"Are you all right with this?" But his eyes asked more than his words. They asked if she still desired him.

"Much more than all right." She reached for him.

235

He tossed away the shirt and lowered himself to her and she let her hands have him.

"Finally we agree on something," she said, and he kissed her, openmouthed, hungrily, his hands tangling in her hair, dashing pins this way and that.

"Each touch of your lips," he said against those lips. "Each caress of your tongue, each moment of your hands on me makes me want more."

"I am all right with more too." She was discovering that a man's spine offered gorgeous shapes for a woman's fingertips to memorize, gentle little undulating mountains, and that the tight muscles of his buttocks encased in thin wool were also magnificently shaped. Touching them did wild, uncontrolled things to her body. He was a banquet for her hands.

He looked into her eyes from about an inch away. "I want to give you pleasure."

"I am all right with that too."

He smiled, a half smile with his mouth, and an entire smile with his sparkling eyes.

He kissed her lips, her throat, then her earlobe. She was sighing and clutching his sides by the time his mouth reached her neck, tingles racing through her and the throbbing ache between her thighs building to a reckless pounding.

Then he touched her breasts and she relinquished every wish she had ever had for anything except to be here, now, with him touching her.

He kissed her through her gown, through the layers of clothing she had donned that morning, which now she understood were foolish contrivances meant to inconvenience everybody. When his mouth covered the peak of her breast, she gasped and pressed her hips to his. Holding her breasts in his hands, he brought his teeth into play. She moaned. It was beautiful, maddening, *not enough*. She wanted his mouth against her skin, his tongue caressing her actual flesh.

As though he knew this, his hand found its way beneath her skirts, first skimming over her stocking to her knee, then to the top of the stocking, his fingertips circling the garter, making shivers race up and down her leg. He lifted his head and, with his gaze on hers, he caressed her thigh.

"You are beautiful, Charlotte."

"What is your hand doing beneath my skirt?"

He smiled, and to see that and feel the heat of his palm on her at once was nearly more than her heart could bear.

He brought his lips close to hers but did not kiss her. "Fulfilling one of my fondest dreams."

"You dreamed about *this* too?"

"I dreamed about everything with you," he whispered.

Reaching up to his face with both hands, she drew him down and kissed him with all of the relief and happiness and anguish and love inside her. That was when he brought his hand fully between her legs and, with the lightest and most astonishing accuracy, caressed her precisely where her body wanted it most.

After that, it was not very long before she fell apart entirely. She knew she made sounds, perhaps several times, and possibly asked for more, again and again. She wasn't entirely certain, but if she did plead aloud, he didn't seem to mind it. He kissed her and touched her perfectly for some time, and when she was trembling and clutching his gorgeous arms and whimpering, and her body was rippling upon waves of heat and pleasure, he kissed her again.

She never wanted to release him.

Gulping air into her lungs, she smoothed her palms over his shoulders.

"I feel as I do after I have run a distance," she said breathlessly.

His smile was slow and decidedly triumphant.

A knock came on the door.

"Shall I dive under the bed?" she said.

He laughed. Taking her face between his hands, he kissed her again, a long, beautiful, leisurely kiss.

"Lady Charlotte Ascot," he murmured against the corner of her lips. "I could kiss you forever."

But of course he had already said that he would not do that. And she had not given him leave to anyway. While the day had brought with it a revelation that she thought could explain his reticence to marry, she must still speak with Serena. Kissing a man who had once been betrothed to a dear friend was one thing, but planning a future of kissing him forever was another altogether.

When he drew away, this time he rose from the bed. Taking up his shirt, he pulled it on, and went to the door.

Through the crack, she heard Lord Fortier's voice.

As he shut the door she sat up and smoothed her hands over her hair.

"Fields wishes to depart for Kingstag at dawn," he said. "He is concerned about more snow in the morning."

"Where are you going?"

"Kentwood."

She stood up and went to him.

"I will not beg you to come to Kingstag," she said. "I will not beg you for anything."

A smile cut across his mouth.

"Anything *else*." She rolled her eyes as heat gathered in the most predictable place, but also very thickly in her chest.

"Good," he said, though softly.

Then he did the most foolish thing: he took her hand, lifted it to his lips, and kissed her knuckles.

"Good-bye, Charlotte." His voice was beautifully rough.

Calling up the fortitude that her Aunt Imogene had praised during their American sojourn, Charlotte drew her hand away with smooth aplomb. Forcing her lips into a smile, she opened the door and left him.

CHAPTER TWELVE

Boxing Day morning

Kingstag Castle, Dorchester

*W*hen Charlotte arrived at Kingstag, the castle was a merry whirl of activity. Throughout childhood she had visited the three Cavendish sisters so often, she felt entirely at home now. A vast medieval fortress with ample modern additions and comforts, Kingstag included rooms aplenty for all sorts of shenanigans. This was a good thing indeed, as Bridget, the youngest Cavendish sister, was producing a play. She had engaged most of the guests to build sets, design costumes, and perform roles, and had entirely taken over the ballroom for the production.

That there was no possibility of a ball at this party suited Charlotte ideally. Dancing would only make her long for a cozy little inn and a spice-scented kitchen and the perfect kisses of a man who preferred bachelorhood to her.

After reuniting with friends she had not seen since before leaving for America, finally she escaped the melee and went in search of Serena. She found her old friend amidst a group of guests.

"Charlotte!" Serena reached out with both hands and clasped Charlotte's tightly. Her eyes light and smiling. "Welcome back to England. How we have missed you!" She seemed as far from miserable as could be. She positively glowed.

"And I you."

"My mother is abed," Serena whispered. "It's only a mild fever, but since Gareth and Cleo are away, keeping everybody happy has fallen to me."

"It seems as though you are accomplishing it splendidly." She couldn't very well drag Serena away from her hostess duties to interrogate her in private as to whether she was in fact heartbroken and only masking it valiantly. And since she had no intention of taking part in Bridget's play, she sought out distraction instead.

She found it with Alexandra. The middle Cavendish sister had taken up a spot in the corner of the ballroom from which with one eye she watched the unfolding of Bridget's haphazard masterpiece and with the other eye studied the gentlemen involved.

"Lord Gosling is exceptionally handsome," Alexandra said, glancing at the charming viscount Charlotte had only just met.

Charlotte nodded. "Mm. Very nice." He was indeed attractive, but nothing to compare to the Duke of Frye's warm, brilliant eyes and dashing smile and perfect shoulders.

"What do you think of Viscount Newton?"

"Also handsome." He was barely Charlotte's own age. "Somewhat boyish." She preferred men four years her senior. One man.

"Serena likes Lord Gosling better. And Mr. Jones. She has spent most of the past several days in the company of one or the other."

Please!

Charlotte tried to school her features to mild interest. "Really?"

"They're smitten with her, of course." Alexandra sighed. "Every man is always smitten with her."

Charlotte did not point out that one man obviously was not—at least not smitten enough to overcome his scruples about marriage.

"You know," Alexandra continued thoughtfully, "if I hadn't seen her right after Frye was here, I wouldn't even believe she was the same person. She was positively downcast. That was when Mama decided we must have this party. But I'm starting to believe Serena is pleased at having been jilted."

"But I thought she was heartbroken."

"If a broken heart can heal so swiftly, I suppose," Alexandra said skeptically. "For believe me, Charlotte, my sister is not heartbroken now. She's positively ebullient."

"But . . ." Charlotte's heart was now pattering far too swiftly. "Why would she have pretended to be heartbroken?"

"Perhaps it wasn't pretending. Perhaps she has simply realized she did not want to marry Frye after all. And she is so much more *interesting* now that she has been jilted. Mr. Jones and Lord Gosling certainly think so."

"Alexa!" Bridget called from across the room. "Do come rehearse your scene at once. We haven't got all day to get this right!"

Alexandra sighed. "The tyrant beckons." With a private eye-roll to Charlotte, she went.

But Charlotte's heart was so full she couldn't even manage a chuckle.

Horace had told her that Serena was not heartbroken over the jilting. Alexandra had now confirmed it.

Swamped with relief and a kind of euphoria that made no sense—after all, whatever affair she had enjoyed with the Duke of Frye was now over—she wandered in a half-daze toward the drawing room. But her eyes drooped as she went. She had barely slept the night before, replaying in her mind every moment she had spent with the jilting duke, every word and touch and kiss. Finally relieved of her burden of guilt and worry over Serena, and quite simply heartbroken herself, at five o'clock in the afternoon she sought her bed.

Gathering up the ducal courage that ten years of observing his ducal father and another fifteen years of actually being ducal had instilled in him, Frye dismounted the hack he'd borrowed from the inn, handed the reins to a groom, and walked up the steps into the Duke of Wessex's castle. His heart was lodged in his throat and his head was shouting at him to get the hell back on the horse and ride away as quickly as possible.

He should not have come. He should have gone straight home to Kentwood, just as he had told Charlotte he intended to do, and begin his life of perpetual bachelordom. That morning at dawn he should not have stood at his bedchamber window at the inn and watched her carriage drive into the snowy distance, then with alarming rapidity convinced himself that he really should go to Kingstag after all. He should not have told himself that he owed Serena an appearance at this party, for the sake of their families and friends, so that in the future there would be no discomfort or blame or unpleasantness of any kind. They had been fond friends for decades. He never wanted her unhappiness. Or so he had reasoned. And he should not have told himself that he needed to ensure that his suspicions about Greyson's feelings for Serena were correct.

Because he could just as easily visit Kingstag after the holidays. And he could just as easily write to Greyson and ask him straight out.

But those justifications had given him an excuse to come here now. Because the truth was that he could not bear another moment apart from Charlotte. It was an unpropitious start to his vow of never seeing her again. But he loved her and this might be the last time he would be in her presence before some lucky bloke snatched her up and carried her to the altar.

Heroic self-denial could wait until tomorrow.

Entering a foyer festooned with decorations, he was swiftly reminded of the reason he especially enjoyed playing the part of common Mr. Church: a duke went nowhere without garnering lots of attention. And a jilting duke could not arrive at the home of his jilted bride without garnering even more.

The foyer swiftly filled with people, none of whom, alas, were the woman he had last seen walking from the Fiddler's Roost Inn as his ribs crushed his heart.

"Good evening, everyone," he said with a nervous gesture of his hat to the crowd. Good God, he was as trembly as a schoolboy reciting his letters. But these were not only his friends and acquaintances; they were also Charlotte's. A perverse part of him wanted anything she heard of him to be glowing.

"You may have noticed there was a bit of a snowstorm out there," he said more steadily, "which made the roads fiendishly difficult to pass through. I hope better late than never isn't just a saying, but a sentiment."

From within the ever-thickening cluster of people, Serena's wide-eyed stare met him.

He bowed and attempted a dashing smile. "Lady Serena. My apologies for my late arrival."

"Frye." She remained immobile all the way across the foyer from him. "How good of you to join us," she said stonily.

Since *dashing* obviously wasn't working, he would try for *mildly clever.*

"I hope I haven't thrown off your numbers," he said.

Finally she smiled. And then her lovely features performed a series of mild contortions, all of which he was unable to read and which was, admittedly, shocking. In twenty years he had never seen her so much as frown.

Then she whirled about and disappeared.

So much for hoping she had forgiven him.

Frye greeted friends and endured introductions. As soon as he could manage it, he escaped the foyer. He had visited Kingstag often enough to know where to find brandy. He headed for the dining room sideboard.

There he found Greyson Jones alone, thoughtfully nursing a glass of port.

"Frye, old man." Greyson stood and came toward him, extending his hand.

Frye clasped his friend's hand and then his shoulder.

"Tell me at once, Grey, is this gathering a dull bore or are you having the time of your life? If it's the former and you are eager to have an excuse to flee, now that I've shown my face and done my duty by our hostess, I will happily invent an excuse to drag you away at first light tomorrow."

The words were a test, and he watched his friend carefully. Greyson moved away, rounding his chair as though he might sit again but instead peering at the floor.

"The truth of it is, Frye, I am having the time of my life. And I've told our hostess as much." He lifted his eyes.

There it was, all the proof Frye needed in his friend's eyes: confidence, certainty, happiness, and just a hint of belligerence. The look said "She's mine now, so don't even think of trying to reclaim her."

A weight slid off of Frye's shoulders.

He grinned. "Fancy a game of billiards, Grey?"

"I will demolish you."

"You will try, I'm sure."

"Actually, in fact, I've got someplace else to be right now—somebody, a lady, to find."

Frye smiled. "I expect you do."

With a grin of his own, Greyson passed him by and went out. Frye set down the glass of brandy and went to find Charlotte Ascot.

*C*harlotte accidentally slept through dinner. Rising groggily, she rubbed the blur from her eyes and went in search of tea. She was wending her way through the labyrinthine corridors when a door opened ahead and Serena came through it, followed closely by Mr. Greyson Jones.

Even in the dim lighting Charlotte could see that Serena's coiffure was in thorough disarray, her gown wrinkled, and Mr. Jones's cravat entirely undone.

Then, Lady Serena Cavendish—whom every gossip columnist and every society matron in England praised for poise, elegance, modesty, self-possession, and exceptional breeding—giggled, threw her arms about the gentleman's neck, and kissed him.

The kiss was neither brief nor superficial.

Breaking apart, they murmured words to each other that Charlotte could not hear and set off along the corridor, holding hands.

Charlotte could not move.

Serena was happy. Obviously very, very happy. Charlotte had never seen her friend so happy, in fact. And she knew Serena would never behave in such a manner if she weren't in love and fully confident of the gentleman's intentions. This was the best possible scenario.

Yet there was so much pain in her chest she could hardly breathe.

She went somewhat blindly the rest of the way to the drawing room. There she found tea, and biscuits that she couldn't stomach, but she forced herself to eat them anyway.

Somewhat restored, she started to actually listen to what the others at the tea table were talking about. Which was how she discovered that the Duke of Frye had arrived at Kingstag.

Then she was looking across the room and into his beautiful eyes.

He smiled.

The pain in Charlotte's chest abruptly dissolved.

He remained where he stood as she set down her teacup and crossed the room and went out the door. She found a nearby corridor unlit by candle or lamp.

He found her there.

"You came," she said.

"I should not have." He halted not a foot away from her.

She leaned her shoulders against the wall. "But you could not stay away from me."

He smiled again.

"It seems that Serena is not heartbroken," she said.

"Now you believe me?"

"I did not disbelieve you before."

"You did," he said.

"I did not."

"You really did."

"We must agree to disagree."

"We rarely agree," he said. "It is one of the things I like excessively about you." His gaze slipped down her face to her chin and throat and neck and all the way to her breasts, which she supposed was reasonable since she had worn this gown precisely because of its minuscule bodice. Desperate for distraction of any sort, she had hoped that it would inspire Lord Gosling to take notice of her. He had, offering her his arm to walk in to luncheon. But his pretty compliments had not inspired any of the heat and tingling that the Duke of Frye's mere glance inspired.

"I think Serena likes Mr. Jones," she said, not knowing quite how to throw herself at him and wishing he would just grab her. "Excessively."

His gaze caressed her shoulders. "He likes her excessively too."

Tingles skittered through her. "Does he?"

His eyes rose to meet hers.

She gasped. "Mr. Jones is the reason you broke off the betrothal!"

"One of the reasons," he murmured. "Charlotte, I could stand here in the dark gossiping with you for hours . . ."

"But?"

"How long will you make me wait to kiss you again?"

Invitation enough.

She threw herself at him.

And quite swiftly she discovered that kissing a man while she was wearing a minuscule bodice was a markedly different experience than kissing him while she was wearing a more modestly designed gown.

She had thought that she would never feel anything so indescribably good as his hand on her most intimate parts. His mouth on her breasts was *at least* as good. Possibly even better. It was only moments before she was considering asking him to do both at once.

His lips returned to hers and she was happy, deliriously happy with this too.

"I did not come here for this," he said, kissing her jaw and throat and beneath her ear and then her mouth again.

She smoothed her hands over his chest and wished she could feel his skin again. All of it.

"Then why did you come here?"

"I had to see you." His hands were tight around her ribs, gorgeously firm and strong, and his gaze was all over her face. "You are even more beautiful tonight than you were this morning. How can that be? How can you grow more beautiful in only eight hours?"

She pressed her bared breasts and her hips and thighs to him, and she lifted her hand to his face to smooth away the creases on his brow. Then she pushed onto her toes and drew him down to her and kissed him. Then she kissed him again. Then again. With her lips and hands and body she told him what she thought of his decision to come to Kingstag.

"We must stop this now," he said in a very deep pitch.

"Why?" She trailed her fingertips down his waist and, brazenly, over the fall of his trousers. "Didn't you come here for this?"

"*No.*" He broke from her and backed away. "Charlotte, I beg of you. Don't."

"Beg?" she whispered over a horribly uncomfortable clog in her throat.

"I am not a saint. I am only a man. A catastrophically imperfect man at that." He raked both hands through his hair. "This curse—this disease—whatever it is that twists my body into convulsions works the same black magic with my thoughts, more often than I can tell you. Sometimes—sometimes I actually believe I am losing my mind."

"I am sorry, Horace. I am." Her voice shook. "Although, of course, I don't see any purpose in imagining a future of possible insanity when you are not actually insane at present." Could a heart actually break in two while it was beating as hard as hers now? "But whatever the long term might or might not bring, I honestly don't know what it has to do with us kissing and touching each other at this specific moment. It is the most glorious madness I have ever experienced."

He laughed. It was a terrible sound, not his rich, gentle laughter that she adored, rather more like the noise of a great wild animal caught in a steel-toothed trap.

"I could kiss and touch you forever," he said very simply.

"Then I think you should at least be able to do so right now."

"For pity's sake, woman," he said, and then he laughed like himself again. But his eyes were still fevered. "Have mercy."

Pulling her garments up over her breasts, she adjusted them. Then, smoothing her hair, she stepped to him and curled her fingers around his wonderfully muscular arm.

"All right, then, Your Grace, let us go play whatever games everybody's playing in the drawing room, and you can subtly remind all the gossips what a fine man you are, despite having jilted the hostess of this party mere months ago."

"Mm. What fun." But he was holding her hand firmly to his side and through his ribs she could feel the hard, quick heartbeats that told her everything she needed to know.

*C*harlotte tossed and turned on her bed.

He wanted her. He was determined not to have her.

She wanted him. She didn't really see why she could not have him.

Nothing in her upbringing or education had trained her for this. But nothing had prepared her for falling in love with him even more than she had been in love with him before, and so much harder than she had imagined possible.

Obviously she must now begin writing her own instruction manual.

Climbing out of bed, she pulled a wrapper over her nightgown, took up a candlestick, and walked barefooted through the darkened corridors of the castle to his bedchamber door.

Her hand was shaking when she rapped on the panel. But that was to be expected.

He opened the door.

Immediately he started to close it.

She stuck her foot in the way.

"Charlotte, don't—"

"Let me in, Horace Chesterfield Breckenridge Church, or I will make a scene that will wake the entire castle."

He opened the door, she entered, and he closed it behind her. He stepped back, away from her, running a hand over his face.

"You cannot just force your way into a man's bedchamber, Charlotte."

"Yet here I am." Her voice shook a little too. She set down the candlestick. "Make love to me. Now."

His hand arrested in midair and his handsome features went slack. His throat worked, but nothing came out of his mouth.

Folding her hands behind her back, she drew a slow breath in an attempt to steady her pulse. He wore only trousers and shirt, not even a cravat or stockings. Despite their tryst on his bed at the inn, she was not at all accustomed yet to seeing him in dishabille, and it was doing deliciously agitating things to her belly and the tips of her breasts.

"I am perfectly fine with your decision to never marry," she said, not entirely honestly. But this was warfare and sometimes war required a little subterfuge. He would understand that. "These past several years in America I have, in fact, been considering doing the same. My father has intimated that he might not be entirely against it." *Not entirely* included the fact that she had never mentioned this to her father. But she would. If she could not have this man, she would not have another. Her family would simply have to live with that. "In any case, I want to make love with you. And I am fairly certain that if we do, it will be wonderful. Now, before you say that I am a bawd or what-have-you—"

"I would never say that."

"Thank you. But before you decline, you need to believe that I have no designs on you. Also, only the two of us will ever know."

"I believe you."

"You do?"

He was completely still, as though paralyzed, yet breathing so hard she could hear it.

"Charlotte, are you—Have you made love with a man before?"

She suspected this was an area in which she would be unwise to employ subterfuge.

"No. I want my first time to be with you. My only time, given that I'm not going to marry. But don't worry," she added swiftly. "I am a very quick learn—"

He dragged her into his arms and his mouth found hers with unerring haste.

Joy burst into pleasure in every corner of her body.

"Is this a yes?" she said when he finally released her mouth to trail the most beautiful kisses along her jaw.

"No," he said, taking her earlobe between his teeth and sending decadent shivers all through her. "This is a hell yes."

He picked her up and carried her to his bed.

It began with kisses. Copious kisses. Kisses on her throat and earlobes and neck and shoulders and the tips of her fingers and her palms and the tender inside of her elbows. Kisses that were soft and hot at first, and soon hungry and deep and that made Charlotte feel she might expire if he didn't kiss *there* and *there* and everywhere all at once.

Then there were touches. Delectable touches. Some in places that she had not even known she liked to be touched. She had never known, for instance, that the caress of a single fingertip along her forearm could make her want to press her entire body against a man—*this* man. And she had never known that slow, light strokes up her calves could cause her knees to part as though she weren't even doing it on purpose.

Then there was the remarkable experience of being undressed. She wore only two garments, both of them uncomplicated by too many fasteners. He made the removal of them a maddening seduction. As he drew back the fabric to reveal each bit of her skin, he kissed her there and touched her.

In a very short time she was breathless, clinging to him and saying words like "yes" and "please" and "oh, yes" and "please now" over and over.

It was then that he invited her to undress him.

A little shocked at first, she quickly decided it was the most fun she had ever had. All over he was smooth, taut, warm skin and contoured muscle. Her tongue wanted to taste it.

"Go ahead," he whispered, watching her lips hover over his chest as she drew his scent deep into her and felt her entire body grow all hot and achy and liquid, especially between her legs.

"Go ahead?" she whispered back.

"Kiss me, Charlotte."

She complied, touching her lips to the hard muscle so gently at first that it only made her hungrier. Then she pressed her lips fully to him, parted them and tasted his skin, and she got even hungrier. And while she kissed him, she did as he had offered: she undressed him. With more kisses and tastes and astonishing discoveries, she lost herself in the task.

When he was finally entirely undressed, and she was staring and could not manage to control the trembling that was taking over her body, he cupped his hand beneath her chin and lifted her face so that she had to look into his eyes.

"We needn't," he said.

"Don't you want to now?"

His eyes had that fevered look again.

"More than I have ever wanted anything, actually," he said in quite a low voice. "But simply holding you is more than I ever thought I would have. So if you are hes—"

She climbed into his lap, wrapped her arms about his shoulders, lowered her lips to his, and said, "You mustn't be distracted from your purpose now, Your Grace."

"I am not distracted from my purpose," he said with a slow smile, kissing her and brushing the hair back from her face.

"Yes, you are."

"This purpose, you mean?" He touched her intimately with his fingers. She gasped, jerked to him, and gripped his shoulders.

"Yes," she said very airily, swiveling her hips to feel the caress even more acutely and because it just seemed to be what her hips wanted to do.

"And this purpose?" he said, and then she was feeling him—*him*—hot and hard at the entrance to her body, and she was suddenly entirely without speech.

She nodded frantically.

Then he was inside her.

It was shocking and astonishing and wonderful and, after a few moments of accustoming herself to it, she decided that she never wanted it to end.

"Charlotte." His voice was ragged.

Sinking both hands into her hair, he kissed her perfectly, passionately, and as deeply as he was embedded inside her body. There was a waiting tension in her, a deep, thick anticipation that made her press her hips to his and the tight peaks of her breasts to his chest. He groaned and took her mouth more fully yet, and the anticipation surged. It was perfect, tantalizing, *delicious*, but something was missing—the wild pleasure she had felt from his fingers caressing her—and she worried that her womanly parts might not be functioning properly now.

His fingers stroked down her neck, over her breasts and to her thighs. Wrapping his hands around her hips, he moved her on him. Then she understood that there was nothing whatsoever wrong with her, or him, or how they fit so perfectly together.

Shortly, there was no understanding whatsoever, only the most sublime pleasure that went on and on and seemed to have no end.

The end did eventually come. Again he put his fingers on her, between them, and in a tightening, winding, agonizing spiral of need and then a crashing, cascading waterfall of pleasure, she discovered a whole new way to thoroughly enjoy him and herself and them together. He captured her whimpers with his mouth. When his body hardened and he stilled abruptly and a low, growling groan came from his chest, she quieted him with her mouth too.

No need to wake the neighbors, after all.

They fell onto their sides on the mattress, she struggling for air and he kissing her lips anew so that the air-getting was at once challenging and delicious. He took her hand and interlaced their fingers, and Charlotte learned the great delight of holding his hand while she was sweaty *not* from running for miles. It was heaven.

When he withdrew his hand from hers to brush her tangled hair back from her face, and his fingertips traveled over her cheek, her lips, and her jaw very tenderly, she had to struggle for air again.

"I never thought I would be allowed this with you," he whispered, lifting his beautiful gaze to hers. "Thank you, my lady."

Thank you?

"It was my pleasure," she replied unsteadily. "Obviously."

"Was?"

"Was?" She blinked. "*Is?* Yes? No?"

The brilliant blue eyes laughed, but they were still a bit fevered. "That is entirely your choice."

Her heart could not possibly pound any harder than at present. "What are you saying?"

"That this is the best night of my life." He said it simply.

Moving to him, she wrapped her arms around him, let him bear her back on the mattress, and made love to him again with everything in her heart.

CHAPTER THIRTEEN

December 27 before dawn

The duke's bedchamber

Charlotte awoke to the bed empty beside her and the soft glow of a single candle across the chamber. Turning over, she found him in the shadows by the dressing table. Atop the table was a traveling bag, and he was fastening the clasps. He was fully dressed, in boots, riding breeches, shirt, neck cloth, and a coat that stretched across shoulders she had memorized with her hands and lips.

"What are you doing?" she said, too few hours of sleep making her words mumbly.

He came to the bed, sat beside her on the mattress, curved his hand around her face and bent to kiss her. His lips were soft and they lingered. She didn't even care that her mouth was cottony. This was a dream. A fantasy. Thoroughly forbidden and auguring the best possible forbidden delights to come too.

She sighed against his lips.

He drew back from her.

"It should be a crime to be as beautiful as you are in the morning," he said.

"It isn't the morning. It is still nighttime. I needn't leave this room quite yet."

He stood. "However, I must." He crossed to the dressing table and took up an overcoat and the case.

"You are dressed for travel," she said.

"I am leaving."

"Kingstag?"

He nodded.

"Now?" She sat up and the bedclothes fell to her waist. Grabbing them, she pressed them to her naked breasts. "Alone?" In the candle's light, Frye could see the distress enter her eyes and it carved a hole out of his gut. "You mustn't," she said. "The sunlight and snow—"

"It will be dark for several more hours. I will be fine."

"But—"

"I can delay my departure no longer."

"But why are you going? So abruptly, that is. Have you business to attend to elsewhere?"

"No."

"No?"

"You know the reason I must leave, Charlotte. To remain would be unfair to you. No—that's wrong. Not *unfair*. Rather, cruel."

She stared at him, her eyes wide and somewhat blank.

Then she swung her feet over the side of the bed. Taking up her clothes from the floor, she tugged her gown over her head. Pulling the other garment on too, she slid off the bed and walked past him toward the door.

"Charlotte—"

She turned to face him.

"I had not imagined this of you," she said firmly. "After what you said, I had not imagined—oh, well, my imaginings were obviously far afield of reality. Thus my surprise now. Well, shock, truth be told."

"You said you understood. That you agreed. That you had no designs."

"I know what I said! I said it only a few hours ago. But then my imagination got active. I will say, though, that at least while I was imagining what I was imagining, I had a very good time with you." She took a thick breath. "A marvelous time, really. I will not forget last night. Not ever, I suspect. Or anything about this Christmas with you, Horace. I will cherish the memory of it. That said, I think it will be best if we avoid seeing each other in the future. If possible."

"Yes," he made himself say.

Her throat constricted in a rough little swallow.

"Your sisters will have their seasons in London," she said, "and there will be parties I must attend. It would be the decent thing for you to avoid events to which my family is also expected."

"I will."

"All right then." She turned decisively to the door again.

"I think I know the back of you better than the front," he heard himself say. The words came from such a profound sensation of grief that he simply was not man enough to hold them in. "Your shoulders and hair and the curve of your hips and not even a word of good-bye."

She swiveled halfway to him. "What are you talking about?"

"You are running away again."

"I am going to my room. Back to my own bed because it is still nighttime. You, on the other hand, are running away. Rather, riding. Neverthe—Wait. *Again?* What do you mean that I am running away *again?*" Her brows twisted. "Are you referring to when *you* bade me abandon you in the mill to run to the inn?"

"I am referring to when you ran away from me in the stable. Then Sheridan's room. Then my room. Then the carriage house. Then the kitchen." The words simply came and he did not bother halting them. He supposed he needed to hear from her the words that would make the coming hell easier to bear. He needed to hear her say that it was not breaking her heart to part from him, that she was actually relieved. "And in Hyde Park two and a half years ago."

Her beautiful lips fell open. "W—What?"

"You have always run away from me, Charlotte Ascot."

"I have not."

"Yes. You have. Since that day. The day you found me in the woods at Cheriot Manor."

"You remember that?" she said in little more than a whisper.

"Of course I remember that. Since that day, every time I have spoken with you, you have run away from me. Literally. You run away."

"I do not."

"Indeed you do, most extraordinarily from Hyde Park after I helped you down from the tree. No, 'how do you do, Frye?' Not even a 'good day.' Not a single word."

"I never imagined you the sort to stand on ceremony."

"That was hardly a ceremonious moment. You were in a *tree*. Seventeen years old, wearing the prettiest pink and white froth of confection I had ever seen a girl wear, and in a rainy London park you were twenty feet off the ground. In a tree."

"My tree climbing offends you?"

"You did not climb into that tree. You flew into it to avoid walking past me on that path. You know you did."

"So what if I did? You should have walked past. It would have been the gentlemanly thing to do. But you insisted on helping me down, to prove that you could speak to me whether I wanted to speak with you or not. Isn't that so?"

"No. Yes. Possibly. For God's sake, Charlotte, we have known each other nearly our entire lives. You were about to leave for America. Yet you didn't even say a word to me. Not a word of greeting or parting or any other word. Why did you run away from me that morning?"

"Well, I couldn't *stay*." She turned her face away and lifted it so she seemed to be looking into the dark corner where wall met ceiling. "You cannot possibly understand," she muttered.

"You might have at least spoken to me."

"And said what?" She pivoted back to him. "That I had a raging tendre for you? That I had adored you since I was a little girl, and that when I grew older and that adoration turned to something much more profound you were all I could think about? That I dreaded meeting you at parties and especially balls because then I would be obliged to invent a torn hem or twisted ankle so that I could avoid dancing with you, because while I could hold fairly steady in conversation with you I was certain I would not be able to hide my feelings if you touched me? Or that I could not bear to be in even the same *park* as you without becoming subsumed in guilt for liking my friend's intended? And that I would rather sail to a tiny island in the Pacific Ocean to attend the wedding of cannibals at which I am the main dish than attend your wedding to somebody else?"

He blinked. "You might have said that. Yes."

"Which part?"

"Any part. Charlotte—"

"Oh, no. I was afraid of this. Please—please don't look at me like that."

"Like what?"

"Like you pity me. Your indifference I can bear. I have long since learned to bear that. But to have your pity would be unendurable."

"Pity is far from what I feel at present. And indifference is the last thing on— Charlotte, how can you not *see* it, even now?"

"I know you aren't completely indifferent to me *now*. You showed your desire for me last night. And at the inn."

"But do you see all of my desires, the legion of my desires for you, that I want more than—that I want everything from you?"

"Everything?" she whispered.

"Everything. Your body, your lips, to be inside you and feel you getting pleasure from me. Yes, of course. But that isn't all. I want your hand in mine, as often as you will give it and for as long as you will allow it. I want your head resting on my shoulder as together we watch the sun set each evening. I want your lips whispering my name for the remainder of my life. And I want your children to be mine, and I want to watch them grow with you. Don't you see that I would give everything I have—my titles, my lands, my very soul—if I could have that?"

Her chest compressed, her breaths swept away. "You love me?"

"So much that it hurts. A good hurt. A hurt I never want to go away. But I cannot curse you with such a life as you would have with me."

"Curse? *Curse?*" Lightning darted across her stormy eyes, and glistening tears were gathering in them. "Do you know what a real curse is? A real curse is loving you and knowing that you could never be mine. That is a curse I know well, for I have already lived it, for years." Hands bunched into fists, she moved toward him. "Horace Chesterfield Breckenridge Church, I have always loved you and I will love you and no other for the remainder of my life. So don't try to tell me that you know all about what sort of life I would have if—"

He caught her up in his arms and she went onto her tiptoes and pressed her cheek against his.

"I want you," she said fiercely, her lips brushing his skin. "Forever and ever."

His arms held her so tightly to him, and he kissed her hair.

"It would not last forever."

"It would. It will." She leaned back and her palms surrounded his face. "You know it will."

His eyes were so troubled.

"Do you doubt my strength?" she said. "My resolve?"

"Neither."

"Then do you doubt my love?"

"Not any longer. Though I'm certain I should. For it cannot be real."

"It is real. Entirely real."

"Charlotte." His gaze held hers. "You will never know when I might fail you."

"Fail me?"

"You will grow to anticipate it at any moment, at all moments. To fear it. You will learn to remain on guard lest it catch you by surprise. And, eventually, you will come to despise me for making you live in that manner. I cannot do that to you. I cannot do that to any woman, but most of all not to the woman whose happiness means more to me than my own."

"I have a story to tell you," she said, stroking the taut line of his jaw.

"A story?"

"It is of a girl who fell in love with a boy who barely noticed her. To make matters worse, he was to marry a friend she held dear and who, she adamantly believed, deserved him. This girl endured years of confusion each time she came into his company, and constant agony knowing that she would never love another as she loved him. For, you see, each time she became acquainted with other boys, other men, none of them were even half as wonderful as he. And so she decided that in order to learn to live without the constant misery, indeed to live happily, she must board a ship and sail as far away from him as she could."

"And she did so," he said softly, bending to set his lips on her brow.

"Don't interrupt me. I am just getting to the good part." She laid her palms on his chest. "She did so, and in that foreign land she tried to forget him, but did not. For she had been mistaken about running away from difficult things. Running away from them did not make them disappear, for when she ran she carried with her the same heart, the same mind, and the same desires. And of course the same love. So, instead, she learned to live with uncertainty and even pain, because that is what one does when one truly loves. For in true love there is joy, and that triumphs over sorrow."

"Does it?"

"Most certainly. Where was I before I began philosophizing?"

"She did not forget him." He nuzzled her brow and his hands were now wandering on her very satisfactorily.

"She did not forget him, but she resolved to find happiness in simply living. It was then that the girl realized she must return home, for even though she was bound to see the young man again and again, now she was strong. Now she knew not only the power of love, but she knew her own power too."

"What happened then?"

She lifted her face. "She got her heart's desire."

"You won't allow me to play the honorable martyr, will you?"

"Martyrs are dreadfully tiresome." She smoothed her palms over his chest. "I would prefer that you play the dashing hero and the dreamy lover." Her eyes glistened. "And the devoted husband."

He smiled. "Was that an offer of marriage?"

"No."

"It was. You have just proposed to me."

"I have not."

"Albeit indirectly," he admitted.

"You suggested it first, a few minutes ago."

"I didn't."

"You did."

"I did not mention marriage."

"Oh. Do you plan to simply install me at Kentwood as the mother of your children? That sounds delightful. I'm certain Her Grace won't mind that at all. And of course neither my father nor Trent will come after you with a shotgun."

"What of Henry?"

"He will; it's true. He has a remarkably strong moral compass."

"Then I suppose I will have to propose to you after all."

She threw her arms about his neck and kissed him full on the lips. "I accept."

"I haven't proposed yet," he said, kissing her back.

"I accept anyway."

"I am now going to go to my knee and do this properly. But you'll have to release my neck first."

"Not for a moment! And I would rather go to the bed anyway."

A tempting half smile slanted over his lips. "Now, that I can agree to."

Sweeping her up into his arms, he carried her to the bed. And there—not on his knee but really much more comfortably—he made her a very handsome offer of marriage, which she accepted.

Years later when they told the story to their children of how they came to marry, they modified that last part of it, for modesty's sake. But in their eyes and voices and entwined hands eloquently shone the true depth of their love.

AUTHOR'S NOTE

I hope you enjoyed Charlotte and Frye's romance! I adore writing stories about long-time star-crossed lovers who finally find their happily ever afters, so I've written several, including each of the novels in my acclaimed Devil's Duke series. To learn about those and all of my books, please visit my website www.KatharineAshe.com where you can also find lots of Book Extras and sign up for my e-newsletter to receive a free short story.

I'd like to share a few words about the historical inspirations for this novella. In all of its tragedy and its triumphs, history fascinates me, especially the history of the early nineteenth century. It was a global era, in which many, many people constantly moved—or were forcibly moved—across oceans and continents in pursuit of education, work, safety, monetary gain, and military domination. I love reflecting this historical reality in the fiction I write.

For instance, for a decade after Haiti's revolution that wrested freedom from the crushing colonial yoke of France, the Haitian constitution was a monarchy. The court of King Christophe included noblemen, many of whom had been educated in France before the revolution. After Haiti's independence, however, Christophe allied himself most closely with Britain, which in 1807 had abolished the slave trade throughout its own colonial empire. Thus Frye and Freddie's friendship: two school boys, neither of them perfectly at home amidst their peers, who turned to each other and forged from their differences a lasting, powerful bond.

Epilepsy is a neurological disorder that induces seizures, which cause a temporary loss of muscular control and unconsciousness. These seizures can take many different forms, although typically individuals experience the same form or forms throughout their lives. Epileptic seizures are often at their worst in childhood and then again in advanced age, but individuals can experience them throughout their lives, too. In the young especially, specific triggers often cause seizures. I chose one of the most commonly recognized triggers for Frye's seizures: flashing light.

In the early nineteenth century explanations for epileptic seizures ranged all over, including the two Freddie offered Charlotte. Many scientists did indeed understand they were due to a disturbance in the physical brain. Haitian polytheists sometimes attributed seizures to spirit possession, and for centuries European Christians believed them to be evidence of possession by the devil or induced as a punishment by God for sinning. Frequent epileptic seizures were frequently seen as markers of insanity, and it was not uncommon for people with epilepsy to be committed to asylums. Those with the condition had to endure not only the seizures themselves but social condemnation, ostracism, and violations of their human rights as well. For instance, since many believed epilepsy was inherited, until 1970 in the UK, individuals affected with epileptic seizures were forbidden from marrying.

Many thanks to the dear people who gave me inspiration as well as technical assistance in writing this novella, including Marcia Abercrombie, Georgie C. Brophy, Georgann T. Brophy, Laurent Dubois, Mariana Eyster, Donna Finlay, Lee Galbreath, Susan Gorman, Rosie Herrera, Mary Brophy Marcus, Martha Trachtenberg, and The Lady Authors—Caroline Linden, Miranda Neville and Maya Rodale—with whom I adore writing books. I offer big hugs and thanks also to Gina DeWitt, Donna Finlay, Susan Knight, and all of the Princesses, and especially to Rebecca Smartis for coming up with the perfect title for this novella.

ABOUT THE AUTHOR

Katharine Ashe is the award-winning and *USA Today* bestselling author of historical romances that reviewers call "intensely lush" and "sensationally intelligent," including her acclaimed Devil's Duke Series, and *My Lady, My Lord* and *How to Marry a Highlander*, finalists for the prestigious RITA® Award of the Romance Writers of America. Her books are recommended by *Publishers Weekly*, *Woman's World* Magazine, *Booklist*, *Library Journal*, *USA Today*, Kirkus Reviews, Barnes & Noble, Amazon, and many others, and translated into languages across the world.

Katharine lives in the wonderfully warm Southeast United States with her beloved husband, son, dog, and a garden she likes to call romantic rather than unkempt. A professor of European History, she writes fiction because she thinks modern readers deserve grand adventures and breathtaking sensuality too. For more about Katharine's books, please visit www.KatharineAshe.com.

~ALSO BY KATHARINE ASHE~

~THE DEVIL'S DUKE~
THE ROGUE
THE EARL
THE DUKE
THE PRINCE

~THE PRINCE CATCHERS~
I MARRIED THE DUKE
I ADORED A LORD
I LOVED A ROGUE

~THE FALCON CLUB~
HOW A LADY WEDS A ROGUE
HOW TO BE A PROPER LADY
WHEN A SCOT LOVES A LADY

~ROGUES OF THE SEA~

IN THE ARMS OF A MARQUESS
CAPTURED BY A ROGUE LORD
SWEPT AWAY BY A KISS

~THE TWIST SERIES~
AGAIN, MY LORD
MY LADY, MY LORD

CAPTIVE BRIDE (A REGENCY GHOST NOVEL)

~NOVELLAS~
A LADY'S WISH
HOW TO MARRY A HIGHLANDER
KISSES, SHE WROTE (A CHRISTMAS ROMANCE)
THE SCOUNDREL AND I
THE PIRATE AND I

If you enjoyed *At the Christmas Wedding*, please consider posting a review of it online for other readers. Thank you!

The Lady Authors invite you to visit them online at www.TheLadyAuthors.com.

~Books by The Lady Authors~

At the Duke's Wedding
At the Billionaire's Wedding
At the Christmas Wedding

CPSIA information can be obtained
at www.ICGtesting.com
Printed in the USA
LVOW13s0108190118
563145LV00018B/884/P